THE DEVIL'S CARESS

THE DEVIL'S CARESS

June Wright

INTRODUCTION BY WENDY LEWIS

**DARK
PASSAGE**

TO
M.M.B.

Author's Note: At no time in this book is any doctor, male or female,
intended to represent a counterpart either living or dead.

A Dark Passage book
Published by Verse Chorus Press
Portland, Oregon
www. versechorus.com

Cover design by Mike Reddy
Interior design and layout by Steve Connell/Transgraphic
Dark Passage logo by Mike Reddy

Country of manufacture as stated on the last page of this book

Library of Congress Cataloging-in-Publication Data

Names: Wright, June, 1919-2012, author. | Lewis, Wendy, 1962- writer of
  introduction.
Title: The devil's caress / June Wright ; Introduction by Wendy Lewis.
Description: Portland : Verse Chorus Press, [2018] | "A Dark Passage book."
  | Identifiers: LCCN 2018005475 (print) | LCCN 2018007343 (ebook) | ISBN
  9781891241758 (ebook) | ISBN 9781891241437 (softcover)
Subjects: LCSH: Physicians--Fiction. | Murder--Fiction. | GSAFD: Mystery fiction.
Classification: LCC PR9619.3.W727 (ebook) | LCC PR9619.3.W727 D49 2018
  (print) | DDC 823/.914--dc23
LC record available at https://lccn.loc.gov/2018005475

INTRODUCTION

I love a good murder mystery, so it was only a matter of time before I came across June Wright. My interest turned to fascination when I realised how popular she had been in her time but how hard it was to get hold of her books! Well, *some* of her books. Of course, Verse Chorus Press is reprinting her novels in chronological order, so the first three were already out there. But I hit the wall with *The Devil's Caress* (1952). Not online. Not in bookshops. Where on earth would I find it?

I tracked down an original edition with dark blue hardcover in the State Library of New South Wales. And then, on a visit to Melbourne, I found another copy – complete with dramatically il-lustrated dust jacket and sensible plastic covering – in the Rare Book Section of the State Library of Victoria. I was thrilled to carefully turn the yellowing pages, visualise the action, and make notes about the characters – 'as odd a collection of medicos as ever snatched an appendix', as one reviewer put it at the time.[1]

I had in mind that I would like to introduce June Wright to a new audience by adapting one of her works to the stage. But which one?

Wright's debut novel, *Murder in the Telephone Exchange* (1948) was a possibility. She was particularly proud of the setting – the Central Telephone Exchange in Lonsdale Street – which was refresh-ingly and unself-consciously Australian. It's likely that the Literary Luncheon for the launch of her book at the Orient Hotel was the first ever such event in Melbourne, a city she clearly loved.

Her second novel was set in 'Middleburn', based on Ashburton where Wright lived as a newly-wed. She wanted to call it *Who Would Murder a Baby?* but this was considered much too shocking by her

---

1   Sweeney Todd's Crime Corner, *The Argus* (24 May, 1952), p. 14.

publishers. The result was the more sedate and Shakespearean *So Bad a Death* (1949), which was serialised in *Woman's Day* with superb Gothic illustrations by Frank Whitmore. Not bad, given that Agatha Christie's *Taken at the Flood* had been serialised the year before.

Much as I enjoyed both novels, they weren't right for the stage. The settings and, in particular, the murder weapons and devious murder methods would fall flat – you'll have to read them to find out why!

Wright's third novel, *Duck Season Death* (2014), was written in the late 1950s and not published in her lifetime, but it should have been. Set in 'The Duck and Dog Inn' somewhere in northern Victoria, it's a wacky parody of the detective genre that is up there with my favourite June Wright novels. But for her theatrical debut I wanted something meatier (and less hilarious!).[2] When I finally found *The Devil's Caress*, I knew I was onto something...

With *The Devil's Caress*, Wright creates an atmospheric psychological thriller about doubt, madness, and the burden of responsibility. The setting shifts to a small township on the tip of a fictional peninsula near Melbourne (not too hard to identify). It is the summer home of the Warings, a rather god-like couple comprising the stately senior physician Dr Katherine Waring – known to all as Dr Kate – and her impulsive surgeon husband Kingsley Waring.

This extraordinary couple live in a film noir-worthy cliff's edge setting, complete with howling winds, crashing waves, and peculiar goings-on in the night. Dr Kate invites the bright young Dr Marsh Mowbray – isn't that a sublime name? – to her home for a well-earned rest. Of course, there is the requisite gathering of interesting persons, mostly members of the medical profession. Uncannily, within twenty-four hours of Marsh's arrival, one of the household is dead. Soon after, another suspicious death occurs and our spirited Dr Mowbray begins to doubt the innocence of her beloved mentor, Dr Kate. Could such a magnificent woman commit murder?

'Doubt is the devil's caress', says Bruce Shane, the mysterious

---

2 I'm looking forward to adapting *Duck Season Death* next.

Left: front cover of the original edition, © 1952 Hutchinson & Co. (Publishers) Ltd.; *right*: June Wright in 1952 (photographer unknown)

stranger in town, who manages to get some of the book's best (as well as some of the most chauvinistic!) lines. Marsh Mowbray is fiercely loyal to Dr Kate, convinced that such a 'remarkable woman' is 'certain to be the victim of envy and misunderstanding'. But when Dr Kate misses a crucial detail in an autopsy – an unthinkable lapse of professionalism – Marsh must face facts. Did Dr Kate miss it through negligence? Or did she miss it for some sinister purpose?

As well as fighting her own fears, Marsh is up against four men who are all adamant that Dr Kate is a devil of a woman. Up-and-coming surgeon Larry Gair is certain Dr Kate has murder on her mind and takes every opportunity to chip away at Marsh's defences (when he's not flirting shamelessly!). Dr Kate's only son Michael no longer respects his mother because of what he calls her 'inhuman intelligence' and seeming incapacity to care. Bruce Shane detests Dr Kate due to past circumstances, and even the local publican Todd Bannister mocks her: 'I wish her luck, bless her ruthless heart'. It does not help that Dr Kate has a restrained, almost regal presence;

perhaps these men would feel more warmly towards her if she cried. Or screamed.[3]

At this point, I can't resist drawing some parallels between June Wright's life and the lives of her characters. The protagonist of her first two novels, Maggie Byrnes, is quick-witted and unafraid to speak her mind. Many people who knew Wright believed Maggie was based on her, although Wright always denied it. In *The Devil's Caress*, I am certain June Wright is there, both in the youthful zeal of Marsh Mowbray and in the more considered wisdom of Dr Kate.

Despite being at the centre of this drama, Dr Kate is an emotionally isolated woman. Although June Wright had a very different life, running a busy household with six children, she was similarly 'isolated' in the sense that her commitment, time, and emotional energy were focused on her family. Wright acknowledged that she began writing for mental stimulation and as a respite from domestic duties, declaring that she would have kept on writing for her own amusement regardless of whether she was published or not.

In *The Devil's Caress* we come to see that Dr Kate carries a great burden of responsibility. June Wright also had a life of enormous responsibility for those in her care, and, interestingly, more than her fair share of dealings with medicos. After the birth of twin boys in 1946, one baby needed major surgery within days then developed pneumonia; the other was diagnosed with severe intellectual disability when he was four. Wright's husband also had mental health issues. His decline was partially responsible for her ceasing writing to take on work that brought in more money. One positive note is that the Wright family's pediatrician took a close interest in her writing; Wright's dedication of *The Devil's Caress* to 'M. M. B.' – Dr Mona Blanch – is testament to this.

The resonance between the 'real' June Wright and her female characters is something that has shaped my approach to her writing. As I have worked on adapting *The Devil's Caress* for the stage, I have read Wright's books, been in touch with her (adult) children,

---

3 Media treatment of the self-contained Lindy Chamberlain springs to mind as a contemporary parallel of a deeply misunderstood woman.

read her memoirs, sifted through family photographs, looked up articles from the late 1940s, and formed my own mental image of her. I imagine June Wright shelling peas and finding a small advertisement for a Literary Competition on an old sheet of newspaper. I imagine her pounding away at a second-hand typewriter with faded ribbon, learning to type as she goes. I imagine her reading while she does the ironing; volunteering for community events not because she has the time but because she is asked. I imagine her seeing Bombe Alaska for the first time at her post-war literary luncheon and leaning towards her agent with a cheeky: 'Why is it not now called Bombe Atomique?'. Most of all I see her as a strong, loving, hard-working, good-humoured woman of great faith, courage and talent. I never met June Wright but I have a gut feeling that she was all those things.

I am absolutely delighted that *The Devil's Caress* is in print again for the first time since 1952. I hope you enjoy reading it.

Wendy Lewis
Sydney, January 2018

CHAPTER ONE

I

It was on a wet windy day, the first Saturday in December, that Marsh drove down to Matthews. Melbourne Weather Bureau had described the beginning of summer as freak weather, but as seasons in Victoria south of the Dividing Range seldom run true to form, few regarded it as out of the ordinary.

Wind shook the little car, and gusts of rain broke against the windscreen. Marsh put up a gloved hand now and then to manipulate the wiper. It was that sort of car. None of the lesser devices functioned properly, and the engine drank up the petrol as it battled against the head wind. A cheap little car which would bring in a few more pounds before she sailed for England the next week to commence a post-graduate course.

She drove steadily and carefully, glancing once or twice at the map laid out alongside her on the seat. Dr. Waring had given it to her after Marsh had accepted the invitation to spend a few days at her summer residence at Matthews. The route had been marked in blue pencil.

The invitation had been a surprise. Katherine Waring was the Senior Honorary Physician at the hospital where Marsh had been in residence for the last three years. Many times during that period she had followed Dr. Waring from bed to bed in the medical wards, absorbing and admiring the skill of the older woman until Marsh's feeling towards her was not unlike a schoolgirl's hero-worship for the head-girl. Not that she admitted it even to herself. She scorned emotions, however secret.

In private life Katherine Waring was the wife of Kingsley Waring, a prominent surgeon. She was a distinguished-looking woman, and might even have been considered beautiful but for the peculiar impassiveness of her countenance. She rarely smiled, and her fine grey eyes were remote and impersonal. She attracted nothing so intimate as friendship, but occasionally a strange partisanship. Similarly, a few hated her for her cold aloof manner without further delving into the reason for their dislike.

With her extraordinary medical ability and sublime detachment of disposition, she represented all that Marsh wanted to be—and would be in another fifteen years. There was a similarity between them of which the girl was unconscious, even as she strove to emulate her.

It was the last Wednesday before Marsh resigned and she wondered if Katherine Waring knew. They were doing the rounds of the wards, Marsh with the charts in her hand and a stethoscope dangling from the pocket of her white coat. The ward sister, Amelia Gullett, a stout bawdy-tongued woman, brought up the rear. Marsh liked her, although she knew she was one of the few who hated Katherine Waring.

Dr. Waring straightened from her bending position over a patient. She held out one hand for the chart. Marsh gave it to her and was surprised to see the honorary glance at her swiftly before she moved away from the bed towards the window. The other two followed obediently.

"Are you tired, Dr. Mowbray?" the honorary asked, without taking her eyes from the chart.

Marsh was startled. She owned privately to an accumulated fatigue, but it was dreadful that Katherine Waring had marked a flagging.

"Your eyes have black shadows under them. Have we been working you too hard?"

"I don't think so," the girl replied confusedly. "I like work."

"Yes, I believe you do. Your career is your whole life, is it not, Dr. Mowbray?" She handed back the chart. "And you leave for London next week?"

Marsh felt an unaccustomed glow. So she did know!

Then Katherine Waring sprang her surprise. "I would like to say good-bye and good luck before you go. Would care to spend a few days at Matthews? It will be very quiet, but the rest will do you good."

"I would like to—thank you, Doctor," she stammered.

No more was said about it, but later, when collecting her mail at the office, she was handed an unstamped envelope. In it was the map and a brief note from Katherine Waring, expecting her for dinner on the following Saturday.

II

The route branched away from the bay-side drive and wandered through the wide sweeping country of the peninsula. Matthews lay on its tip, facing the ocean. Marsh passed through one or two tiny hamlets, apparently deserted. The country was remote from the everyday world. The desolation did not disturb her, but the continual wind and the rain increased her weariness of mind and body.

About three miles from the township she slowed her steady speed. A car almost as battered as her own was drawn up at the roadside ahead, its bonnet open to the weather. A young man was bending into it. Hearing the approaching engine he straightened up. As Marsh cut it off and slid down the hill he moved to the centre of the road. The rain dripped from the limp hat-brim on to the sodden shoulders of his coat. He took up a pose and raised one soaking trouser leg to reveal a hirsute limb.

"Can I help?" Marsh asked curtly, her foot hard on the uncertain brake.

The young man grinned cheerfully. "To think that I have been brought to this! Asking assistance of a woman driver."

"What's the trouble?" she inquired without enthusiasm.

"To be quite frank," the young man replied, "I don't know. When I opened up the bonnet I had hopes some little voice would pipe and say, 'Here I am, fix me.' Do you think you would know?"

"No," said Marsh. "But I'll give you a tow."

"No rope," he said mournfully. "Mother wouldn't let me join the Boy Scouts. I haven't so much as a piece of string with me. What about you? Were you ever a Girl Guide?"

Ignoring the facetiousness, she said: "Is Matthews the nearest town with a garage? I'll take you there."

The young man promptly put one leg over the door of her car and settled his damp body on the outspread map. Marsh took a crank-handle from the floorboard and passed it to him in silence. He sighed loudly and got out.

"The trouble with you and me," he confided, when they were under way, "we don't know enough about cars to afford buying cheap ones. Are you going to Matthews?"

"Wasn't that implied?" she said, putting up a hand to the wiper again.

"What I mean is—will you be staying there?"

"I am having a short holiday," she enlarged.

"Holiday?" He glanced out at the rain. "Great weather you choose! Great place too, for that matter. Unless," he added, "you play golf. Do you?"

"No," said Marsh.

"Fishing," said the young man wisely.

"No," she repeated.

"Walking?" he asked incredulously.

"On occasions."

"Golf and fishing are the only recreations Matthews has to offer. If you don't do either of them you're in for a dull time. Do you play anything at all?"

A slight smile came into the girl's grave eyes. "The piano."

"Jazz, swing or boogie-woogie?"

She shook her head. The smile had deepened.

"You don't mean Mendelssohn and fellers like that!"

"I prefer Bach and Brahms," Marsh replied, glancing down at her fingers gripping the wheel lightly.

The young man sank back, stunned. He seemed to be considering something deeply. Presently he said: "Take a bit of advice from a local lad. Turn right around and go and have your holiday somewhere else. You can drop me off here. I will walk the rest of the way."

"That is an heroic offer, Mr—"

"Bannister. Todd Bannister. We have the local and one and only pub. The Tom Thumb."

"Well, thanks for the tip, Mr Bannister, but I would like to see

Matthews. What is the matter with it?"

The rise in the road was steep now. Marsh changed into second gear. The little car climbed protestingly. On the left of the road the land sloped away to a bay; a broad steady expanse of water rimmed by desolate swamps which formed the township's eastern foreshore. The rain spattered against the windscreen viciously. At the crest of the road the wind became violent. It shook the car, almost threatening to overturn it.

"Matthews!" announced her companion succinctly. "We've been here for a year now. It never seems to stop blowing. That is one of the things that matter."

"What else is wrong?" she asked, amused.

"Apart from the wind I don't object to the position. Taken by and large you might even call it pretty. But dead! The place hasn't changed over the last fifty years. Do you realize this is the only decent road that runs through the town? No sewerage—no water. In summer you have to wash in a cup."

"Sounds rather quaint, even if it might be considered unhygienic," Marsh commented.

"It may be quaint," the young man said gloomily, "but it is not too good for business. The whole trouble is people around here don't want to progress. They run a Retarding Society, not a Progress Association. Matthews could be made into a splendid little resort, but the powers that be won't have it."

"Who are the powers that be?"

"A small group of ruddy quacks. Years ago some bright boy, seeking a respite from carving people up, hit on this spot. Members of the medical profession are two a penny down here now. The place is mushroomed with their weekend mansions. If you address every person you see on the links or down at the jetty as Doctor, you won't cause any embarrassment."

Marsh drove on in silence. Presently they reached the little township.

"Is that your place?" she asked, slowing up.

"That's the hostelry. Care to come in and let me give you a drink out of gratitude for the Girl Guide deed?"

She shook her head. "I don't think so, thanks."

Todd Bannister got out of the car. "I hope Mother won't see me—accepting lifts from strange girls. Shall I be seeing you again? Where are you staying?"

"With one of the powers that be," Marsh told him, releasing the brake.

"For Pete's sake, are you? Whatever did I say? Which one?"

"With the Warings, at Reliance."

The young man stuck one finger in his mouth, rounding his eyes in horror. "The biggest power of the lot! How I hate dear Kingsley!"

"Good-bye," she said.

"Hey, wait a minute! I don't know your name. I must be able to tell Mother something. Otherwise she might start imagining things."

"Mowbray," Marsh supplied. "You'd better get off the running-board."

"Miss or Mrs.?" he asked, glancing at her gloved hands.

"Doctor," she said gently, and put the car into first. Bannister jumped aside in haste. She looked sideways as she moved back on to the road. The young man was still staring after her.

III

Marsh drove slowly through the tiny village. Reliance lay at the other end somewhere, where scrub and ti-trees covered the rise to the cliffs. There should be a sandy track through the bush which would lead to the house, but she drove to the end of the metal road without finding it.

The road stopped almost at the cliff's edge, where the ocean fore-shore was indented into a small rocky inlet. Marsh, with one foot hard on the brake again, sat for a while looking down on it. The rain was still coming down strongly. Great sheets of it, visible against the tall shadow of the cliffs, were being swept across by the wind. The water of the inlet was tumultuous, a grey swirling mass. It beat against the rocks, sending up clouds of spray, and smashed its way to the tiny crescent of sand below. A solitary gull was held immobile above her car. It stayed poised for a moment before it turned tail to the wind, as though giving up trying to get to the cliffs the other side of the inlet.

These cliffs were quite barren; a contrast to the thickly wooded land on Marsh's side and above the inlet. They sloped inland in a series of folds and dents caused by abortive water-courses. Under their towering protection a miniature mole ran into the sea from a boat-house built into the solid rock.

Marsh turned her attention from the view to the map on the seat beside her. Todd Bannister's damp clothes had rendered it almost indecipherable. She put the gear into reverse and backed a few yards. She was pulling the wheel hard to turn when something caught her eye on the bare hill the opposite side of the inlet.

A man on horseback was climbing to the cliff's edge. She watched them frowningly. The wind was strong enough to send the animal off its balance. It seemed a foolhardy project and she caught her breath as the horse was forced to the very edge. For a moment or two the rider held his mount at the top of the cliffs, gazing out towards the ocean. Then he turned and cantered back down the slope. He disappeared into a path through the bush above the inlet.

Marsh turned the car about and waited. Presently the rider came through the ti-trees at a hard canter. He reined in as he saw the car blocking the entrance to the track. Under the skilful pressure of knee and hand the horse passaged to alongside the car. Water ran off the animal's coat and the rider's leather jacket and whipcord breeches. He bent to glance into the car.

"Can you tell me the way to the Warings' place?" the girl asked above gale.

The horse was fidgeting badly. The man's leg seemed clamped to its wet heaving side.

"I am a stranger," he said curtly. "I do not know anyone in Matthews. What is the name of the house?"

"Reliance."

The rider frowned. "There is a turning a hundred yards or so back. I think that will be the one you want. Drive slowly. It is easy to miss."

"It was," Marsh retorted. "I didn't come here just to admire the view."

The man glanced behind him, down to the heaving sea. "This is a very dangerous point. One day someone will walk straight off the road on to the rocks down there. Then maybe they will put up a railing and a warning notice."

His knee released its pressure, and he touched the horse's flank with his heel. The animal leaped forward at once.

Marsh's car crept along. Her eyes searched the right side of the road for a break in the undergrowth. Presently she discerned the track, irritated that she had missed it in the first place. It was getting late, and she was never late for appointments as a rule.

The wheels moved heavily over the grey sandy surface of the drive. It curved in and out of the scrub, following the contour of the ground for about half a mile before the grotesque shapes of the ti-trees gave place to tall ordered pines and a harder-soiled area in front of the house. She pulled up and got out, thankful that the pressure of the wind and rain was lost against the huge swaying pine-trees. She felt very tired.

A figure moved forward from the shadow of the house. A shambling heavy body with arms that swung loosely from hunched shoulders. It loped over to her. A stupid face grinned wetly.

"Is this Reliance?" Marsh asked, surveying the boy uncertainly.

He nodded his big head. "Dr. Kate's," he announced in a proud voice, lifting one of his arms towards the house.

Marsh turned to drag her cases from the boot of the car. The imbecile wiped his slobbery mouth on the back of one hand and picked them up. Then a door in the house opened and Katherine Waring came along the verandah swiftly. In her dinner dress of dark red velvet she was an even more arresting figure.

"How are you, Dr. Mowbray?" she asked cordially. "Come inside. You must be very cold. Sam, take the doctor's bags up to her room."

"Which room, Dr. Kate?" asked the boy, his small red-rimmed eyes blinking up at her.

"I showed you this morning, Sam. Go upstairs. You will know when you see it."

The boy clumped through the house, his voice raised in a sing-song chant.

"I hope he did not startle you," Dr. Waring said to the girl. "He shows occasional signs of intelligence. He is an interesting case."

Marsh followed her along the verandah. It ran round two sides of the house with long French windows opening on to it.

"In here," said Katherine Waring, stepping over the sill into a small book-lined room lit only by a lamp. "A glass of sherry will do you good. Then you would like a bath. I have told Jennet to keep dinner for you."

"I am sorry I am late," Marsh said, moving over to the fire. "I missed the turning." She drew off her gloves and held her fingers to the blaze. "One would never think this was the first week of summer."

"Matthews is a draughty spot," Dr. Waring remarked, handing her a glass.

"So the young man I gave a lift to said. A Mr Bannister from the hotel."

"Bannister? Oh yes, the new people. Mother and son."

"They have been here a year," Marsh said, looking up in surprise.

A slightly more reserved expression overlaid Dr. Waring's fine face. "Anyone who has lived here less than five years is counted as a newcomer."

Marsh sipped her sherry in silence. She felt a small rebuke and hoped Katherine Waring did not think she made a habit of giving lifts to strange young men.

Then her hostess said in a warmer voice, "I am so glad you came."

"I was glad to come," the girl stammered. She finished the sherry and placed the glass on the tray.

Katherine Waring moved to the door. "Sam will have your bath ready. Go straight upstairs. You can meet the others after you have had your dinner. I will send up your tray in half an hour."

She led the way along the passage to the stairs. Another lamp, beautifully wrought in copper, stood on the bottom newel. She lit it and adjusted the wick. "Your room is the second on the right. You'll forgive me if I don't come up. The others are still in the dining-room. They will be wondering where I am."

"Please go back," Marsh replied, wondering just who the other members of the household were. She did not like to ask as Dr. Waring had not enlarged upon names. It was not in her nature to waste words on premeditated introductions or to discuss others loosely in order to prepare the meeting.

Marsh was glad of the respite. She felt too tired to appear suddenly as a congenial companion at the dinner-table. The long drive and the wild weather had left her almost exhausted. Her room was comfortable and attractive. Her bags, one containing her clothes, the other her attaché case, stood near a door which opened into an adjoining bathroom. For a moment she pressed her fingers against her aching eyes. Then she gave herself a little shake and began to undress.

IV

She had finished her bath and was about to slip into a reseda-green dinner dress when a tap came at the door. She put on her dressing-gown again.

"Come in," she called, tying the sash.

The door swung open slowly as a girl backed her way in. She was carrying an immense tray. She nodded, but did not smile.

"Dr. Kate said if you felt all in to go to bed and have this. She doesn't expect you to come down if you don't want to." She did not look at Marsh as she spoke. "Will I put the tray here on the table?"

"Yes, that will do. Haven't I seen you somewhere before?"

"I'm Betty Donne, Dr. Kate's nurse at her rooms. Do you think you have all you need? I must go down now. I promised Miss Jennet I'd help her."

But she did not go at once and Marsh waited for her to speak. Then the young nurse muttered something inaudible and darted out of the room. Marsh closed the door after her, shrugged slightly and then turned her attention to the dinner.

It was an odd sort of meal but exquisitely served. Everything seemed highly seasoned and the sweet was a shade too sweet, but she attacked it with an appetite hitherto dulled by plain hospital fare. Finally she pushed aside the tray and finished her dressing, sipping the rich coffee as she carefully attended to her appearance. Then she picked up the tray and opened the door.

She descended the stairs and went down the passage to find the kitchen.

It was a big warm room and full of tantalizing smells. Betty Donne, an apron tied over her dress, was scraping plates. She was not doing it quickly. She would pick up a plate, run a knife over the surface once and then stop, as though the noise might prevent her from hearing something of the conversation that wafted through the servery from the dining-room. She glanced at Marsh vaguely as she put her tray on the table and turned her head away again.

A plump little woman immaculately dressed in a white overall was lifting a heavy boiler from the stove.

"Let me take that," Marsh said at once, seeing the woman's trembling wrist.

"No, really I can manage. Well, just over here, thank you, Doctor. Do mind your lovely dress. Did you enjoy your dinner?" She darted over to inspect the tray. "Oh, I am glad. Kate told me about you. I'm Jennet, you know."

Marsh said doubtfully, "Yes, I guessed—"

"I know what you are thinking. I've always kept house for Kate, but I'm a sort of cousin, too. Such a distinguished pair!"

"Hush," said Betty Donne suddenly. Marsh swung round, her brows lifted. The nurse flushed, but she bent her head closer to the servery.

"Hush yourself," said Miss Jennet good-naturedly, "because I want to listen to *The Morans*. Do you like the radio, Doctor? I follow six different serials." She spoke with pride.

"Not very much," Marsh replied absently, observing the intent face of the nurse. Miss Jennet went on chattering in the background until she found her station, but she did not hear her. She, too, was listening to the voice in the dining-room; a man's voice, slightly raised in tone and with a hint of perpetual patronage.

"Medical errors should be acknowledged for debate and censure, not excused in a wealth of detail or hidden away amongst subsequent successes. If a doctor cannot bring himself to admit a mistake then it is the duty of a colleague to expose it."

There was silence for a moment in the dining-room before another man's voice said: "All very well, King, but the fellow who does the exposing is going to make himself unpopular. Let sleeping dogs lie, I say."

"A comfortable motto, but not a very brave one, my dear Henry."

"You mean to say you would have the courage to denounce another man to the world!"

"Or woman. Let those of our profession who are infallible remain god-like to the public. But the many others should be exposed so that the hero-worshipping of patients will be tempered a little."

The radio in the kitchen suddenly rose to a roar.

Betty Donne whirled around furiously. "Why did you do that?" she asked in a fierce voice.

"Do what?" asked Miss Jennet, startled.

The nurse's hands were trembling. "Nothing," she muttered. "Never mind."

She began to scrape the plates again, and Miss Jennet, after a moment's distress, returned to her soap-opera.

The diners were filing out of the adjoining room as Marsh closed the kitchen door behind her. She stayed in the shadows until the living-room door farther along shut them in. Then she made her way along slowly. Before she reached it the door reopened and Kingsley Waring came out. She did not see his face in the dimly lit passage, but she recognized the voice again as he spoke some word excusing himself as he went past her.

There were five persons in the big living-room when Marsh entered. The sound of the sea was very clear and occasionally fine points of spray came out of the darkness to spatter the broad windows which covered the view to the ocean. The front of the house had been built into a fold of ground almost at the cliffs' edge.

Katherine Waring sat behind a coffee-table near the huge log fire at one end of the room. She looked up as the girl came in and smiled. It was a comradely personal smile that made her feel she was the one person Dr. Waring wanted to be there. She went over at once.

"Did you get coffee with your tray? Perhaps you would care for some more. Let me introduce you to the others."

Marsh turned to face them, her green skirt flaring out gently. The glowing fire was behind her and the lamplight was soft on her serious young face.

"My sister-in-law, Mrs Arkwright, and Surgeon-Commander Arkwright. Delia, this is Dr. Marsh Mowbray."

Marsh looked down on the pair seated together on a couch the other side of the fire. Mrs Arkwright raised her eyes from her knitting, nodded, and then lowered them again. She did not speak. Henry Arkwright got up. He was a big handsome man, very conscious of the naval insignia in his lapel and the responsibility of extraordinary courtesy that went with it. He stumbled across his wife's extended feet with an outstretched hand.

"Glad to see you on board," he said heartily. "Will you splice the main brace with your coffee?"

"A liqueur," Dr. Waring supplied. "Brandy or *crème de menthe*?"

"Just the coffee, thanks."

Katherine Waring turned her head. "Miss Peterson, will you have a liqueur?"

The young woman leaning over the piano at the opposite end of the room straightened up and sauntered over to the coffee-table. Her white crepe frock clung tightly to her thin body, outlining the shape of each leg as she walked.

"Evelyn Peterson, my husband's nurse, Dr. Mowbray. You have met Betty. She took up your tray."

Miss Peterson extended one narrow hand. The fingers were long and curved. The thumb and first fingers were bright with nicotine, the third was smudged at the tip with lipstick. Only the little finger was its proper colour but this seemed more claw-like than the others. She gave Marsh a long lazy look.

The fourth member of the group stopped playing and shut the lid of the piano. Marsh frowned slightly at his approach.

"Dr. Gair—Dr. Mowbray."

"We know each other, Dr. Kate," Dr. Gair said. "Quite well—almost intimately, one might say."

Marsh gave the young man a steely glance and opened her mouth to speak. Dr. Waring was regarding her closely. Gair got in before her. "We shared the same corpse for a year. Third year, Marsh, was it not?"

"How do you do, Larry," she said, in a closing-the-subject sort of tone.

"I will never forget that corpse, Dr. Kate," Laurence Gair remarked. "Or Marsh. We had to cut away chunks of fat before we could get to the intestines. Remember, Marsh? We couldn't agree on whether he had died of occlusion or over-eating."

'I remember," she replied bluntly. "Particularly the way you used the scalpel. I thought at the time you were destined for the abattoirs."

"Larry is Kingsley's junior partner," Dr. Waring interrupted, in a smooth voice.

"Oh yes," he declared airily. "I have advanced considerably since those days. What about you? Are you about to improve your lot, too, Marsh?" He glanced sideways from her to Katherine Waring.

Marsh was puzzled and annoyed at the note in his voice and the way the deep cynical lines either side of the mouth deepened. Before she could speak Katherine Waring had interposed again: "Dr. Mowbray leaves for England in a few days. I know you will all wish her luck in the difficult post-graduate course she is undertaking."

She turned back to the girl. "Will you play the piano for us? I should like Larry to hear you."

She must have heard me at the hospital, Marsh thought. I didn't think she knew.

Gair bowed gracefully, as though acknowledging verbal defeat. He led Marsh towards the piano. "Don't let her down, Marsh. I would be so disappointed. And here comes the devoted handmaid! What an entourage she maintains!"

He was referring to Betty Donne, who had come in hastily and was making straight for Dr. Waring. She seated herself on a floor cushion at her feet. Katherine Waring bent over her, asking some question. The girl shook her head in reply and put an impulsive hand on the older woman's in some gesture of comfort or reassurance. When Dr. Waring gently moved her hand away the flush deepened in the nurse's cheeks and she glanced at Marsh in a way that caused her to fumble and hesitate in her playing.

Surgeon-Commander Arkwright got up from the couch abruptly. "You play marvelously!" he called to Marsh. "Do you mind if I watch? Very keen on music."

He came round the back of the couch where Evelyn Peterson stood, her liqueur still in her hand. Her dark eyes were veiled and she lifted her glass to hide the little smile that broke over her lips. Arkwright lurched against her clumsily.

"I beg your pardon, my dear," he said in his boisterous voice. "It must be King's excellent brandy. I'm half seas over. Never do to upset a trim craft like you."

Mrs Arkwright said, without looking up: "Henry, some wool is on the table over near the door. Will you pass it to me?"

Why Marsh wanted to watch the group near the fire she did not know, but each time someone spoke her gaze would dart to Katherine Waring's face as though to see the older woman's reaction and thereby gauge her own attitude towards these people. As if sensing Marsh's gaze she turned and smiled. That smile of friendly camaraderie she had bent on her when she came into the room. The girl experienced the same warm feeling of a personal contact with her that set her apart from the others in the room.

"Don't stop," Arkwright requested. He had been standing in the curve of the piano and leaned nearer. She moved her hands to the keys again, struck a chord and then stopped. Footsteps sounded on the verandah outside the long-curtained window behind her. They moved without furtiveness, but Arkwright looked towards the window uneasily and then back at Marsh.

"What was that you were beginning to play?" he asked loudly.

"A lost chord," she said, getting up from the stool. "Do you mind if I stop now? My fingers are stiff. The ivory has made them cold."

Arkwright directed another look at the window and then followed her back to the fire.

"Sit here," Gair offered. He stood up, one hand fumbling in his pocket amongst keys and loose change. "I must excuse myself for one moment. There is something I forgot."

Marsh sat down, facing Betty Donne. The nurse's face was hectically flushed. Her eyes, wide open in a startled fashion, followed Gair's progress from the room.

"Sorry, sir," Gair said, brushing against Arkwright as he passed. "I deserve to be keel-hauled for being so awkward. I'll keep more to starb'd in future."

No one smiled, but Miss Peterson let a slight husky laugh escape her. When the door closed on him, Betty Donne got up and went over to the ocean windows. The rain was beating hard against the black glass, but she stared out as though the view was binding in its beauty.

Slightly redder in the face, Arkwright took a seat next to his wife. "Shall I wind some wool for you, my dear?" he asked. "Perhaps Miss Peterson would help me."

"I have enough, thank you, Henry," Mrs Arkwright replied, in an acid tone.

"If this weather keeps up you will have us all begging for knitting to do, Delia," Katherine Waring observed. "This is one of the wildest nights I have experienced here."

Evelyn Peterson crossed her legs and lit another cigarette from a stub. "I'm sure I'd find something better to do than knitting," she said, in her drawling throaty voice.

Marsh looked at her with a distaste reflected from Katherine Waring's face. The tight dress and the slow undulating movements were flagrant. Arkwright found it impossible to take his eyes from her.

Then Laurence Gair came back, with raindrops glistening on his sleek hair. He ignored the group by the fire and went to the windows. Like Betty, he stared out at the blackness and wetness of the night.

The desultory conversation lapsed. The only sounds came from the crumbling logs and the click of Delia Arkwright's steel needles, companionable noises which seemed oddly out of place. Marsh, stealing a look at Katherine Waring, saw the older woman's eyes moving from one to the other.

Betty Donne was sitting bolt upright on the floor cushion, her hands grasped tightly together. The firelight played on her feverish face. Miss Peterson's lower lip was a full sulky curve. Her eyes were lowered as she pressed back the cuticle of her right fingers with the nails of her left. Arkwright fidgeted next to his wife, who remained knitting and ignoring everyone. He found it impossible to keep still and got up several times—for a drink from the tray near the door or to put another log on the fire; finally for a pack of cards. He cast one last look at Miss Peterson's silken extended foot and then began an idle patience.

Marsh's gaze came back to Katherine Waring. The doctor was staring at her intently; a measuring, speculative look. The girl smiled at her warmly and confidingly, but this time Dr. Waring glanced away without response.

At last Laurence Gair left his position at the window. As he passed the piano he struck a swift harsh chord with one hand, set the lid down with a bang and made for the door. There he turned.

"Good night, everyone. I'm turning in. King said he would not be in again, Dr. Kate."

"I see, Larry. Good night."

Arkwright gathered the cards together. "I'm for my bunk, too. Are you coming, Delia?" She finished the row before she rolled up her knitting, piercing the ball with the needles.

Evelyn Peterson stretched herself, yawning like a bored cat. "The party seems to be breaking up. It's a pity King couldn't come back to hold it together. 'Night, folks!"

Marsh saw Betty Donne's hands clench. As soon as the door closed on Miss Peterson's graceful back she turned to Katherine Waring.

"You look very tired, Betty," Dr. Waring said at once. "Go to bed like a good girl. Thank you for helping through dinner."

The girl closed her mouth, nodded to Marsh and left the room.

Marsh stood undecided, with her back to the fire. She felt reluctant to leave. She wanted Katherine Waring to talk to her for a little while.

"How is the exhaustion?" Dr. Waring asked, as she walked to the drinks table. "You looked better when you came downstairs. I am going to give you a tiny dose of brandy. It will help you to sleep. Doctor's orders, but don't make a habit of it."

Marsh took the big glass between her hands. The liquid went down her throat like silk. "What a wonderful place you have here!" she remarked, for want of something better to say. The wind and rain and the crash of the sea on the rocks below the windows had been very clear in the silence between them.

"I hope the noise of the ocean won't disturb you. We have become so accustomed to it now. The wind makes the house alive with peculiar noises, too. Don't let any sound you cannot interpret worry you. I suggest you go to your room and stay there until breakfast. Betty can bring up a tray."

"1 would just as soon come down," Marsh said, surprised.

Dr. Waring moved to the door. She held it open. "You have been working hard, Marsh. Make the most of this opportunity to rest. Good night, my dear."

"Good night, Dr. Kate." The familiarity escaped her after hearing the older woman address her by name. It was the first time she had ever done so, and the warmth with which she had spoken stirred Marsh.

At the foot of the stairs Katherine Waring paused to light a candle from the lamp. The girl took it and began to mount the stairs. At the landing she turned.

"Good night," she said again, and then added politely as an afterthought, "I was sorry not to meet Mr Waring."

A strange expression passed over the upturned face of the other woman. Then it became serene and reserved once more. Marsh continued up the stairs with an odd sensation of discomfort.

V

Her clothes had all been unpacked and neatly arranged in drawers and cupboards. There was a hot-water bag in the turned-down bed and a pair of Marsh's severe white silk pyjamas lay ready. In the adjoining bathroom her few toilet articles had been placed side by side on the ledge over the hand-basin. No gesture of comfort had been omitted, even to the pile of magazines and light literature on the bedside-table.

A gust of wind, sucking the curtain out of the casement window, roused Marsh from the lethargy that had overcome her. She crossed to the window and the curtain blew inwards against her face. She held it aside with one hand. Her bedroom overlooked the red-soiled yard where her car was still parked in the shadow of the pine-trees. The thick evergreens formed a natural garage and would prove an adequate protection against the weather.

A flickering light from the house, probably a torch, swept across the yard as though to reassure her concerning her car. It was a quick, faint illumination but Marsh's eyes widened in a startled fashion. She was certain that someone was sitting in the driving seat of her little runabout.

She leaned out of the window, the rain beating down on her head and shoulders, but it was impossible to see anything. Presently she drew back and began to get ready for bed.

It was a comfortable bed, far different from the narrow hard mattress at the hospital. Marsh relaxed with a deep sigh. It was good to remember that there was no chance of being called in the middle of the night to go to a patient. She was to stay there until that little tense nurse of Dr. Waring's brought her a breakfast tray. She gave another sigh and lolled over on to her side.

She was warm and drowsy when the first disturbing noise occurred. She turned on to her back and opened her eyes wide in the darkness. Somewhere, not far away, a horse had whinnied. She recalled the stranger on horseback whom she had watched climbing the cliff. He was an odd person to go riding in such inclement weather. Marsh rolled back again and tried to recapture the warm drowsy feeling.

The effect of Dr. Waring's brandy had worn off. The idle thought of going downstairs to get another passed through her mind. She had been so relaxed and sleepy, and now the feeling had gone. She began with sheep jumping over a fence and worked through a series of other monotonous tricks to reciting *Materia Medica*. This last usually proved infallible.

Suddenly she was jerked into a tense listening position.

Between the rise and fall of the wind came an unmistakable sound of someone outside crying. It was as continuous as the crank and whine of the windmills the other side of the yard, but whereas one could become accustomed to the sound of the windmills, the steady moaning was infinitely disturbing.

"What a place for a rest cure!" Marsh muttered grimly, heaving herself up and feeling for her dressing-gown.

She had no idea of what she was going to do. Getting out of bed was a purely mechanical movement; as though she was back at the hospital and a patient was restless and disturbing the ward. She fumbled for matches and relit the candle, feeling a certain sympathy for Todd Bannister's complaints.

Shading the candle, she opened her door. The passage was dark and very still. It seemed unnaturally quiet, as though behind each of those closed doors the occupant stood waiting and listening. She crept down between them to the stairs.

The candlelight flickered dangerously as the draught swept up the stair well. Marsh steadied it, curving her hand completely around the flame, and began to descend.

At the foot she paused and listened. The sails of the mills still clanged harshly as they spun round in the gusty wind, but the moaning had stopped. She stood undecided. Her feet were cold and her nerves were on edge. Then an overwhelming urge for another brandy took hold of her, and she forgot about the crying. It may have been her imagination. No one else had been disturbed by it to her knowledge. She would find a drink and go back to bed.

A faint thread of light lay at the end of the hall. Kingsley Waring must still be in the library.

The library was the first room she had entered at Reliance. She had been cold and stiff from the long drive and had not observed her surroundings over-keenly. Only the fire and the wine had been of importance, although she did recall Katherine Waring opening an immense cupboard and selecting a particular bottle. All the liquor must be kept in that cupboard. The drinks in the living-room had been served from a tray.

Marsh blew out her candle, placed it on the table at the foot of the stairs and went forward. The door of the library was slightly ajar, but she knocked gently before pushing it open. A wave of sweet warm air rushed into her face.

The fire in the open place was a blazing stack of logs. A deep leather chair was placed with its back towards the door. From it a pair of long legs were stretched upwards to the mantelpiece. Marsh could see the top of a dark head and a slim twitching hand curved around a glass. Before she could speak a huge black dog arose from a shadowy corner and growled.

"Down, you brute!" said the man in the chair.

The animal retreated. The feet were removed off the mantel and the dark head peered around the corner of the chair. "What the hell do you want?"

The voice was slow and slurred. The face was a surprisingly young one, although deeply lined. A pair of dull eyes stared Marsh up and down deliberately, almost insultingly.

"I thought Mr Waring was here," Marsh said.

The young man laughed raucously, causing the dog to stir and make a noise in his throat. He got to his feet and went over to the cupboard.

"He's not here. He went out. He will be disappointed when he finds out what he missed. Drink?" He held up a bottle.

"Yes," said Marsh, before she thought. She passed over the young man's insulting inference. "Brandy."

She took the glass and drank quickly.

The young man stared at her with narrowed bloodshot eyes, "Who the hell are you?" he asked rudely.

She told him her name. "One of Dr. Kate's little pets," he suggested, with a sneer.

Marsh moved over to the fire and spread out her hands to the roaring blaze. "And who are you?"

"I," said the young man, punctuating his words as he drained. his glass, "I am the son and heir, Michael Waring. More brandy?"

"No," she answered curtly. "And you'd better stop, too. You're far too young to be drinking spirits."

Amelia Gullett, the ward sister at the hospital, had told her of Michael Waring. Barely twenty two and already he drank like a fish. His behaviour at the University, where he was supposed to be engaged on a medical course, was notorious. Only his parents' standing had saved him from disgrace and expulsion. At the rate he was going, even the Warings' influence would fail.

He was still staring at her, but a spark had come into his dull eyes. "Young, am I?"

He lurched over and seized her by the shoulders. "Tender in years, maybe, but not in experience. Take a sample of this."

Before she could turn her head Michael Waring kissed her hard on the lips. It should have been a silly adolescent show of defiance, but somehow, even while he held her, Marsh realized he was right. There was a viciousness about him that seemed almost decadent.

She gave him a push that made him break away and go reeling towards the armchair. He fell into it, cocking one leg over the arm and watching her mockingly.

"Father didn't miss much, after all. Another of Dr. Kate's little disciples, are you? So aloof—so untouchable!"

"Good night," Marsh said. She could see a likeness to Katherine Waring in the boy's drunken face, and felt sick.

"No, don't go. I want to talk to someone. To unburden my soul, as it were."

"Good night," she repeated, and made for the door.

Michael turned his head and spoke sharply. "Rex! The door!"

The big dog got up from its corner and padded across the room. It lay down across the doorway and eyed Marsh unwinkingly.

"Call him away," she ordered. "I must go back to my room. Whatever would your mother—"

"Whatever would my mother say if she could see her little pet alone with her own son like this?" he taunted. "Sit down."

She hesitated, glanced at the dog and then sat down. "You talk of Dr. Waring as though she were another person—no relation at all."

"My mother? What a wonderful woman! A remarkable woman! Am I right?"

"I consider her so," Marsh said stiffly.

"And my father? He is a wonderful man?"

"So I am told. I have not met him yet."

"Am I not fortunate to have two such remarkable persons as parents?"

Marsh did not speak. The note of mockery in Michael Waring's voice became overlaid with a tone of bitterness.

"Being the son of two such remarkable persons it is to be hoped that I become as fine and wonderful as them. It is a goal worth striving for—an ambition regarded with envy by all. I have unusual opportunities to become something great. There is nothing I can't wish to be. And I wish"—he put his head back against the chair and closed his eyes wearily—"I wish I was an imbecile like Sam. Quite happy and quite unconscious of the subtle cruelty of the world."

He remained there with his eyes closed in silence. Presently he opened them. "You can go to bed," he said in a tired voice. "Come here, Rex!"

Marsh got up. Pity for his youth and his wretchedness stirred beneath her disgust.

"What about you?" she asked. "You look worn out."

He turned his head and grinned up at her impudently. "Is that an invitation? Don't tell me you're losing your aloofness!"

"You talk like a dirty-minded schoolboy," she said coldly. "Your mother—"

"Oh, get out!" said Michael Waring angrily.

CHAPTER TWO

I

Marsh awoke with an indefinable sensation of shame. Her throat felt dry and rough. There was an ache between her shoulder-blades and another incipient one behind her eyes.

It was barely daylight, although it was nearly seven. The rain had eased but the wind still blew fiercely in from the ocean. The sky was heavy with clouds. It was just the sort of morning for those who could to stay in bed, but Marsh got up and pulled back the blankets as though to withstand temptation.

She went straight to the bathroom and turned on the shower. The water came down in a gentle spray. She surveyed it resentfully. An embryonic headache called for something stronger than tank pressure.

It was hard to conceive in that particularly hard and cold morning light that she, the reserved and unemotional Marsh Mowbray, had behaved with such indiscretion the night before. With her aching head and burning throat, she could not understand now the powerful urge that had caused her to leave her room and to go downstairs in search of drink; especially after Katherine Waring's light admonition and her advice to ignore all strange noises.

Marsh's eyes darkened with remorse. Dr. Kate must never know of her midnight prowlings or of her meeting with Michael Waring.

She donned the severe grey suit she had worn the previous day and picked up her trench coat. A good brisk walk before breakfast would do much towards restoring her equanimity.

The bedroom floor was still quiet, but when Marsh reached the bottom of the stairs she heard someone moving around in the kitchen. There was the cindery smell of a fuel stove burning and the pungent odour of freshly made tea.

Miss Jennet glanced up as the girl passed.

34

"Dr. Mowbray!" she called, looking distressed. "Does Kate know? I mean—she said I was to prepare a breakfast tray for you."

Marsh came into the kitchen. "I am going out for a walk before breakfast. It is such a—" She stopped. What she was about to say would have been quite ridiculous, as one glance through the window would have told Miss Jennet. "May I have a cup of tea?" she asked lamely.

The cups lay on a tray, each with its triangle of bread and butter, ready to be delivered to the members of the household.

"No milk in mine," Marsh said hurriedly. She could not bear the thought of tasting anything with a fat content. Her palate needed cosseting for a while.

"Just as well you came down, then," Miss Jennet chatted on. "I know what all the others like; although it is so difficult, what with Kingsley and Mrs Arkwright—though she doesn't like it to be known. But, after all, she can't help it, can she? It isn't as if a disease is a bad habit. But I'll remember no milk for you."

Marsh felt too lethargic to start on an explanation that she usually took milk in her tea, but she just did not want it that morning. She sipped the hot liquid and watched the little woman fill the other cups.

"Four. Miss Peterson. Oh dear, I wish Kingsley wouldn't bring her here. Five, six. Poor Michael! Where's my bottle of aspirin? I'll put it on his saucer. Seven. That's the lot."

She turned to rummage in a cupboard for the aspirin. Marsh listened dully to her chatter.

"Don't you want to do something when you see people making everyone miserable? It's all so foolish and so easily fixed. Kate could, you know, but she is so funny sometimes. We grew up together. She has always been like that, but I love her. She's the sort of person you'd die for, if you know what I mean. Have you finished your tea? No milk or sugar. I'll remember."

"Thank you," Marsh said, and set down her cup. "If Dr. Waring should inquire for me, tell her I went for a walk. What time is breakfast?"

"Eight-thirty. I'll tell Kate. She never gets angry, you know. But you feel awful if you do something she doesn't want you to do. It might rain again. Would you like to take an umbrella?"

Marsh thought it was an idiotic suggestion. You don't take umbrellas when you go out to walk. Anyway, the wind would have it inside out in two minutes. She nodded to Miss Jennet and left.

Outside on the verandah lay the big black dog, Rex. His eyes were closed but he opened them the instant he heard the footstep. Marsh stopped and surveyed him carefully, wondering if he remembered her.

He lay there with an unmoving gaze. Marsh took courage and advanced. The dog stood up on his front legs and bared his teeth with a growl. She glanced around her in irritation. The beastly animal lay in her path. There was no other exit from the verandah, unless she was prepared to vault the railing on to a flower-bed. She considered such a move would be a sign of cowardice and indignity. It would never do to let Michael Waring's dog know he had her bluffed.

The imbecile boy came across the courtyard, his long arms hugging a pile of logs. The sharp wind had reddened his eyes, and his nose and mouth were running freely. He was not a pretty sight but the girl watched him with relief. The wood was probably for the kitchen fire, which meant he would have to get past Rex himself.

The dog turned his head and thumped his tail as Sam approached. The boy grinned and shouted something unintelligible.

"Can you call this animal off?" Marsh asked. "He won't let me get by."

Sam looked at her with vacant eyes as he mounted the steps to the verandah.

"Tell him to move," Marsh said, ashamed of her irritation at the dull expression when she remembered Katherine Waring's superb patience the evening before.

Sam grinned again and lumbered along the verandah with his heavy load. Presently he came back with a length of plaited leather in his hand. Feeling in the thick hair about the dog's neck he slipped on the leash and handed the other end to Marsh. She took it and at once Rex lunged down the steps, pulling her along.

"I hadn't bargained for this," she said aloud, bending back

36

against the dog's weight. She looked back to the house. Sam was jumping up and down, shouting excitedly and throwing his arms about. The door from the kitchen opened and Miss Jennet came out. When she spoke to him the boy quietened and followed her meekly inside.

Marsh had no plan where to go. At first she was inclined to let Rex lead her where he willed. Then the thought that such laxity might lead to indiscipline caused her to shorten the leash and to force the dog's movements to suit her own. They came out on to the road, Rex pulling to the right. By this time Marsh had made up her mind to visit the point where she had stopped the car the previous evening. She proceeded along in some discomfort, the wind against her. Presently, in the face of such obstinacy, Rex gave up his abortive attempts to follow his own inclinations and padded alongside amiably. With the change of front Marsh was stirred to a faint liking for the black beast.

The sea was still raging on the rocks below the open point. Marsh stood near the edge, Rex still and silent beside her. Somehow the clean rain-washed air and the dog's obedience did much to dispel the jumbled emotions she had set out with. She stayed there for a few moments to test out Rex's loyalty and then stooped to release the leash. The dog did not move from her side.

Marsh regarded him with a certain misgiving. Such blind unreasoning homage might prove embarrassing. She plucked a branch from a nearby ti-tree, stripped it and flung it along the road with a word of encouragement. Rex went off at a bound. She followed slowly, a smile of grudging amusement on her lips. Amazing what one could do with animals. She must get a dog when she came back from England.

Rex came back to drop the stick at her feet. As she stooped to pick it up, the hair rose on the animal's neck and a low growl sounded in his throat. Marsh watched him uncertainly. Then she heard footsteps coming along the track that wound round the inlet. She slipped her hand through his collar as he barked and made a jerk forward. Out of the tangled ti-trees came the stranger who had ridden his horse along the cliffs the evening before.

He lifted his eyes and saw Marsh standing in the road. His gaze passed over her impersonally as though she was one of a crowd. The girl tugged at Rex's collar, but the dog would not budge.

"In trouble again?" asked the stranger.

"I don't think so," Marsh replied, annoyed at the man's impatient tone. He passed on without another word. She clipped the leash back and tried to pull Rex into movement.

"Of all the ridiculous creatures!" she told him. "What's the matter with you?"

At the bend in the road the stranger stopped and turned. He came back.

"I'll try," he offered, putting one hand on Rex's head. His fingers caressed the dog firmly before he jerked the leash. Rex arose.

"And I was just thinking I understood dogs," Marsh said laughingly.

The man ignored her remark. He did not even look at her as he handed her the leash, but strode on ahead, this time without a backward glance.

II

Vexed at the stranger's surliness and not wishing to repeat the performance, she permitted Rex to pull her where he willed. They went off the road into the scrub. The thickly growing ti-trees made it very quiet, but as they climbed out of a gully the sound of the sea became clearer. At the top of the rise it turned abruptly into a roar, and Marsh stood on the edge of the cliffs again with the surf lapping angrily around the rocks far below.

The cliffs sloped away towards the left almost to sea level, forming a small cleared plain. At first she thought this clearing was a freak of nature until she noticed the red and white flags standing in patches of vivid green grass, and the white sand-boxes standing in the protection of windbreaks made of dried ti-tree branches lashed together with wire.

She stood for a long while surveying this strange man-made

playground. It extended to the narrow rugged headland which separated the bay from the ocean. Then the dog lifted his head to the wind. He gave one short bark and jerked away the leash lying slackly in her hand. He went off at a long loping stride, his head now bent to the ground. The big black body diminished in size as he made straight for the headland.

Another bark was borne on the wind. It was a strange sound, almost a howl; as though the dog were in pain. With a vague thought of rabbit-traps, Marsh broke into a run.

She found him standing just outside a windbreak where the ground rose up to a hillock, and nosing unhappily at a pair of feet clad in rubber-stopped golfing brogues which extended from the entrance of the shelter.

Marsh was accustomed to bodies wrapped cleanly in white hospital gowns, lying in beds equally immaculate. Even her term on duty in the casualty ward, borne by her with some distaste, was not as bad as finding an untidy body needing urgent medical attention lying exposed to the weather in complete isolation.

The owner of the rubber-stopped brogues was a man a little past middle age. He lay on his face with his arms flung above his head. She turned him over with difficulty, bending her ear to the damp shirt. There were still signs of life, although his condition was poor. She could detect a faint heart-beat in spite of the noise of the wind whistling through the branches of the break. Kneeling on one knee she scanned the face anxiously. It was a handsome one, topped by a growth of thick silvery hair. In health it would be a rugged face, but just now the jowl hung loosely above the open shirt.

She stripped off her raincoat and the jacket of her suit to tuck around the unconscious man. She did not waste time trying to find out the trouble as there was no sign of visible injury, but she knew she must get help at once. The patient must get warm if there was to be any chance of strengthening the weak pulse.

Gripping him under the arm-pits she pulled him right into the shelter and adjusted the wraps again. She turned her head sharply as something caught her eye near the dog, who had been sniffing around inside the shelter. It was a bundle of clothing; a raincoat, a muffler and a tweed jacket and matching cap all folded neatly into a pile.

The dog would not let her go near them. He growled and squatted menacingly as she tried to take up the leash.

"All right, damn you!" Marsh said, and went off at a run.

She was a long way from Reliance, and to make the situation more uncomfortable it had commenced to rain. The whole width of the links and the ti-tree spinney lay in front of her, so she turned in the direction of the red roof visible above the pine-trees which marked the landward boundaries of the course.

She stumbled across roughs and over smooth fairways, ploughing through sandy bunkers and leaving her heel-marks for golfers to curse. Her thin shirt was wet on her back and the wind stung her arms below the short sleeves. Presently she came to a narrow car-track, made of loose stones. This, she discovered later, ran in and out the fairways for the convenience of the green-keeper. Grateful for the guide she ran along the heavy surface. After a short distance the track was barred by a gate with a notice on it requesting that it be closed after use. Marsh went through, ignoring the polite order in her haste.

The road had widened and was now a metal surface. At once that conveyed something to her. Todd Bannister—the hotel—the only decent road in Matthews. The red roof she had seen belonged to the Tom Thumb.

She slowed her pace to long swinging strides. Although the case called for speed there was no necessity to rush like a mad woman. Her appearance was already against her, so there was all the more reason to act in a dignified manner suitable to the profession.

The hotel seemed deserted, but she finally found a woman sweeping out the bar parlour. Chairs were stacked on the tables and a smell of beeswax and turpentine overlaid the odour of beer and spirits.

"Breakfast in a quarter of an hour," said the woman, taking up a mop and plying it with vigour. "No drinks until ten."

Marsh stood at the threshold, shaking the rain out of her hair.

"Is Mr Bannister about?" she asked. "I want to see him at once. It is most important."

The woman stopped mopping and turned to give her a longer look. "I am Mr Bannister's mother. What do you want?"

Marsh was getting cold. She had found a desperately sick man lying on the golf-links and had given up her clothing to him to run through the rain for assistance, and now some suspicious woman was detaining her with idiotic questions.

I want Mr Bannister to come with me at once," she said curtly. "There is a man lying unconscious on the links. He must be brought to shelter immediately. I am Dr. Mowbray."

Mrs Bannister gazed at her sceptically, trying to absorb this fantastic tale. Then she placed the mop neatly alongside the broom. "I will go and call Todd," she agreed.

"Please hurry," Marsh said, on a sneeze. "And could you lend me a coat or something?"

"You'll find one in here," Mrs Bannister replied, opening the cupboard under the stairs as she passed.

Screened by the open door the girl peeled off her sodden shirt and skirt. A pair of khaki overalls stained with paint and grease was hanging in the cupboard. She put them on and wrapped a man's overcoat nearly twice round her slim body, pulling the collar high to hide her bare neck. She backed out of the extempore cubicle and shut the door.

Lolling against the wall of the passage was the man who was now identified in Marsh's mind as the stranger on the horse. His eyes went over her impersonally enough, but she was ready to pass some withering remark when Todd Bannister came down the stairs.

"Hullo, Doc! Mother said you wanted help. Is it true you have a patient lying in one of the bunkers? What an odd place to put a patient."

"This is no time for jokes," Marsh said crisply. "Can you bring the car? And I want some blankets. Mrs Bannister, have you any hot water ready? If so, please fill any hot-water bags you can lay your hands on."

Todd Bannister said: "Dear Doc, you know where my car is. Have you forgotten our meeting so soon?"

"Todd, get a car from the garage at once. Mr Scott won't mind," Mrs Bannister ordered. "Mr Shane, you go with this young lady. She will probably need more assistance than Todd can give."

"Mother!" said Todd Bannister reproachfully.

Marsh turned her back and spoke to the stranger. "There is a sick man lying on the links. Judging by his clothes he must have been there all night. I would be glad if you could help me bring him to shelter."

"What is the matter with him?" Shane asked, following her down the passage.

"I don't know. I haven't examined him yet. Pneumonia, maybe."

She paced up and down outside the hotel impatiently until Todd Bannister arrived with a car almost as old as the one he had left on the road outside Matthews. He kept the engine running as Marsh and Shane got in.

"I see you two have met. Sorry about your breakfast, Bruce, old man, but it is better to start the day off with a good deed. Succour the wounded, you know."

Marsh said seriously, "There was no wound that I could see."

Mrs Bannister came to the window to thrust in an armful of blankets and nearly burned Marsh with a hot-water bag.

"Todd!"

"Mother mine?"

"Now, be sensible, Todd, and help Dr. Mowbray."

"Don't think that I have dragged myself out of bed just to take her for a joy-ride," he retorted.

Mrs Bannister stood back with a nod, and the car moved off.

"Follow the car-track through the golf-links. I will tell you when to stop," Marsh said.

Shane asked: "What do you propose to do with this man? Where are you taking him?"

"Where is the nearest hospital, Mr Bannister? We'd better go straight there."

"Thirty-odd miles away, my fair physician. We don't need hospi-

42

tals in Matthews. The place abounds with doctors holidaying with their pretty nurses. Didn't you find that out last night?"

"Then we'd better bring him back to your hotel," she declared.

"Mother will be mad at you." Todd shook his head at her in the mirror.

"I'm sorry about dragging you into this, Mr Shane, but I could not manage alone. You do understand?"

Shane, who had been whistling absently under his breath, brought his gaze round to her. "Quite," he said.

"Absolutely. Definitely. Indubitably," Todd Bannister said in mincing tones.

Having exacted a certain retribution for the stranger's churlishness, Marsh did not rebuke him. She was busy picking out the shelter in the distance.

"Stop here," she ordered. "Now, Mr Shane, just bring one blanket. I will roll the patient in it. It will make him easier to carry. Follow me and quickly, please."

Bending her head against the rain Marsh ran in a direct line towards the tee. The dog had disappeared but the man was lying where she had left him. One hand had moved free of the jacket she had tucked under his chin. She marked the alteration with a slight thrill. It gave evidence to some sign of strength in the condition. She bent her head over the region of the heart, longing for a stethoscope.

"In here," she called, as Todd Bannister and Shane climbed up the hillock. She took the blanket and rolled the sick man over expertly to spread it beneath him. Shane knelt on the opposite side, anticipating her plan of a cocoon wrapping.

A smothered exclamation from Todd Bannister, standing at the man's feet, caused Marsh to glance up. "What?" she asked.

Bannister's face was very white. She noticed the dark grooves under his eyes.

"The King of Matthews! Didn't you know? It's Kingsley Waring."

Marsh's hands stopped still for a moment. She glanced from Todd to Shane, who had eased his hand into Kingsley Waring's shirt. He was frowning heavily.

"There is still a faint heart-beat," she told him curtly.

"Quickly now. You take this end. And bring those clothes with you. I think they must belong to Mr Waring."

She had the other blankets ready in the car as the two men came up with their burden. They were panting slightly. Beads of sweat stood out on Todd Bannister's forehead. Kingsley Waring was heaved into the back seat. Marsh climbed in after him and began to unlace the brogues. She held the hot-water bag against the stockinged feet.

Out of nowhere Rex the dog appeared. He came up at long loping strides holding some object in his mouth which he dropped on the running-board of the car.

"Get going," Marsh ordered impatiently. "The dog can find his own way home."

Todd Bannister hurried to the driver's seat, but Shane paused to pick up the dog's find before he climbed in beside him.

"Where to, please?" asked Todd. "While I don't mind succouring the sick at my place, I do think His Majesty, and not to mention Mother, would dislike it heartily. The Bannisters and the Warings never did see eye to eye."

Marsh watched the sick man's face. "It really is Mr Waring?" she asked. "Dr. Katherine Waring's husband?"

"Sure is. He looks muchly the same as usual. Bit pale about the gills, of course. But surely that doesn't disguise him."

"Disguise him? Oh, I see. You are wondering why I had not recognized him. I missed being introduced last night. Drive straight on to Reliance."

Waring's head moved slightly and she lifted one drooping eyelid. The pupil was enlarged.

"Todd," Shane said suddenly, "where is Saracen?"

"Who, old boy?" Bannister asked, steering the carefully.

"My horse. I stabled him at the hotel last night."

"Sure you did. Isn't he there still?"

"No. I went to see him before I came into the hotel."

"Must have broken stall, Bruce. Don't worry, he'll turn up. But you know the old one about locking the stable door?"

"I do, and Saracen was in the stable when I locked it."

"Very odd. Very odd, indeed. Must ask Mother about it. Still, the place is fairly decrepit. Your nag might have kicked the bolt somehow."

Shane was silent for a while. "Yes, probably that is what happened. He must have tried to find his way back to the cottage. He cast a shoe on the links. The dog found it."

He lifted up the relic Rex had brought to the car. Marsh gave it a cursory glance and turned her attention back to Kingsley Waring.

The car turned into the track which led to Reliance. The heavy rain of the previous night had changed the sandy surface into a quagmire. Todd Bannister continued as far as he dared. As the car pulled up Marsh awoke from her abstraction to ask sharply: "What are you stopping for? Don't you know this is a matter of life and death?"

"Don't be terse, my querulous quack. No can do. Look at that mud. We'll be bogged. And not even for the King of Matthews can I let that happen to Scott's car. He has an uncertain temper before breakfast."

Marsh gave one look and got out of the car. "I'll go on to the house and get a stretcher brought back," she said, banging the door.

She squelched along, keeping as much as she could to the drier sides of the track. It was impossible to run. The mud was like a quicksand. She reached the house with her shoes caked.

III

Betty Donne was standing on the verandah looking out over the courtyard, but when Marsh called to her she started violently.

"Where is Dr. Kate?"

"She hasn't come downstairs yet," the girl replied. She looked at Marsh again and came forward quickly. "Where have you been? You look shocking. What has happened?"

She gripped Marsh's arm, her fingers biting through the thick cloth of the ancient overcoat she still wore.

"I found Mr Waring out on the golf-links. He is in a pretty bad way."

45

"Dead?" Betty Donne asked, in a fierce voice.

"Not yet," Marsh said, shaking off the girl's hand as the grip loosened. "I had him brought home in a car. We couldn't come any farther because of the mud. Is there a stretcher anywhere?"

"There is one kept in the lab, but it is locked. Mr Waring has the key."

"There is no time to go back and search his pockets now," Marsh said, irritated by the nurse's negative attitude. "Here! Take one of those deck-chairs to the car. It will serve. I must find Dr. Kate."

Betty Donne watched her go to the door of the house. "Hurry!" snapped Marsh, as she saw the girl pause. "The man may be dying."

Suddenly Betty Donne began to laugh. It was a low sound, but held a threat of hysteria. Marsh came back with a menacing tread. When the nurse saw her eyes she stopped laughing, picked up the folded canvas chair and hastened down the steps.

Half-way up the stairs to the bedroom floor she met Laurence Gair. He was wearing dapper sports clothes and surveyed Marsh's dishevelment with one raised brow.

"Good morning, colleague," he began.

She seized his arm. "Larry, ask Miss Jennet to prepare hot-water bags and to bring them up to Mr Waring's room. He is very ill. Don't ask any questions. Just do as I ask, like a good chap."

Gair opened his mouth, then shut it and went downstairs with a shrug.

Guessing wildly at Katherine Waring's room, she knocked at a door at the front of the house. As the evenly modulated voice answered she went in. Katherine Waring sat in front of her dressing-table coiling her long hair into the nape of her neck. Her eyes met Marsh's in the mirror, and the girl had one awful glimpse of her own appearance. Her face was pale and her eyes enormous under straggling wet ringlets of hair.

Dr. Waring turned round quickly. "My dear Marsh, whatever have you been doing? Where did you get those dreadful clothes?"

"At the hotel," she said hurriedly. "Never mind them. Dr. Kate—"

Katherine got up. "What is the matter? Why did you go out?"

There was something in her tone that reminded Marsh of what Miss Jennet had said. She sounded reproving.

She made a gesture with her hands as though to say explanations could come later. "It's your husband, Dr. Kate," she burst out. "I was out for a walk, but I did not know it was Mr Waring. He looks terribly ill."

Katherine Waring put down her brush and moved to the door. "King? Where is he?"

"They are bringing him up from the car. He must have been out all night. Didn't you know? Didn't you wonder where he was?"

The older woman gave her a fleeting glance. "No, I did not know. King goes for a walk every night. That is his room on the other side of the passage."

"Oh," said Marsh, "I see. Excuse me, I'll go and tell the men where to come. Larry is getting hot-water bags."

They came up the stairs as she spoke, Betty Donne leading the way. Shane had been relieved of his part by Laurence Gair, who carried the farther end of the improvised stretcher with the patient's feet pressed against his chest. Katherine Waring watched the scene from her doorway. She did not move or speak, and her face was quite blank.

Betty Donne went ahead into the room to prepare the bed. She looked up at Marsh through the open door. "High or low, Doctor?" she asked, in a brisk nurse's voice.

"High," said Marsh and Gair together. Marsh glared at him.

The patient was propped high with pillows. His breathing had become more audible but he was still unconscious. Marsh detected a hoarse note which sounded ominous. Then Miss Jennet came running up the stairs, her arms laden with hot-water bags, Marsh's own amongst them. Her face was troubled and she glanced in a concerned way at Katherine Waring.

Gair had been bending over the sick man. He straightened up and came to the door. "Dr. Kate, where does Kingsley keep his glucose? We will have to give it inter-nasally."

Glucose? Marsh thought. He must be a diabetic. I should have guessed. He must have had too much insulin.

"Glucose, Dr. Kate," Larry snapped impatiently. "Do you want King to go out under your eyes?"

But still she did not move, nor did she make any sign of having heard him.

With a muffled sound of exasperation Gair strode into the adjoining bathroom, Marsh at his heels.

"What about the laboratory?" she suggested, watching him search through cupboards and drawers.

He pounced on a coil of rubber tubing. "We'll need that," he said, taking it back into the bedroom. Then he began a search through Kingsley Waring's discarded clothes.

"I locked the lab myself last night," he answered Marsh, "and gave King the key. He always carries it with him." He held up the sodden slacks by the ends, shaking them vigorously.

"Damnation!" he exclaimed. He shot another anxious glance at the patient and strode to the door. "Dr. Kate—" he began.

Katherine Waring had left her position at her bedroom door, and was rapping gently at another one farther down. She held up one hand at Gair for silence.

"Delia, are you awake? Can I come in for a moment?" She opened the door.

Presently she came out again, with a jar in her hand.

"Here you are, Larry," she said, giving it to him. "Marsh, go and change your clothes. You have done your part for the moment."

IV

Marsh went back to her room, relieved and happy. Hitherto she had felt that Kingsley Waring's life depended on her and that the responsibility was hers. But now Dr. Kate was arranging matters and all would be well.

She stripped off her ludicrous clothes, wondering if her grey suit would find its way back to her. Todd Bannister had gone without a word after he had left Waring on his bed. The skirt would still be at the Tom Thumb. Somehow Marsh knew Mrs Bannister would see that it was dried, pressed and returned folded to avoid creasing. She looked the type. But the jacket and the trench coat—she could not remember if they had brought them in the car still wrapped around the sick man, or whether they had been abandoned in the shelter.

She lifted her head out of a towel with which she had been drying her hair and frowned at her reflection. There was something odd in the way Kingsley Waring's outer clothes had been folded neatly and placed in a corner of the windbreak. He must have had a hypoglycaemic attack while out on his nocturnal walk. Knowing himself about to be overcome he must have made for the nearest protection. But why take off his clothes?

Footsteps had sounded in the passage outside Marsh's door, and now a voice broke across her troubled thoughts.

"Miss Donne!" She recognized Evelyn Peterson's husky voice.

Betty answered shortly: "Yes? What is it you want?"

Kingsley Waring's nurse came along the passage so that the two girls were immediately outside Marsh's room.

"What is the matter with everyone this morning? People rushing up and down have interrupted my beauty sleep."

"Perhaps you should go to bed earlier," Betty suggested, in a meaning tone.

Evelyn laughed softly. "Perhaps. Did I hear aright? Is King ill?"

"Very ill. Maybe dying. I shouldn't know. I am only the nurse."

"So you are the nurse, are you? I think not. I will attend him. After all, he is my chief. You keep to your own side of the fence."

"Dr. Kate inferred—"

"I don't care what she said. I am going to nurse King."

Betty Donne spoke deliberately. "Mr Waring doesn't need your type of nursing now. He is a sick man."

Marsh heard a quick indrawn breath. Then Evelyn laughed again. It was a nasty sound. "You little devil, Betty Donne. I'd like to scratch your face for that."

"Try—and see what happens."

"I will one day. You've been asking for it. You and your sanctimonious Katherine and—yes, that frozen-up Mowbray wench."

Betty said coldly: "Go and dress yourself. You are wasting your time on me."

There was a slight scuffle of feet and Marsh opened her door quickly. She had had experience with bickering nurses before. Betty was holding off Miss Peterson by the wrists. The latter was white with fury and her thin hands looked particularly claw-like.

"Stop that!" Marsh ordered. "Miss Peterson, go and get your clothes on. You may be needed later."

Betty released her grip and slipped away without a word. The other girl retreated, rubbing her wrists and muttering angrily. Her dusky hair was tangled, not unattractively, half across her face, and Marsh could understand what had prompted Betty Donne's suggestion that she should go to her room. The house might be alive with persons to whom the human anatomy was an open book, but there was such a thing as innate modesty.

Katherine Waring, coming down the passage from her husband's room, nearly collided with her. Evelyn paused defiantly. Dr. Kate's eyes went over her.

"Get into whites, please, Miss Peterson. I want you on duty in Kingsley's room."

The girl half turned towards Marsh and gave her a triumphant smile.

Marsh reopened her door. "One moment, Dr. Mowbray!" She paused.

Katherine Waring came into her room.

"Shut the door and sit down for a moment." Marsh obeyed. "I think you will find working with Miss Peterson better than with Sister Donne. After all, she is my husband's nurse. He thinks highly of her."

Marsh stared at the older woman. "I?" she asked. "You mean you want me—"

"Yes, Marsh, you. I won't and can't attend King. Apart from ethics, I could not do it. Larry is essentially a surgeon. This case calls for a physician."

"What about Dr. Arkwright or someone else? I was told Matthews was over-run with notable doctors."

"I want you, Marsh. I have every confidence in you; more than in any other doctor here. I beg of you to do what I ask." She paused and dropped her eyes. "This is very hard for me to say, but King has tried to kill himself. He wants to commit suicide."

CHAPTER THREE

I

Marsh tried to absorb this announcement before she thought or spoke. It was hardly credible that a renowned surgeon such as Kingsley Waring should want to take his own life. His name was famous, his career at its peak. Suicide was such an appalling mess of a death. Of course, there were some unfortunates who were mentally ill—Marsh had had two such experiences at the hospital—but a wealthy distinguished man like Waring! There seemed no reason for such an attempt.

She badly wanted to ask Katherine Waring the reason, but dared not. Ordinarily a doctor had every right to demand an explanation of every detail of the prospective case, but somehow this was different.

The reserved unemotional tone had gone from Katherine Waring's voice when she had spoken. Marsh had never heard her speak thus before. It was almost as though the aloof honorary she had known intimately in the medical world was beseeching her for a favour. The position was fantastic.

Dr. Waring spoke first. "Marsh, you are so trustworthy, so discreet. I cannot let King die like this. You are a good physician, Marsh. I have been observing you for a long time now. You have a great career in front of you. Let this be the beginning. "

A sudden thrill of excitement passed through her. She had never before felt anything like this exhilaration of spirit; neither during her long hard years at the University, nor in the grinding monotonous term at the hospital. She thought she had lost the gift of spontaneity. But she answered Dr. Waring in her usual calm deep voice.

"I will attend your husband, Dr. Kate."

The older woman touched her shoulder for a brief moment. "Thank you, Marsh. I will give you all the assistance I can. King kept a medical chart. It is in the laboratory. You may find it of some use.

But first, have some breakfast. Things have probably become slightly disrupted in the kitchen, but ask Jennet to serve you at once."

The girl hesitated. "I would like to see the patient first. And Larry should know about your decision."

"A good doctor should keep herself fit," Dr. Waring declared, with a disarming smile. "Go and have something to eat. I will see King, and tell Larry about arrangements."

"Very well," she agreed reluctantly. Brushing aside a small feeling of rebellion she went downstairs.

Miss Jennet was not in the kitchen, but a clatter of crockery from the dining-room indicated that she was setting the breakfast-table. A smell of burnt fat pervaded the room, and the teacups that had stood on the table waiting to be filled were there again. This time they were stale with dregs and the triangular pieces of bread and butter were now crumbs or half-eaten crusts.

In front of the hot range, quiet and comfortable as an animal, stood the imbecile boy. Between his hands he held a long, shining, carving knife. He was passing one finger along its fine edge in a caressing way that was not nice to behold. The sharp edge made no impression on the thick hard skin of his finger. A soft crooning sounded from his wet lips.

"Sam!" Marsh said. Her voice rang out along the stone-floored kitchen.

The boy lifted his arm holding the knife. It was an action that implied defence. He turned round, the blade of the knife glittering in contrast to his dull eyes. He saw Marsh and grinned, shambling over to meet her. She watched his approach warily.

She realized she had frightened him and lowered her voice. "Sam, put that knife on the table, please."

The boy regarded her without a change of expression. Still grinning he came nearer, holding the blade like a dagger ready to throw.

"On the table, please, Sam," she repeated firmly.

He glanced down at the knife in his hand. Then his eyes came back to Marsh. They looked cunning at first, then bewildered and frightened. He was at the end of the table now, not eight feet from where the girl held her ground in the doorway. He was as dangerous as a panic-stricken animal is dangerous. She dared not take her eyes from him.

"Very well, Sam. Give it to me."

She held out her hand steadily for the knife. The imbecile's eyes blinked rapidly, and he smiled again, lifting his arm.

A quick footstep sounded behind Marsh as she moved sideways. Another minute and the boy, bewildered by her commands, would have thrown the knife straight at her head.

"Sam!"

It was Michael Waring. He went unhesitatingly to the boy's side and slid one arm along the lumpy shoulders.

"What game is this, Sam? What a fine knife! A beautiful gleaming strip of steel, so sharp and destructive and yet so lovely." His voice fell to a whisper as he gently ran his fingers down the imbecile's hands and gripped the handle of the knife without exerting any pull away from him. The knife was released, and Michael dropped his arm.

"Thank you, Sam," he said, as though in appreciation of a gift. The imbecile grinned happily and loped past Marsh out of the door.

"Did you frighten him?" Michael asked angrily. "You fool! What have you done to him?"

"I did not mean to frighten him," Marsh answered coldly. "I saw him playing with that knife and told him to drop it."

"You must have done something," he insisted. "Come on, tell me. Sam wouldn't act like that without cause."

"I did nothing. The boy should be locked up. He is dangerous. Has Dr. Kate seen him like that?"

"You blab to my mother and I'll root your tongue out. Sam is all right for those who know how to handle him. I'd rather see him dead with his brains out than sent to some foul institution. He shouldn't be locked up any more than Rex should be."

Remembering Rex's contrary behaviour earlier, Marsh decided that the dog had something in common with Sam. She forbore an acid comparison as Michael was still surveying her darkly.

Suddenly he smiled. "Have you seen my father yet? I waited up as long as I could to tell him about your visit, but he did not come in."

"Yes, I have seen him," she replied steadily. "What time did you go to bed?"

"About two or three. I can't remember clearly. Are you so interested? I thought my father was your concern."

"He is—very much my concern. I found him this morning lying on the golf-links. He had been there all night."

Michael's eyes narrowed and his mouth was a tight line. His hands were clenched in the pockets of his dressing gown.

"Are you trying to tell me he has been murdered?"

For a moment the girl was speechless. The question had stunned her even more than Katherine Waring's pronouncement.

"What are you saying?" she managed to whisper. "Are you mad? Your father had a hypoglycaemic attack. He is very ill."

Michael brought his clenched hands out of his pockets.

"Is he dying?"

"I can't tell you yet. Pneumonia might develop."

"Is my mother going to attend him?"

"No," said Marsh. "I am. Excuse me, please. I must have some breakfast and go to him."

Michael looked at her oddly. "You will do everything Dr. Kate says, of course."

"Your mother is a physician of wider experience than I. Naturally I will be guided by her advice."

She went over to the table. There was some toast in a rack near the stove and a tall silver coffee-pot.

"You fool!" Michael said again savagely, and slammed the door behind him.

Miss Jennet came hurrying back into the kitchen, clicking her tongue in distress. She made no secret of having overheard Michael Waring's heated words from the dining-room.

"You must not let Michael upset you," she assured Marsh. "He is a very hasty boy. He paints, you know. So temperamental. Let me pour your coffee. Honey or marmalade?"

"Marmalade, thanks. Is he any good?"

"I am not sure," answered Miss Jennet, as she busied herself at the stove. "He shows me his work occasionally. I find it startling, but

I don't pretend to be any judge. I do hope he behaves for a while. Poor Kate! And so like her, don't you think?"

Marsh grunted. She found Miss Jennet's chatter irritating. She so obviously prided herself on being able to see below the surface of the minds of others.

"So—so visionary, the pair of them. But Kate won't get temperamental. Is Kingsley very bad? Will he die?"

She turned round as she spoke, her face puckered with fear and misery like a child's before it bursts into tears; a child who wanted the world to be happy and suddenly found it was not.

Marsh got up and went round the table to her. How many times had she done this at the hospital; the firm kind hand on the shrinking shoulder and the firm kind voice asserting that everything that could be done was being done. Such cold hackneyed words, and poor recompense for the patient gratitude you received.

II

Katherine Waring was coming down the stairs when Marsh left the kitchen.

"Did Jennet give you something to eat? Good. Come now and I'll get you King's chart."

"Did Larry find the key?" Marsh asked, following the older woman out on to the verandah.

"The key? Oh, you mean King's. No, this is a duplicate."

The girl thought it was strange that Dr. Kate had not produced it during the frenzied search through Waring's pockets, but she said nothing. Her sympathy went out to her hostess in her tribulation and surmounted the little doubts in her mind. Katherine Waring was carrying a load that was unknown to all save her. She alone had been privileged to learn Dr. Waring's unhappy suspicions.

The laboratory was a square brick building, which lay apart from the house in the ti-tree spinney. It consisted of one large room with a smaller one leading out of it. Along one wall ran a stainless steel bench, holding test-tubes and chemicals in sealed bottles.

The other two sides of the room were lined with book-shelves that reached almost to the ceiling. A surgery divan lay on the left of the entrance, and a filing cabinet and a sterilizer were on the other side. The smaller room was used as a store-room and occasionally as a dark-room for inspecting X-ray plates.

Kingsley Waring might be a surgeon, but his interest in his profession was catholic. It embraced all spheres that went to make up the magic art of healing.

"There is everything here that any doctor could wish for," Katherine Waring said, as she specified the contents of the laboratory. "In that cupboard are the drugs. A limited supply of each, but enough for one patient's prescription. You may use whatever you want."

"Thank you," said Marsh, and crossed the room to examine the labels.

"In the store-room," Dr. Waring went on, in an even tone, "are the oxygen cylinders."

Marsh swung round abruptly. Words of sympathy and understanding crowded in her mind, too inarticulate to voice. She stammered slightly: "No—Dr. Kate. I trust it won't come to that."

Katherine Waring watched her struggle for expression. A smile hovered around her mouth. Then her eyes dropped away from Marsh and her lips took on a firmer line. The girl followed her gaze to the bench. On it, with its point resting in a fold of cotton-wool, lay a hypodermic needle.

"You know how he did it," Katherine Waring said softly. "A stronger injection of insulin. I think he wanted to die when he was walking on the cliffs. Poor King!"

The girl was silent. There was nothing anyone could say.

"Marsh!"

"Yes, Dr. Kate?"

"Do you think it would be better if we let him die? King wanted it so. What would you say, Marsh, if I asked you—"

"No," she said violently. "I could not have a hand in that."

Dr. Waring turned her back. She opened a drawer in the filing cabinet, and began to finger through folios.

"You know I could not do that," Marsh repeated. "Neither could you, Dr. Kate."

Katherine Waring lifted out a card. "I am not asking you to, Marsh," she said gently. "Here is King's chart, and the key of the laboratory. Do your best for him."

Surgeon-Commander Arkwright was coming up the path as they left the building. His face looked ashen in the dull cold light, and was further enhanced by a grey stubble which he had not yet removed.

"I have been looking everywhere for you, Kate. What is all this about King? Miss Peterson told me he was out all night on the links."

Dr. Waring motioned Marsh to walk ahead. The path was narrow.

"It is quite true what Miss Peterson said, Henry. An attack caught King when he was out on his walk last night. You know he always takes one before going to bed."

"I have considered that habit of King's unnatural for a long time, and last night was filthy. How did the attack come on? He told me at dinner he had had his needle."

"I don't know, Henry. Perhaps he forgot to take it," Katherine Waring replied vaguely. Marsh had the impression she was attempting to baulk Arkwright's intention to get to the bottom of the matter.

"King wouldn't forget," he said stubbornly. "I saw him heading this way before dinner. What probably happened is that he miscalculated his dose and had an insulin reaction."

Marsh glanced sideways to catch a glimpse of Dr. Waring's face.

Arkwright went on: "Another habit I never approved of in King is this experimenting in lines outside his own sphere. You can't do everything in medicine."

Still she made no comment.

"Well, what are you going to do, Kate? Get King to a hospital in town?"

"It is impossible. The track from the house to the road is impassable by now. He will stay here. Dr. Mowbray has my instructions."

"King won't like that," Arkwright said. "You know what he thinks of women doctors, if you don't mind me mentioning it."

"Yes, I know, Henry. Dr. Mowbray is thoroughly capable. She will be in charge of the case."

Arkwright fell silent at the note of finality in her voice.

Betty Donne was waiting on the verandah again as they approached. She drew Dr. Waring aside and Marsh heard her say quietly: "Mr Morrow has called, Dr. Kate. He heard about Mr Waring in the village."

Katherine Waring's face seemed to harden suddenly.

"Thank you, Betty. Where is he?"

"In the library. May I bring you a tray there? You haven't had any breakfast yet."

She replied to the nurse's solicitous suggestion a little impatiently and went indoors. Marsh, who was scraping her shoes free of mud, glanced up to find Betty's eyes on her. There was such an expression of dislike in them that she felt disturbed.

Henry Arkwright slid a hand under her elbow as they entered the house. He bent his head towards her confidentially. She could smell his stale breath and see the grey bristle on his chin and jowls more clearly.

"I know it is Kate's idea," he murmured, "but if you feel like slipping your moorings at all, I'll take over King. After all, a girl like you, a very attractive young girl, can't have had much experience in diabetic cases."

She thanked him for the offer and tried to edge away. Then Delia Arkwright came down the stairs with her knitting in her hand, and he moved away at once. Marsh took the opportunity to escape, and went up to look at her patient.

III

Laurence Gair was still in Kingsley Waring's room when she entered. He was rummaging through a tallboy, scattering clothes on to the floor. She eyed him coldly and suspiciously, but he did not appear abashed.

"Mind your own business, dear Marsh," he said, pushing the clothes back and shutting the drawers.

"I intend to," she retorted. "You may go now, Larry."

"Go? What do you mean?"

"Just what I said," Marsh said calmly. "Mr Waring is my patient. If I want to consult you, which is hardly likely, I will send Miss Peterson to tell you. Just now, I would like to examine my patient without any strangers present."

Gair looked angry. "What is this, Marsh? You have no right—"

"Dr. Waring's instructions," she interrupted. "I believe she told you the arrangements."

"Told me? She said nothing about it."

Marsh turned to the bed. "If you see Miss Peterson, tell her to bring my case from my room."

Gair came up to her swiftly. He was breathing hard. "My dear Marsh, I don't want to hurt you, but I will if you don't stop this nonsense. Get away from that bed."

She regarded him steadily. "If you try any strong-man stuff, Larry, I shall put in a report to the Medical Board. Dr. Kate has asked me to attend her husband, and that is the end. You may as well be resigned to it."

"Katherine Waring told me nothing of this. She came in, but she did not tell me. Are you sure you have it right? Aren't you just a little inexperienced to be handling a case like this?"

"Sneering does not help you, Larry. I am a physician, and I know more about diabetes than any surgeon does. How would you set about the case? Start cutting him up on the off-chance that the sugar will show itself in an abdominal cyst? You surgeons are never happy without a scalpel in your hands."

Suddenly his anger left him, and his face returned to its smiling captious mask. "You always were a rude girl, Marsh."

Marsh opened her mouth to retort, but a knock came at the door. Evelyn Peterson came in carrying a case. She had dressed herself in a tight-fitting white uniform but her dark unruly hair was uncovered. Marsh eyed it censoriously as she took the case. She snapped open the lid and took out her stethoscope, slipping it round her neck.

"Will you go now, please, Larry?"

"No," Gair retorted. "I want to talk to you."

Miss Peterson looked from one to the other with interest, and pouted when Marsh told her to leave the room but to stay within call.

Turning her back on Gair she drew back the blankets and commenced her examination. From the heart she moved up and down the lungs, listening intently. Her earlier prognostication was verified. The exposure to which Kingsley Waring had been subjected had brought on pneumonia. She began to plan her treatment and picked up the chart Katherine Waring had given her. In order to prescribe correctly she had to see the amount of insulin Waring might have taken on previous occasions.

"What is that you have?" Gair asked, as she removed the stethoscope to around her neck again. He had been quiet during the examination. Marsh had almost forgotten he was still in the room.

"Mr Waring's record," she replied, running her finger along the closely written lines.

"Where did you get it?" Gair demanded.

"Dr. Kate gave it to me," Marsh said, without looking up. "She got it from the laboratory. I do wish you'd go, Larry."

"I'm not going until I find out a few things. Firstly, how did Dr. Kate get into the laboratory? I locked that door last night and gave the key to King. You might recall my going out suddenly."

"Dr. Kate had a duplicate."

"Why didn't she produce it earlier, then?"

Marsh did not reply. She began to scribble on the prescription pad to still the tiny tremor of doubt that was moving around in her mind again. There was silence for a moment before Gair spoke quietly: "These are the rest of his clothes. They had been left on the verandah. When you came in, Marsh, I was making another search for the lab key. I wanted it because, surgeon or not, I fancy those oxygen tubes will be wanted. Look at this!"

He was holding up a bunch of keys on a ring. "Marsh, I swear to you I returned these to King last night after I had locked the lab. But the key I used is not among these."

"Dr. Kate said she had a duplicate," she said quickly. "Do you want me to doubt her word?"

"The key is not the only thing missing," he went on. "You, as

61

a physician, must know that all careful diabetics carry with them a supply of glucose in some form or other to ensure against a loss of consciousness from an overdosing of insulin. King is more than careful. Why, he even keeps to an unnecessary diet."

"Of course I know," Marsh interrupted shortly. "Well?"

"King always carried his in a small silver box. I believe it was once a snuff-box. He was rather proud of it. Where is it now, Marsh?"

"What are you trying to say, Larry?" she asked, looking at him squarely.

He shrugged and turned aside. "I am trying to give you some sound advice, but I know I am doomed from the start. Katherine Waring is up to no good, Marsh. I am convinced of that. Be a sensible girl and let me look after King. If he were conscious he would want it."

"No, Larry. He is my patient."

Gair sighed. "Marsh, you fool! Don't you realize what I am trying to tell you? You are only a tool of Dr. Kate's. You will do everything she says. Do you want to become implicated in such a scandal?"

"Stop talking ambiguous nonsense," she said, keeping her temper in check. "If you can't come to the point, get out."

"Very well, Marsh, if you want it straight. I think Katherine Waring is attempting to murder her husband."

Marsh dropped her eyes to the pad under her hand. She was thinking of the correct and the most non-committal reply to make. Had she not been the confidante of Katherine Waring, this no less astounding accusation would have been easy to meet.

"Well?" Gair asked impatiently. "What do you say to that?"

"I repeat—get out! I have been ordered to do a job, and I intend to do it."

Gair ran his hands through his hair in exasperation. "Marsh, are you blind or so besotted with Katherine Waring that you would help her kill her own husband?"

Her temper was rising. Discretion, more familiar to her than wrath, was forgotten.

"The job I intend to do is to make her husband well again," she said fiercely. "I am the only physician in Matthews Dr. Kate can trust. And if you knew what she was suffering you would hold that vile tongue of yours. Why should she want to murder her husband? Kingsley Waring tried to kill himself last night."

Gair glanced frowningly from Marsh to the patient in the bed and back again.

"Now, for the last time," she said, taking advantage of his lowered guard, "get out."

He moved to the door. When he turned round he had recaptured his customary suavity.

"You poor simpleton, Marsh. Do you really believe that? And she wants you to save the man she loves, I suppose. Don't you know what everyone else knows? They haven't lived together for years."

"There are other things besides physical love. Companionship and their work."

"They haven't even worked together for years. They are two separate magnificent entities that happen by chance to share the same house."

Marsh did not speak again. She tried to think she was not interested in what Gair was saying.

"If King gets better it will be amusing to see what he does; not that I think for one minute he will be allowed to recover. His death is going to be the perfect murder, because no one who knows about it will be able to do anything—even if they were willing to risk the scandal. Dr. Kate will see to that. Yes, Marsh—I, too, will hold my tongue. What good would it do me to do otherwise? But I intend with all the persuasion and coercion I can muster to make you realize just how rotten Katherine Waring is under her high-bred exterior."

The girl continued to ignore him. "Marsh," he said abruptly, "you funny little loyal creature, I think I could almost love you."

She looked up at last, but Gair had slipped out of the room before she could speak.

IV

In the bed Kingsley Waring was showing faint signs of consciousness.

Marsh watched him anxiously. The task Katherine Waring had set her was going to be difficult. She wished desperately for her to appear to check the plans for treatment. If the patient had been an ordinary one at the hospital, just a sick body with no background or personal associations, she would not have felt like shirking responsibility. But the patient was a well-known figure and this was his own home.

She took out her thermometer. In spite of his desperate state, Waring seemed to understand what was required of him. He did not fight against her touch, but rather co-operated eagerly; or so it seemed to Marsh, who noted the struggle with a slight frown. She took the temperature and the respiration count and marked them on the chart. Then she went to the door.

Outside, the passage was empty. "Miss Peterson," she called.

Someone was moving about in Katherine Waring's room opposite. She crossed the hall and tapped at the door. "Dr. Kate? May I come in?"

Evelyn Peterson opened the door. "Were you wanting me?" she asked coolly. "What are you doing in Dr. Kate's room?" Marsh demanded.

The nurse was quiet for a moment. She was deliberating an answer which was obviously going to be a lie. "Dr. Waring asked me to tidy her room."

"I did not hear her come upstairs."

"You don't hear everything, Dr. Mowbray." The girl's tone was impudent, but held an underlying significance which stopped Marsh from delivering a rebuke. She tore a sheet off the pad and handed it to her.

"Get this from the laboratory immediately."

Evelyn's lower lip pouted at the peremptory command.

"I am not used to being spoken to like that. I volunteered for this job, and I don't intend to be pushed around."

"You are nursing for me now," Marsh answered. "You will have to get used to my manners."

Kingsley Waring and Larry had ruined the girl as a nurse. She could do with a term at the hospital.

When Evelyn had gone downstairs, Marsh could not resist a glance into Katherine Waring's room.

"Tidying it!" she exclaimed to herself, surveying the open drawers, and the bed a litter of books from the bedside table. The nurse had been searching for something amongst Katherine Waring's belongings.

Marsh straightened the room. Dr. Kate was going through enough without adding this new disturbance to the list. She experienced an odd sense of impropriety as she folded and laid away clothes, and replaced the books. Footsteps came up the stairs and then along the passage. Thinking it was Evelyn Peterson back again she continued with her work. Presently she glanced up to the doorway. Delia Arkwright stood there, watching her suspiciously.

Caught unawares, Marsh made a halting explanation, not unlike the nurse's cooler reply. "Dr. Kate's room was so untidy. I thought I'd straighten it."

"Henry said you have the care of my brother," Mrs Arkwright said. "Do you think that is wise?"

"What do you mean?" Marsh asked sharply.

Mrs Arkwright ignored her question. "Henry is agreeable to relieve you of the task. It would be better for everyone concerned."

Marsh looked around the room to satisfy herself that everything was in order, and then walked towards Mrs Arkwright with purposeful steps.

"Listen," she said, in a firm voice, "Dr. Waring asked me to attend her husband. I accepted her invitation. That is all. Would you do me the favour of making that quite clear to everyone below-stairs?"

For a moment Mrs Arkwright's expression of perpetual disdain vanished and she looked more like an irate fish-wife. She struggled against an inclination to behave like one.

"You have excessively bad manners, young woman. I insist on seeing Kingsley."

"He is very ill. He will not know you."

"Hasn't he regained consciousness?"

The girl thought she detected a faint note of relief in the woman's voice. "He has come out of the coma," she admitted, reluctant to talk of the seriousness of Waring's condition.

"I will see him," Mrs Arkwright repeated.

"Very well. Come with me."

The patient was moving restlessly on the bed, and his eyes were open. Marsh watched for a sign of recognition as Delia Arkwright came up to her brother.

"Kingsley," she said authoritatively, placing her fingers on the sick man's hand.

The hand moved and he began to mutter. Marsh went to the other side of the bed, keeping a close watch on Mrs Arkwright as she bent over to catch the words. She did not like this at all. It was all so unprofessional. Lay people should know better than to demand entrance to a sick-room, even though they might be close relatives. Relatives were a nuisance.

Evelyn Peterson came back with a covered kidney dish. She saw Mrs Arkwright and said quickly: "What is he saying? Can you hear anything?"

"Nothing intelligible. Are you nursing Mr Waring?"

"Any objection?" asked Miss Peterson truculently.

Marsh broke in: "I must give the patient an injection, Mrs Arkwright. Will you go now, please?"

She stepped back from the bed and withdrew as far as the end of the room, as though to show she would leave when she was ready and not before.

"The old harridan," Miss Peterson murmured, from her side of the patient.

The muttering had started again, and now and then a word was distinguishable. The door opened quietly and Katherine Waring came to the foot of the bed. She watched her husband's face without expression as he struggled to speak.

"Every doctor . . . mistake," he panted. "My duty . . . my duty," and the voice lapsed again into a mutter.

"There is no point in your staying, Delia," Katherine Waring said. "Dr. Mowbray will keep you informed as to Kingsley's progress."

"Progress? Isn't he dying, Kate?"

Marsh glanced up from her work quickly. She felt that by looking at Dr. Kate she could spare her the impact of the crude question. But Katherine Waring did not wince, neither did she reply to the untimely question. She merely moved across the room and opened the door. The action was significant enough and Mrs Arkwright went with as much dignity as she could assume.

"And don't come back," Miss Peterson said under her breath.

Marsh tried to think of something fitting to say to Katherine Waring and failed. Instead she discussed her plans for treatment just as though they were back at the hospital. The older woman listened attentively, nodding approval but rarely making a comment. When Marsh faltered slightly over her suggestion to have the oxygen cylinders on hand, she inclined her head more slowly. Presently she left the room, and Marsh heard her door shut opposite. It did not open again until a gong was touched softly on the ground floor, signifying lunch.

She sent Evelyn to have something to eat, and the nurse and Dr. Waring went along the passage without a word between them. Marsh did not dare leave the patient. He had grown more restless and needed watching. He had become more talkative, too, and now and then a flash of full consciousness entered his eyes. She could see he was puzzled by her presence.

Half an hour went by and Evelyn Peterson came back along the passage with Katherine Waring. This time a few low words were spoken outside the door before Dr. Waring went to her own room again.

"You are to go down for some lunch," the nurse said. "Dr. Kate's orders."

Marsh got up. "The patient's condition is unsettled. You must stay here all the time with him."

The girl reddened angrily. "Do you see this, Dr. Mowbray?" she asked, pointing to the badge pinned at the low neck of her uniform. "I did not earn that for nothing."

"See that you continue to," Marsh retorted coldly, from the doorway. "And while you are under my instructions, please do not answer me back."

V

She ate her meal in solitude. Once or twice Miss Jennet put her plump worried face through the servery to inquire after her wants, but beyond that she did not see any other members of the household. She had expected to be bombarded with questions regarding her patient's progress and suspected that the reason for being left alone was due to Dr. Kate's intervention. Presently, unaccosted, she returned to the sick-room.

She paused outside for a moment, glancing over her shoulder at the closed door opposite. Was Dr. Kate still convinced that her husband had tried to kill himself? Marsh knew that the possibility of his recovery was remote. It seemed a waste of time and energy to go through the form of treatment when he wanted to die and would most probably do so. She gave herself a little shake, ashamed of her musings.

Kingsley Waring's breathing was audible even through the door. He must have rallied slightly, for Evelyn Peterson was speaking to him.

"Where did she put them?" the nurse was asking.

"King—answer me. Where did your wife put them? In her room? King, I beg of you—it's Evelyn. Try to remember."

Marsh opened the door quickly. The girl was bending low over the sick man, her hands on either side of his head. She was shaking it to and fro.

"Are you crazy?" Marsh demanded furiously, running forward. "What are you doing to him?"

She pulled her away roughly, and sent her reeling across the room. Waring's appearance was shocking. She felt for his pulse.

"Send someone for the oxygen," she shot at the nurse. "And don't you come back. Tell Donne I want her."

Evelyn Peterson's voice rose sharply. "I must get him to speak. Let me near him. Please, Dr. Mowbray."

"Are you a fool? This man is dying. Get that oxygen at once."

"If he dies she will ruin me. He must tell me what she has done with the papers." The nurse's face was desperate as she made a move to get past.

Pushing the girl out of her path Marsh went to the door. Laurence Gair was mounting the stairs and she called to him in relief.

"Larry, the cylinders in the lab. Get someone to help you with them quickly. Mr Waring is nearly gone."

She crossed the passage. "Dr. Kate," she called, rapping at her door. Without waiting for a reply she went back to Waring to do what she could for him.

The next half an hour was a nightmare to Marsh. She barely raised her eyes from the bed and Kingsley Waring's face, but she knew Katherine Waring was there and Betty Donne. While somewhere on the outside Laurence Gair hovered. Then she felt Dr. Waring's hand on her shoulder and she realized that the immediate danger had passed.

All through the afternoon her attention was fixed on the gauges on the cylinders. Betty Donne went down for her dinner, but when she came back there was no instruction for Marsh to do the same. Dr. Kate knew she could not leave the patient now. It was only a matter of time.

At the hospital, with the patient an unknown personality, the situation was viewed cynically. The sooner death came the sooner one could get one's meal. It seemed so futile to Marsh to keep checking the cylinders and injecting stimulants, when she knew for certain it was of no avail. She had only to remove the oxygen mask for a longer interval and all would be over. Then Kingsley Waring would be happy and she, Marsh, could go about the business of living.

She endeavoured to shake off this defeatist mood. While there was a flicker of life it was her duty to encourage it. Waring's life was neither his own nor his doctor's to be thrown away like a disused mechanical instrument.

He was conscious enough now to obey her instructions. One

hand clutched feebly at the long tubing as though clinging to a life-line. He seemed to Marsh to be regretting his attempt at suicide. Once or twice he tried to speak and she called Katherine Waring from her room. Each time she stayed at the foot of the bed, not uttering a word and without attempting to touch her husband. The intervals she spent in the room were brief, but she came quickly when Marsh sent Betty Donne to call her.

With nightfall the wind rose again, and the rain rattled against the window-panes. The surf below the house seemed to boom and break in time with Waring's breathing.

Marsh was very tired. The sheer monotony of the two sounds wore her down. She began to wish desperately for the end, but when Betty Donne offered to relieve her for a brief spell she answered her sharply and stayed where she was.

It must have been about ten o'clock when the music started. The sound of someone playing the piano broke in on Marsh's conscious-ness slowly. Waring had started to mutter again, and in trying to catch his word she was irritated by the waves of music that floated up from the living-room. It was music that she was familiar with, the same movement she had played the previous night. It opened with sombre diatonic chords and then drifted into a slow and poignant *andante*.

She spoke to Betty Donne. "Go downstairs and tell that indecent person to stop playing at once."

The nurse went out of the room. Marsh waited for the music to stop. She was standing right over the sick man, with her head turned away as she listened.

Then Kingsley Waring spoke. The mask had slipped from his face. He gasped for breath and with his eyes on Marsh's face jerked out vehement words between pauses.

"You . . . devil, Kate. I . . . I've . . . always loved . . . you."

The girl turned on him swiftly. His eyes were wide open for a minute, then they flickered and fell half-closed. His lips moved but no sound came from them. She snatched up the mask and placed it back on the exhausted face. The cylinders hissed.

"Breathe in, Mr Waring," she ordered sharply. "Breathe in . . . breathe in."

Betty Donne entered the room quietly.

"Get Dr. Kate again," Marsh said to her. "Why is that person playing still? Didn't you go downstairs? Who is it?"

"Michael," the girl replied. "He won't listen to me. He is drunk."

"Filthy swine," Marsh said under her breath.

This time Katherine Waring did not come to the foot of the bed. She stayed in the doorway, staring at the figure on the bed with its face nearly obscured by the oxygen mask. She glanced at Marsh, feeling her eyes on her. Then she moved over to the bed and lifted the mask for a moment. A slight spasm of pain crossed her fine features as she saw the changing face of her husband.

"Dr. Kate—" Marsh began, her voice deep with emotion. The other woman looked at her again. The girl strove to speak.

"Michael," she jerked out. "Do you think . . . Ask him to stop playing. Miss Donne says he is drunk."

Katherine Waring nodded slowly and left the room.

With her finger on Waring's flickering pulse Marsh waited. It should happen soon now. The room had grown suddenly quiet. Betty Donne stood like a statue on the opposite side of the bed, but she shuddered when a noise came from the dying man's throat.

The music stopped abruptly, breaking off in the middle of a bar. Then came a discordant crash of chords as though Michael was banging the keys with closed fists.

The mask had slipped again from Kingsley Waring's face, and Marsh did not replace it. The eyes were half-closed above still eye-balls. The mouth slowly sagged open.

CHAPTER FOUR

I

It was after midnight when Marsh finally left Kingsley Waring's room. She fumbled her way down the passage to her own room like a drunken woman. The house was quiet, as quiet as the death-room she had just left. Somehow she had managed to stay erect until all the others had retired, Katherine Waring in a state of control which Marsh would have regarded with apprehension in any other.

Her feet felt leaden as she tried to tiptoe, and when she located her own room and pushed open the door she reeled against the jamb in exhaustion. Fully clothed she collapsed on to the bed, her mind and body sodden with weariness. She tried to rouse herself and put up one hand to turn down the lamp, but the effort was too much. She was asleep almost before her relaxed hand dropped back.

She did not awaken until Miss Jennet's gong sounded for lunch. Downstairs the rest of the household, quiet and subdued, were gathered in the living-room sipping pre-luncheon sherry; all except Katherine Waring. She was still in her room, and Marsh, going down after a hasty toilet, met Betty Donne bringing up a tray.

The nurse was very pale now, but her eyes still shone with a peculiar brightness. Her movements conveyed a fussy eagerness. All she wanted was to wait on Dr. Waring, run errands for her and make herself indispensable.

Marsh found a silent group in the living-room. Surgeon-Commander Arkwright was the only one attempting to say anything, but as he spoke in such a hushed tone and repeated his conventional clichés so often no one listened. His wife sat beside him, her hands working together as though she missed the knitting she had evidently discarded for the time being. Michael Waring watched her fidgeting hands with hazy eyes. Marsh was shocked at the appearance of his young face, so deeply lined and puffy with drink. He held a cigarette in his shaking hand and ash was scattered all over his clothes.

At the windows looking out to the ocean Laurence Gair stood with his back to the others. Miss Peterson was alongside him, addressing him in low tones.

Marsh, who had been standing in the doorway reluctant to join them, glanced over her shoulder as Betty Donne came hastily down the stairs. She still carried the tray and there were traces of tears on her face. She hurried into the kitchen.

Then Katherine Waring came slowly down, stately and remote in her black dress.

They all turned towards her as she entered the living-room, and Henry Arkwright rushed over to her side, clumsy with sympathy.

"My dear Kate, my very dear Kate. A shocking blow! Like losing the ship's rudder. But you must keep your flag nailed to the mast. A splendid fellow, King!"

He wanted to throw a supporting arm around her shoulders, but she held him off by giving him one hand while she extended the other towards Delia Arkwright, who took it without a word. It seemed to Marsh that Mrs Arkwright was waiting for words of condolence from Dr. Kate, obstinately refusing to be the first to sympathize.

Michael Waring lurched to his feet as Katherine Waring looked at him gravely.

"My dear mother," he began, drawling the words, but something in her gaze stopped him from saying anything further. He fell back into his chair with a mutter.

She waited for Gair, who came forward slowly and touched her hand for an instant. "King was a great surgeon. He will be missed very much."

Still at his side Evelyn Peterson spoke up defiantly. "I am one of those who will miss him the most."

"I am sure you will," Katherine Waring answered gently, and Arkwright gave a slight cough. The lines either side of Gair's mouth deepened.

"Marsh, my dear," said Katherine Waring. Her voice was soft and meant for her alone. She pressed the girl's hands.

"Dr. Kate, I—"

"You did all you could. You did a grand job, Marsh."

Miss Jennet came to the door, easy tears spilling out of her eyes when she saw the drawn face above the stark black dress. Dr. Waring patted her hand gently and led the way to the dining-room, her head high and her shoulders firm and straight.

"Magnificent woman!" Arkwright muttered to Marsh.

"Shouldn't remain a widow long. They say Simon Morrow—"

Marsh moved away from him in disgust.

Luncheon was not a very pleasant meal. Almost at once, Dr. Waring began to speak of funeral arrangements. It would take place the next day.

"I know King would have liked to be buried in Matthews," she said, not looking up from her plate. "Perhaps, Henry, you could finalize matters in that direction."

"Certainly, my dear Kate, certainly. You couldn't have thought of a better notion. King loved this place."

"I want the funeral to be private. I know you all would like to stay for it, but afterwards ..." her voice trailed off.

No one spoke. She turned to Marsh, who had been avoiding Gair's sardonic gaze. "It seems a pity that this tragedy should interrupt your well-earned holiday, Marsh. I shall be here for a while, and if you should care to stay on it would make me very happy. Will you, Marsh?" Her tone was almost compelling.

When the girl agreed to stay the mockery went out of Gair's eyes and he frowned. He addressed his hostess.

"Forgive me, Dr. Kate, but I must ask your permission to remain here for a short while. I was working on something for King in the laboratory. I am sure he would want me to finish it. We must carry on the way he wanted, mustn't we?" He spoke easily, and Katherine Waring inclined her head.

"Very well, Larry."

"Naturally," he went on, "I must ask for Miss Peterson's assistance. There is such a number of notes to check. She knows King's handwriting so well, don't you, Evelyn?"

The nurse, who had been sitting pale and silent, hardly touching her meal, suddenly gave Gair a dazzling smile.

"I certainly do, Larry."

Dr. Waring glanced from one to the other, the thin line between her brows deepening.

"Sister Donne could be of the same help," Delia Arkwright stated flatly. "There is no reason why Miss Peterson should be detained."

Betty Donne, who had been listening tensely, interrupted eagerly, "Oh yes, please, Dr. Kate."

"You keep out of this," Evelyn said angrily. "I know the job Mr Gair wants done. You couldn't do it."

Gair pulled the carafe towards him and poured water into his tumbler. "If it is all the same to you, Dr. Kate," he bowed towards her, and also to Delia Arkwright, "Miss Peterson would be more suitable. Knowing King's handwriting so well," he added, a malicious gleam in his eyes.

"How long will the work take?"

"I am afraid I cannot tell you," he replied, his eyes on Marsh again.

Then Miss Jennet came in with the coffee. When she reached Michael she whispered to him. He looked up at her, and rose to his feet.

"What is it, Jen?" Katherine Waring asked. "Where has Michael gone?"

The little woman said apologetically: "I knew he wouldn't mind, but I have run out of wood in the kitchen. He has gone to get it for me."

"Where is Sam? That is his work. We must keep him to his tasks if he is to show any advancement. I told you that before, Jennet."

She began to back out of the room. "Yes, I know, Kate. But I can't find Sam anywhere."

Dr. Waring frowned. "When he comes in, send him to me. He must learn a sense of responsibility, and the jobs I have set will help him that way."

She got up from the head of the table. "Has everyone finished? Marsh, I want you in the library. Will you excuse us, please, Delia?"

"Perhaps the boy has run away," Arkwright suggested, as he got hurriedly to his feet.

Miss Jennet, who was still at the doorway, agreed eagerly.

"Such a relief for you if he has gone, Kate dearest. You know, he has been behaving in such a funny way lately, I can't help thinking something—" Her excited voice suddenly faltered as she looked up at Katherine Waring. "I must get back to the kitchen."

Marsh went to follow Dr. Waring, but Betty Donne slipped in ahead of her. "Dr. Kate?"

"Yes, Betty? What is it? I am in a hurry."

The girl's flush was rising again. "Dr. Kate, please let me stay here with you for a while. At least until the others go."

"My dear girl," Dr. Waring said, regarding her closely. "You look quite feverish. Are you all right?"

"Yes—no. Yes, I'm quite well. Please let me stay." There was a beseeching note in the girl's voice.

"Very well, Betty," she agreed, after a short hesitation. "Perhaps you could go and help Jennet in the kitchen."

The nurse swallowed. "Anything you want, I will do, Dr. Kate." She shot a look of animosity at Marsh as she turned away.

II

The library was cold and just a little stuffy; as though it had not been aired properly since the night Marsh found Michael Waring there. Dr. Waring pulled the windows down at the top, drawing back the heavy drapes. A fire was set in the open hearth and she knelt before it and waited until it crackled and blazed. Then she rose to her feet and went to the cupboard.

"Drink? What would you like?"

"Not for me, thanks," Marsh said. She watched the other woman pour herself one.

"Sit down, Marsh." She pulled a chair nearer to the fire. "Cigarette?"

"Thank you, Dr. Kate." The girl sat down, her eyes following her hostess as she moved around the room. Presently she came to stand behind her chair and Marsh looked at the fire instead.

"About the death certificate, Marsh."

"Yes, Dr. Kate?"

She moved again and placed her empty glass on the table. "You will be able to give one, you know. You treated King. You haven't written one up yet, have you?"

"No, I wasn't quite sure—"

"There need be no post-mortem," Dr. Waring interrupted. "You have nothing to worry about. You are entitled to sign the certificate."

"Very well," Marsh said, half-rising. "I will do it now if you like."

Katherine Waring went to the desk at once. "It need only be a simple affair," she said, taking a sheet of paper from a drawer. "Here is a form. Come and sit down." She guided Marsh to the chair in front of the big table. "I hope this pen will suit you."

The girl took it and studied the paper in front of her.

"Cause of death—pneumonia," Katherine Waring dictated, running one finger along the line.

Marsh dipped the pen into the ink and held it poised above the form. "Pneumonia?" she queried, glancing up. "Do you think that will be enough? What about the diabetic condition?"

Dr. Waring moved her hand from the desk and placed it on Marsh's shoulder. "King died from pneumonia. The events leading up to it are of no importance now."

The girl frowned at the form, hesitating. The pressure on her shoulder was light but firm. Quickly she wrote the word on the certificate. Dr. Waring removed her hand and wandered about the room again. When Marsh finished signing her name, Dr. Waring was pouring another drink at the cupboard.

"Just leave it on the desk," she said, without looking round. "I will give it to Henry. He will need it when he makes the funeral arrangements. That will be all."

Marsh left it folded neatly in the middle of the big cedar desk. At the door Katherine Waring called her name. She turned eagerly.

"Yes, Dr. Kate?"

She gestured towards the desk. "Thank you, Marsh."

Marsh went slowly upstairs. Her mind was clouded. She did not have a conscious thought, and yet she moved as though deep in thought. For a long time she sat on her bed, staring in front of her. She felt strangely unhappy but she could not define the impression further. In an endeavour to shake off the mood, she got up and went along to Kingsley Waring's room. Although she and Betty had performed the necessary and unpleasant tasks immediately after the death, there were still some matters to be attended to.

She opened the door quietly and stood for a moment looking at the body on the bed. It lay with a spotless sheet drawn right over the face; a vision of horrible immaculacy and neatness. Averting her gaze she went into the bathroom to clear up the litter that had been left there the previous night.

The bathroom, white and chill, was a replica of the one attached to her own room. She found herself staring at her reflection in the mirror above the basin. Her eyes were wide and dull, and her hands hung aimlessly at her sides. How long she stood there she could not remember and she was aroused by the sound of someone entering the bedroom.

She peered through the crack of the door. It was Betty Donne.

The nurse's cheeks were hectic and her eyes gleamed as she stood at the foot of the bed. The sheet had been folded back exposing Waring's face, which looked grey against the whiteness of the linen. The girl was smiling, the corners of her mouth pressed downwards. Then she started to whisper, addressing the grey sunken shell of a man on the bed.

Marsh strained to hear the macabre little monologue.

"It has been done and I am glad. I hope you know I am glad you are dead. You were never fit to touch her or even to be with her. You are gone and she is better off without you. You never were as great as she is. You tried to drag her back and hold her down, but you can't do that now." The nurse took a deep quivering breath. "I wonder if you realized what was happening. I hope you did. Everyone else realized it, so I think you must have, too. Were you frightened of death? I like to think you were. I like to think of you cringing and whining inside."

Marsh could stand no more. She pulled open the bathroom door, and the two girls stared at each other in horror. Betty Donne's hands went to her face, and she glanced from the corpse on the bed back to Marsh again. She was panting and trying to speak.

"Get out," Marsh said. She crossed to the bedroom door and slipped the key on to the outside. "Get out quickly before you go completely insane."

The nurse ran past her, her hands still covering her face.

Replacing the sheet, Marsh left the room, locking the door behind her. She went over to Katherine Waring's room, placed the key in a conspicuous position and then went swiftly down to her own. She picked up the nearest coat she could find. It was the one she had borrowed from the Bannisters' hotel, but she did not care. She pulled it around her firmly as she descended the stairs.

Laurence Gair stood at the foot. "Marsh!" he said urgently. "I must talk to you."

She brushed past him. He called after her, but she took no notice.

The big dog, Rex, got up with a sinister slowness as she stepped out on to the verandah, and she checked her haste. The animal's leash lay on the back of a deck-chair. She snatched it up and clipped it to the collar. She was in no mood to bear with the dog's whims, but she had to get away from Reliance.

They went through the ti-tree scrub, the dog keeping up with her pace. The track was still heavy although the rain had passed over and patches of blue sky were visible through the whitening clouds. The wind blew strongly but the sea had calmed a little.

At the road the dog stopped abruptly. His ears rose up to two sharp points and a low growl sounded deep in his throat. Henry Arkwright was walking towards them. His eyes were on the ground but he looked up when he heard Marsh trying to urge the dog on. Least of all would she be able to endure Arkwright's nautical platitudes.

"Beastly brute," he observed, coming up to her. "Won't pass anyone he knows. I can't imagine how King ever let him get like this. Give me the leash."

"I don't want him. Could you take him back with you to the house?"

Arkwright shook his head doubtfully. "I'll try, but Rex wants his walk." He bent over the animal, holding the dog's jaw. "Been down to the village. Everything is shipshape for the funeral. I suppose you signed the certificate?"

She nodded. Arkwright did not look at her. "All for the best", I dare say. What treatment did you use on poor King?"

"You have no right to ask me that," Marsh said, a small flame of anger starting to rise up in her.

Arkwright glanced up for a moment and then bent over the dog again. "Don't go overboard, my dear. You are so young and inexperienced I was surprised that Kate . . . I am sure you did your best."

"Will you try to move Rex now?" she asked coldly. "I want to go for a walk."

As though sensing the antagonism in the air Rex moved off abruptly. He pulled the leash from Arkwright's hand and circled around with his nose to the ground. Marsh followed without a word to Arkwright. The dog had paused and was trying to pick something out of the sandy soil bordering the road. It was a long slim piece of steel, a knitting-needle, and she bent to pick it up. Even before she recognized it Arkwright was behind her. He snatched it out of her hand.

"It belongs to my wife," he said, his face fiery red. "She must have dropped it."

Remembering Delia Arkwright's empty hands before lunch, Marsh was surprised at his agitated manner. She left him with Rex running around him barking loudly.

She had walked for some distance along the road before she directed her footsteps. The flight from Reliance had been instinctive. Unimpulsive by nature, it took Marsh as long to shake off impressions as it did to absorb them. Tightening her coat again, she looked down at it with a new significance. The little township was now in view, the red brick hotel standing out amongst the weatherboard cottages.

III

The bar of the Tom Thumb was filled with fishermen, roughly clad silent men with calloused hands clutching their tankards. In contrast to the taciturnity in the public bar the private saloon was a babble of noise. Marsh threaded her way through the tables where sporting men sat drinking with sleek-looking women, past peaked yachting caps and leathern golf-bags, to a table in a corner.

A man glanced up from nearby as she sat down. She observed a look of recognition although she did not know him herself. With him sat Shane, dressed in his whipcord breeches and leather jacket. He had seen her come in, but his dark grim countenance had not changed expression. Both men were drinking slowly and what little talk passed between them was not started by Shane.

Todd Bannister's mother came through the swing doors from the bar, expertly carrying a loaded tray. She set it down, answering the badinage smilingly. Shane's companion signalled for her attention. He must have been someone of importance for immediately the drinks were served she went to his table. Her straying glance fell on Marsh, and the smile vanished. After a few words with the man she came over to her.

"Mr Morrow says would you care to join them?" she told Marsh, whisking a damp cloth over the table.

The girl glanced towards them indifferently. They were an ill-matched couple; Shane with his surly expression and rough clothes and Morrow in impeccable tweeds. He had a thin almost effete face and a faintly superior air. He was smiling at her, waiting for her to come. She nodded to him curtly, for she remembered Katherine Waring knew him.

"I didn't come here to drink," she replied. "Convey my regrets to Mr Morrow. But I would like to see Mr Bannister for a moment."

Mrs Bannister did not want Marsh to talk to Todd. He was busy in the bar, but she could convey a message. Even as she spoke Todd burst into the room. Voices calling his name greeted him on all sides. He appeared to be popular and answered with his usual half-impudent manner. He caught sight of Marsh, and immediately a delighted look spread over his mobile face.

"If it isn't my little medico marvel! All right, Mother, she won't hurt me. Please let me talk to her for a while."

Mrs Bannister gave him a friendly pat, but a faint shadow seemed to cross her placid face.

Todd drew up a chair. "Delighted to see one of the bereaved household. There is another out yonder getting nicely plastered. Celebrating, I suppose."

"Michael Waring?" Marsh guessed, disturbed.

"The same. The lad will end in his grave before he puts his hands on the ducats."

"Is he . . . is he talking?" she asked.

Todd brought his bright gaze to bear on her. "Why are you worried about his conversation, I wonder? No, as a matter of fact, he is dead silent. A glassy eye and a cleaved tongue, you know. What's the matter with you?"

"Nothing. Please don't talk so loudly. That Shane man is behind us."

Todd swivelled round in his chair. "So he is! Hullo there, Bruce. Good-day to you, Mr Morrow."

"Is that Simon Morrow?" Marsh whispered. "The surgeon?"

"Sure is. Looks like being the big noise round here now—that is, if his health is good."

He spoke lightly, but Marsh frowned at a note in his voice. She began to play with the brightly polished brass ash-tray.

"He called on Dr. Waring after we brought her husband home," she remarked.

"Did he now? He must have been after some business. He's our local coroner."

The girl's hand jerked, and the ash-tray nearly fell off the table. She snatched at it nervously. "Why do you talk in that loose indiscreet way?" she asked. "It's not funny."

He caught her shaking fingers and held them firmly.

"What's the matter, Marsh Mowbray? You've changed. The last time I saw you, you were a cool efficient person, busy aiding the sick.

Today you look like an uncertain sixteen-year-old. Have a drink and tell Uncle all."

Before she could protest he had leapt up and was edging his way through the tables agilely. She watched the slim figure with its neat small head vanish through the swing doors.

Perhaps she could do with a drink. It might stop her jumpiness. The fact that Simon Morrow's eyes were constantly on her was making her nervous. And when Mrs Bannister came into the room with another tray of drinks, and looked at her in a grave appealing way, she felt that one drink would not be enough. She was glad when Todd came back.

"Here you are!" he said cheerfully. "My own invention. Guaranteed to brace the nerves and stimulate the imagination." He seated himself and lifted his glass. "Now what shall we drink to before we get down to business?"

Marsh sipped her drink. "Nothing. And there is no business to get down to."

Todd's eyes began to sparkle. "I have it! Mr Morrow, will you join me in a toast?"

The man at the next table turned his head at once, and raised his glass in reply.

He had been listening, Marsh thought resentfully.

Todd stood up. "The king is dead!" he announced. "Long live the queen!"

The chatter in the room subsided a little. Curious eyes were directed to them. Simon Morrow set his glass down again without touching its contents. He turned back to Shane and began to talk quietly.

"That fixed him," Todd whispered to Marsh. "The queen will have to battle hard against the pretender. I wish her luck, bless her ruthless heart."

It had fixed Marsh, too. She had remembered all at once that Todd was just a casual acquaintance she had picked up on the road to Reliance. She had let her confusion of mind run away with her.

"I must go," she said abruptly, and got up.

"You haven't finished the beautiful drink I gave you," Todd

protested. "Neither have you even begun to pour forth your heart to Uncle."

"I am going," she repeated. "Thanks for the drink."

"Didn't you like what I said about your hostess?" he asked shrewdly. "Haven't you found her ruthless?"

"Listen, Mr Bannister—"

"Mother won't mind if you call me Todd."

"Dr. Waring is an outstanding person. Your opinion of her is one of the many attacks and misunderstandings a distinguished person has to bear. Those who are closest to Dr. Waring can judge her for themselves. Where is your mother?"

"You don't really want her, do you?" he asked, in alarm.

"I want the clothes I left here the other day."

Todd Bannister's face fell. "And I thought you'd come to see me—even if it was just to blow off steam," he complained. "Mother is in the bar. Go outside and I'll get her for you."

The girl said awkwardly, holding out her hand: "I did come to see you in a way. I have had a few bad nights. I thought you might help blow the cobwebs away."

His smile was ecstatic. "Like a sea breeze? Come down again, won't you? And you will call me Todd, won't you, Marsh? I mean what I said about Mother not minding."

It was hard to know where sincerity began and pretence left off, but she had to laugh at his prattle. "Like a sea breeze," she agreed.

But when she met Mrs Bannister in the lobby she was not at all certain about Todd's assurance. The woman was cordial but distant and seemed to eye her surreptitiously. She produced the skirt Marsh had abandoned. It was pressed and neatly folded, and she hurried away to get some paper to make a parcel.

When she came back Marsh was staring at the aspidistra at the foot of the stairs. It was a good one of its kind, but she did not know that. She did not even see it.

"What's the matter?" Mrs Bannister asked quietly.

Marsh roused herself. "Nothing," she replied. "Nothing. I—I am very tired. There has been trouble at the place where I am staying. I suppose you heard."

"Yes, I heard." She started to wrap up the skirt. "What did Todd—my son, say about it? About Mr Waring's death?"

Marsh was surprised. "Not much. I can't remember. I doubt if he mentioned it at all." She stared at the parcel Mrs Bannister held, trying to snatch at an elusive thought. "Oh—thanks very much." She put it under her arm and turned to leave.

"Dr. Mowbray!" Mrs Bannister said. The girl paused and looked back. "Dr. Mowbray, don't think it rude of me, but when are you going back to town?"

"I don't know. Not yet, anyway. Dr. Waring asked me to stay on."

Mrs Bannister came nearer. Her voice was lowered. "You don't have to stay unless you wish. Why don't you go now? You came down here for a rest and a holiday. A bereaved household is no place for that. Go back to town."

Trying to understand the woman's curious vehemence, Marsh said gently, "Perhaps I could come and stay here."

"No," said Mrs Bannister, backing away. "No, I don't want you." She turned and hurried back to the parlour.

Shrugging, Marsh stepped out into the wind.

IV

The air was fresh and salty on her face as she walked briskly along the road. Her mind had become clearer and more dispassionate, and she now felt ashamed of her precipitous flight from Reliance. She had run away not only in body but in her mind, which was a far more despicable and cowardly deed.

Death, even to those more familiar with its insignia, was never pleasant, she told herself. There was a horrid excitement attached to it which caused repercussions to those connected with it. An unholy thrill that lowered discreet barriers and caused people to say or do things almost the same as they would under alcoholic or drug influence.

She had been foolish in interpreting impressions as genuine reactions. She had run away because she, too, had come under the spell of that morbid excitement when she had allowed her imagination to control her intellect. Looking back on her state of mind she acknowledged honestly that doubt had been the predominant element. Doubt concerning none other than Katherine Waring herself.

The absurdity of the thought, overwrought though she had been, caused her to smile. It was as she had said to Todd Bannister: a remarkable woman like Katherine Waring was certain to be the victim of envy and misunderstanding. She had to suffer because of her distinction. Even those closest to her had to be guarded against in some measure.

Marsh's heart went out to her again, full of warmth and admiration. Satisfied, her mind ceased its analytic prowlings. She walked steadily on, wrapped in a dream of hero-worship.

Had the girl been able to maintain that attitude of blind faith, Katherine Waring's position in her life would have remained unaltered. If she had gone straight back to Reliance then, she would have been able to withstand Laurence Gair's cynical innuendoes, Arkwright's false heartiness, and the unbalanced demeanour of the nurse, Betty Donne. She could have endured the boy Waring's uncouthness and the flamboyant Miss Peterson's presence without trying to find a reason for their reactions to Kingsley Waring's death.

It was such a small thing that stopped her as she was about to turn into the track leading to the house; a few bars of melody being whistled absently. Her forehead creased as the idle tune nagged at her memory and disturbed an unpleasant chord which seemed to belong to her former confusion of mind. The comfortable feeling of isolation and detachment gave way, as Marsh glanced back involuntarily and saw that the whistler was Shane.

It hurt her pride having to address this uncivil male. She considered most men egotistical and patronizing, but she had never before met one who so palpably ignored her.

Shane saw her motioning gesture and stopped.

"Well?" he asked curtly, one foot already in advance of its fellow. He returned her gaze without interest.

Marsh had had no subtle dealings with the opposite sex. She asked what she wanted to know bluntly and without finesse. "Why did you come to see Kingsley Waring the other night?"

Shane's face altered. He no longer regarded her expressionlessly. "My good girl, what are you talking about?"

She stepped in front of him. "Please wait for a moment. I have something to tell you. You came to see Mr Waring the night before he died. You walked round by the verandah to the library window. We heard your footsteps. I want to know why you came."

"You are a very direct young woman," Shane said. "What makes you so sure it was I?"

"Because I was playing the piano when you arrived and that particular sonata is not yet so well known that you should whistle the melody by sheer coincidence. You also whistled it when we went to get Waring from the links. I want to know why you did not admit you knew him and why you took care not to come into the house."

"You play quite well," Shane said.

"You admit you were there that night? Why did you make your visit so secretive?"

He looked down at her thoughtfully. "There seems no point in denying I was there since you have it proved to your satisfaction. But I refuse to answer impertinent inquiries of forceful young women."

"I am Dr. Mowbray," Marsh said. "I attended Mr Waring."

"What does that mean? Am I to read some special significance into those two momentous statements? Personally I don't like women doctors."

The girl said angrily, "If you were a doctor you still wouldn't like us, but you would respect our capabilities."

"If I had been Kingsley Waring's doctor," Shane replied softly, "I wouldn't have let him die."

"What do you mean? That statement is not only momentous but ridiculous."

He shrugged. "Take it as you like. I was being enigmatic. An effect of consorting with the oligarch of Matthews."

She guessed he was alluding to Simon Morrow. "What did he say? A man of his standing should be more careful. I gave Kingsley Waring the only treatment possible. No doctor could have done more. It was not my fault that he died."

Shane eyed her narrowly. "Take it easily. You'll go to pieces if you go on like that. Walk along quietly for a while."

Marsh took a deep breath. "You haven't answered my questions yet."

"I don't intend to," he retorted. "If you can give me good reasons, I may."

She turned to him eagerly.

"Well?" he asked promptly.

The girl lowered her eyes. She dug her hands into the pockets of her coat and kicked at the loose soil of the road. "I can give you no reason but my peace of mind," she said quietly.

"That is not good enough. Tell me why your peace of mind is disturbed."

"No," said Marsh. She had told him too much already, but there was a limit to her indiscretion.

She attacked again. A half-forgotten incident occurred to her. "Your horse? Did you find him?"

She felt the man beside her check his stride. Then he began to walk faster so that she was almost running to keep up with him.

"Saracen? Yes, he came wandering back to my cottage with a strained fetlock. He must have done the damage kicking the door of the hotel shed."

"You don't believe that," Marsh declared. "Someone took him from the hotel that night and rode over to Reliance. I heard a horse whinny quite close. Was it you?"

Shane glanced down at her. "It could have been," he said provokingly.

"It was you. You were the man waiting in my car under the pine-trees. You followed Waring on horseback when he went for his walk and your horse cast a shoe on the links. Rex found it. Why?"

"Why what?" Shane asked coolly.

"Why did you follow Waring?"

"I didn't say I followed him. Because your deductions are feasible does not mean that they are correct. Like all women you want to satisfy some speculative emotion while you are still trying to convince yourself there is no need to. Under those conditions I refuse to help you in any way. Rid yourself of your mental meanderings and I may. Just now you are wasting my time."

Marsh ran after him. "If you could just tell me what I want to know I will be satisfied. Please, Mr Shane! It means a great deal to me."

He had reached the point where the road ended and the track leading to his cottage followed the shape of the cove around the cliffs.

He stopped impatiently. "Even if I answered your questions you would still be full of fears and uncertainties. Doubt is the devil's caress. Face up to facts, girl. Why do you stubbornly cling to your fancies? I can guess what is troubling you and so will everyone else if you are not careful. Take my advice and leave Reliance."

He turned and went quickly along the track.

Marsh stood on the point and watched him go. She had been a fool to attack Shane. It had gained her nothing while he had learned more than she wanted him to know. Far better if she had ignored the provocation and gone straight back to Reliance. The fact that someone had whistled a tune she had played was a flimsy basis for accusation. She felt not only depressed but foolish.

Far below her the sea broke over the rocks torn from the cliffs' side. The swell swept forward, swamping the huge fragments and sending up spray nearly into the girl's face. Then the waves would recede, the water streaming away to leave the rocks bare and glistening before the next onslaught.

Her eyes were absently following the monotonous movement of the tide when suddenly she caught a glimpse of something at variance with the setting of rocks and water. It looked like a bundle wedged between two boulders.

Again and again the current dragged at it and it weaved to and fro as though trying to find a way out to the deep sea. Before the next wave came she saw that it was a hideously distorted bundle. Spume clouded the sea to prevent her from distinguishing what it was.

Then the water streamed away again, leaving it easily recognizable as a human body.

CHAPTER FIVE

I

Shane's figure was still visible through the ti-trees. He had almost rounded the little cove when Marsh shouted after him. Her voice was flung back by the wind and she watched him helplessly.

He could not have heard her but at the last break in the scrub he turned round.

"Shane! Shane!" she cried again, waving her arms to attract his attention and pointing below her to the weaving body in the sea.

He did not come back to the point where the girl stood. He had caught the meaning of her frantic gestures and could see the body from a place in the centre of the cliffs where wind and water erosion had cut a deep ravine, making a rough pathway to the narrow beach below. He beckoned to her to meet him and she ran along the track.

He looked angry and impatient, as though he would rather have dodged this unpleasant task. "We can get down here and climb across the rocks. Give me your hand."

Marsh shook her head briefly. She clambered down the ravine, setting her feet firmly and digging into the grey sandy soil with her fingers. Shane followed her, his heavy body sending the loose earth flowing.

She reached the sand first, landing clumsily on her knees. This time he made no attempt to assist her. She ploughed over the beach and splashed heedlessly through the water to the first group of rocks. The man cast a comprehensive look at the route ahead and took a different direction, nearer to the cliffs.

The sea rushed at Marsh as she climbed and stepped from rock to rock. Once it enveloped her to the knees and she clung to a nearby ledge as it swirled about her, dragging at her feet. Shane, farther ahead, saw her.

"Come in, you fool!" he shouted. "Follow my way."

With her eyes fixed on the ground she calculated each step across the rough passage. The roar and perpetual motion of the water on her right made her feel slightly dizzy. The going was slow and infinitely tiring. She lifted her head and saw that Shane was now some distance ahead. He was half-hidden by a boulder and had paused. She guessed he must be near to the body, and made her way towards him laboriously.

An incoming wave sent him reeling back against the rock. He was standing ankle deep in the water that had risen on the platform where the body drifted to and fro like a balloon.

"Damnation!" he said softly to himself. "Damnation!"

"Who is it?" Marsh asked. "Do you recognize anyone?" She began to climb down beside him.

"Careful!" Shane said quickly. The sea rushed in again and the girl was flung back hard against the rock. The sudden impact jarred her spine. Shane pressed upon her, his arms outstretched to clutch the rock on either side. The water reached her waist this time and she felt her feet slipping from under her. As it receded Shane moved.

He bent over the imprisoned body, his hands fumbling in the water to release it. He had it free and dragged farther up the platform before the next wave.

"Climb up," he ordered Marsh curtly. He stripped off his leather jacket, trussing the body from head to hips. With the belt bound tightly around the sodden figure he hauled it over one shoulder.

Marsh crouched on the rock above watching him. With a sudden heave he managed to roll the body off his back to the girl's feet. She began to fumble at the belt.

"Not yet, you stupid girl!" Shane said angrily. "The tide will be above here shortly. Get to the beach."

He hauled up the flaccid bundle and the tedious trip across the rocks started again.

Marsh kept to the rear, allowing Shane to pick his own route. The sea came and went, each wave rising higher than the previous one. The journey was slower than before. The weight of the body, clumsy and heavy with sea-water, made the man in front, powerful though he was, breathe heavily. Sometimes a low angry mutter escaped him.

Marsh followed closely, her eyes on Shane's steps marking them for her own.

They were nearly at the last of the rocks when a box slid out of the bundle and rolled to a crevice. Shane did not look round as the girl bent to pick it up.

It was small and oblong, the lid inset with mosaic pieces of iridescent metal; a pretty article. She paused to open the spring lid curiously. Inside was a quantity of wet white powder.

A stab of fear passed through her and she shut the lid, slipping the box into her pocket. She glanced guiltily ahead at Shane. Only his head and the hideous burden on his back were visible above a rock. He turned, jerking his head impatiently, and she hurried to catch up.

At last Shane let his burden fall on to the sand.

"Who is it?" Marsh asked again, and her voice was not quite steady.

"Open up and see," he suggested. "Or is the tough woman doctor squeamish? It won't be a pretty sight."

She knelt down beside the body and ripped out the belt from its buckle. Her hands were stiff as she fumbled at the jacket. She turned the heavy sodden thing from side to side and at last flung the coat away.

Shane was right, but she made no exclamation at the hideous sight. Sam was still recognizable in spite of his battered face.

"Well?" said Shane. He stood above her, his eyes sardonically amused. "Do you want to vomit?"

"It's Sam, from the Warings' place," she said, getting up. "He was an imbecile. He must have fallen from the top of the cliff."

The man directed a brief glance at it. He said, almost absently, "Maybe they will rail off the point now."

He moved towards the body and dropped on to one knee. Marsh watched his face.

"Yes, you said that, didn't you?" she said slowly. The wind whipped her short hair across her eyes, and she put up one hand to tuck it away. "You told me the point was dangerous; that there would be an accident one day."

Shane did not reply. He was moving the heavy broken head to

one side. For a moment the girl thought it would break away from the trunk. The man studied the ugly thing frowningly. Then he released it and buried his hands in the sand to clean them. He stood up.

"An accident?" he said at last. "Yes, a railing will be put up now."

He picked up his coat and laid it over Sam's body, securing it with stones. It lifted now and then in the wind and looked to Marsh as though the chest of the dead boy might be rising in breath. She found herself shaking as she watched Shane's deliberate movements.

"You'd better go and tell them at the house," he suggested.

"Yes," she replied, clenching her teeth. "I must do that. Will you wait here while I get help?"

"No, I am going now. Your odd-job boy met with a fatal accident, that's all. He was only an imbecile, anyway. Why should I stay?"

He strode off towards the ravine, and Marsh was left on the lonely beach with the hideous corpse at her feet.

Presently she pulled herself together and followed Shane's path up the cliff. She went slowly. There was no need to hurry. It wasn't like the last time when there had been some hope. Kingsley Waring had been still alive, whereas Sam was quite unmistakably dead. This body was a less pretty sight than the last one.

She picked her way carefully to the track at the top of the cliff. The parcel she had brought from the hotel lay at the point where she had dropped it when she had signalled to Shane. She put it under her arm again and continued on to Reliance slowly as though returning from a stroll.

II

Miss Jennet was on the verandah as she approached the house. She had come out of the kitchen to collect some of the logs Michael Waring had stacked in the wood-box. She startled Marsh by saying: "Sam hasn't come back. I was so certain he would be in his bungalow."

Her training at the hospital, where death was treated with profound secrecy even in the middle of a crowded ward, stopped

Marsh from blurting out her news. Katherine Waring should be the first to know.

"Where is Dr. Kate?" she asked, as she mounted the steps.

"In the library. Are you all right, Doctor? You look quite strange. So tired-looking! Let me get you a cup of tea."

The girl brushed past her and went through the house and along the passage to the library. She knocked at the door, but entered before Katherine Waring had time to answer.

Katherine was seated at the desk and glanced up, frowning at the intrusion. When she saw Marsh she put down her pen.

"My dear girl, where have you been? I thought you went up to your room after lunch."

Marsh dropped into a chair and covered her eyes with one hand. "I went for a walk. Down to the hotel, I think. Yes, the hotel. On the way back—"

"The hotel. The Bannisters?" The woman's voice was smooth.

"They had my skirt," Marsh explained, uncovering her eyes and surprising Dr. Waring's narrowed gaze.

"Marsh, you look quite exhausted again. You must not go off for such long walks like that."

"Dr. Kate," she said wearily. "Something appalling has happened. The boy Sam—"

The older woman started up from her chair. "Sam? What about him?" Her face had assumed a taut expression, unlike its usual serene reserve.

"A terrible accident," Marsh faltered.

"Are you saying Sam is dead? What happened? Where has he been? Marsh, tell me at once."

"He must have fallen over the cliffs. Do you know the point where the macadam ends? I'm afraid he is dead. His body is on the beach."

"The beach?"

"A man called Shane whom I met the other day carried him there. I saw the body on the rocks from the point."

Katherine Waring sank on to her chair again. Her hands gripped either side of her desk. For several minutes there was silence. Then she asked abruptly: "Does anyone else know? Have you told anybody?"

"No, I came straight to you."

There was another long pause. Marsh tried to rouse herself. "Dr. Kate, it will be getting dark soon. Will I ask the men to go for the body? Perhaps Larry and Michael will—"

"No," said Katherine Waring. "Not Michael."

"Why not Michael?" asked a voice behind Marsh.

The woman at the desk rose again. She put out one hand towards the handsome moody boy standing unsteadily in the doorway. Marsh had never seen her self-control fail her before and it caused her a twinge of discomfiture. She averted her gaze.

"Why shouldn't I go?" Michael Waring asked, advancing into the room. His drunkenness had augmented his bitterness towards his mother. "Jennet told me something was up. Marsh Mowbray has found another desperately sick man on the links, has she? Another diabetic who has most unfortunately mislaid his glucose."

Marsh's hand flew to her pocket. She felt the outline of the box through the thick material.

"Michael—" Katherine Waring's voice was not quite steady.

"Don't try and spare my feelings," he flung at her savagely. "Who is it this time?"

Marsh jumped to her feet. "Be quiet! Your mother has had enough to stand without your callow behaviour. Will I tell him, Dr. Kate?"

She nodded, and moved over to the window where she stood with her back turned while the girl spoke. "Sam fell over the cliffs. I found him. I am sorry, but he is dead."

Michael Waring's face went white. He lurched forward and gripped the back of a chair. Ignoring Marsh he addressed his mother's averted figure.

"Sam!" he said. His voice was low and furious. "Sam! The poor idiot boy who never hurt anyone. The poor faithful creature whom you coaxed and trained like an animal. Just to be useful and to be called to heel as an experiment. He wasn't even an object of casual affection to you like Rex. How could he be? He had no brain worthy to appeal to that inhuman intelligence of yours."

"What have you done?" the boy went on. "He was a human being, but you dismissed him as something less than human; someone lower than an animal."

"Get out of this room," Marsh said, slipping between the mother and son. "Get out or I will hit you as hard as I can across the mouth."

Michael looked down at her angry face. A scornful smile touched his mouth. "You poor damned simpleton! You think you know her, don't you. Where is Sam?"

"On the beach of the cove at the end of the road. Will you get him?"

He nodded abruptly and left the room.

Katherine Waring did not move, but stood staring out of the window at the sea. Presently her bowed shoulders straightened and she dropped her hands slackly to her sides.

"Get me a drink, Marsh," she ordered quietly. "Whisky. You'll find it in the cupboard."

"Yes, Dr. Kate." She went to the cupboard and found the bottle.

"Double, please, Marsh."

The girl poured more into the tumbler and carried it over to the window. Dr. Waring took it and drank quickly. She gave back the glass and walked to her desk with her head still averted.

"Sam has been with us for a long time. He and Michael almost grew up together. They were the same age. Michael developed a peculiar fondness born of pity for him. This terrible accident has been a great shock. He is such a child in some ways. He has none of the control we have learned by hard experience, Marsh."

"No, Dr. Kate."

"I have always been most interested in Sam's case. I think my work on him might have had a slight success in later years. Not complete control over his faculties, of course, but he would have been able to enjoy this life more. You have heard of such cases, Marsh?"

"Yes," said the girl.

Katherine Waring sat down. She moved some papers together, her attention held by them. "Would you ask Henry to come here, Marsh? As Sam has been with us for so long I would like his funeral to take place with King's if possible."

Marsh advanced slowly to the desk, one hand at her pocket again. She stood in front of Dr. Waring straight and tensed; as though she were the one ready to receive the blow instead of delivering it. She drew the box out of her pocket and placed it on the desk without speaking. It lay within Dr. Waring's vision, although her head was bent over her papers. She did not look up, but one hand went out towards the box. She drew it nearer to examine, and then opened the mosaic lid.

"Where did you get this?" she asked, in a whisper.

Marsh bent over the dividing width of the desk. "Sam had it. It fell out of his pocket as Shane carried him to the beach."

"Did this man Shane—"

"No," interrupted Marsh. "And I did not tell him."

Katherine Waring nodded. She was stirring the sodden powder with one finger. "An odd toy for Sam to pick up. I wonder where he got it."

"Dr. Kate," the girl said desperately, "don't pretend with me. That is glucose."

Dr. Waring shot a quick look at the strained young face above her.

"Larry told me your husband always carried his glucose in an old snuff-box. He couldn't understand why—"

"Hush!" the other interrupted swiftly. "You shouldn't listen to Larry's gossip. Yes, this is King's box, but you mustn't let your imagination run away with you, Marsh."

The girl's fingers gripped the desk. "There is something else I must tell you."

Two cool hands were placed over hers. "No, not now, Marsh. Wait until you have thought matters over. You came down here suffering from overwork. You have come up against two distressing experiences; first King and now Sam. You are bewildered and confused—and no wonder! Wait for a while, I beg of you, Marsh. Wait!" Dr. Waring's voice caressed the last word like a hypnotist's.

"I have thought things out," Marsh said rapidly. "Dr. Kate, your husband did not intend suicide. I am sure of it. He was fighting for his life all the time I treated him. He wanted to live. This," and she indicated the snuff-box, "proves it. The coma was brought on by the violent exercise of his walk through the boisterous weather and he had mislaid his precautionary glucose. Sam must have found the box somewhere."

Katherine Waring was silent. She removed her hands.

"That is what happened, Dr. Kate," Marsh persisted. "Your husband's death was a tragic accident. It couldn't have been suicide or—or anything else."

She waited anxiously for Katherine Waring to support her convictions.

"Of course you are right, Marsh," she agreed smoothly. "Just two tragic accidents, King and Sam. Now, my dear, ask Henry to come to the library."

Marsh left the room with a light step. Since her opinion had been endorsed without question by a highly experienced physician, who was she to doubt even her own theory that Waring's walk was the sole contributory cause of his coma? The mere force of Katherine Waring's personality was a counter-irritant to any uneasy stirrings below the surface of her mind.

Laurence Gair found her singularly unimpressionable when later he followed her upstairs to change for dinner.

"Marsh, my poor darling!" he murmured, sliding one hand under her unresponsive elbow. "Such a messy corpse! I am sorry I was not on hand to help you. But I believe you had more than adequate assistance with the strong silent stranger of Matthews. Who is he, and what does he here?"

"I have no idea," the girl replied. "Excuse me, Larry, but I must dress."

His hand slid down to her wrist. "Not yet. I want to talk to you. There are one or two points I want to bring to your notice. Remember my vow to persuade and coerce?"

"I do, but I am not interested, Larry."

His eyes narrowed. "It becomes difficult when you are fresh from Dr. Kate's hands. What an influence that woman has over you, you mad girl."

"Larry, be quiet!" Marsh whispered fiercely.

"I know, I know," he said airily. "She is my hostess. Now that King is gone I have no right to be here except on sufferance. By the way, did you observe my neat *rapprochement?*"

"If you mean that story you and Evelyn Peterson cooked up together at lunch—I did. I wouldn't be surprised if Dr. Kate called your bluff."

He laughed softly. "She won't dare. She's afraid of me."

"Don't be ridiculous."

"It's true. She's afraid for me to stay and afraid to let me go just yet, until she finds out what I intend to do. It is an interesting situation. Now, about those points."

Marsh jerked her hand away. "Go away. Tell Miss Peterson your bedtime stories. She should suit you better than I. Her position in this house is even odder than yours."

"Evelyn? Oh yes, I know all about our hot-blooded Evelyn's doings. She told me, and she is not going to budge from Reliance until she has what she wants. But whereas she wants a definite article, my desires are more nebulous." His eyes went over her face.

Marsh pressed her mouth into a straight line. "If you are after some disgusting love-making, Larry, I am not the type."

He laughed again. "Your attitude is an exact replica of Katherine's, Marsh. Studied detachment faintly backed by hostility."

Marsh opened the door of her room. "Another disparaging remark about Dr. Kate and I will dislike you even more intensely, Larry."

She slipped into her room quickly and shut the door.

III

At dinner that night Dr. Waring sat in her usual place, pale and tired but with no change in her courteousness. She made no reference to the fresh tragedy.

It fell to Henry Arkwright, blundering in hearty sympathy, to pass some remark about Sam's accident. He found it impossible to resist, although to whom his condolence was directed was a matter of conjecture. Unless it was to Michael, who had been glowering at his mother from the foot of the table and immediately told him savagely to shut his crude mouth. His Aunt Delia turned to Dr. Waring to demand an apology for such manners. But before Katherine Waring could speak, Betty Donne, who was waiting on the table, intervened by checking Mrs Arkwright's sweet course. She glanced at the head of the table for approval of her opportuneness.

Michael threw down his table-napkin and left the room.

The incident passed over, but Marsh continued her search from face to face. What she was looking for she did not know; any more than she knew why she was scrutinizing each one. When she came to Laurence Gair she found him staring at her, and made a mental resolve to dodge any future tête-à-tête he might be planning.

The unpleasant proximity of table companionship was broken up by Katherine Waring's suggestion to have coffee in the living-room, and as they all filed out Gair managed to reach Marsh's side.

"I must talk to you," he whispered. "Be reasonable, Marsh. There are some things you must know."

"Larry!" Dr. Waring called. "Perhaps you will get the liqueurs from the cupboard in the library."

"Blast the woman!" he muttered. "She did that on purpose."

"Another night and a fire won't be necessary," Dr. Waring observed pleasantly. She sat down to avoid Arkwright's heavy hand of sympathy on her shoulder.

"Why do you say that, my dear?" he asked, his bulging eyes showing an interest out of proportion to the casual remark.

"Henry, sit down here," Delia Arkwright said, from the couch. "Kate can't get to the coffee-table."

"I beg your pardon, my dear. I never thought—"

"It doesn't matter, Henry," Dr. Waring interrupted. His extreme solicitude did not appear to irritate her. "What I meant was the weather is likely to clear. You know what Matthews is. Bleak one day and furiously hot the next. You might be able to get in some sailing before you leave."

"Yes, yes. I suppose we must be going in a couple of days. Are you sure you wouldn't like us to stay on board for a while, Kate?

There are a few more distressing details of which I might be able to relieve you."

She smiled faintly. "I will read the will before you and Delia go."

Arkwright reddened. "My dear, I assure you—"

"Of course not, Henry," she interposed again, and then as if to change the subject she asked her sister-in-law where her usual knitting was.

Mrs Arkwright replied tartly: "I never knew you were interested in knitting, Kate. I have always considered it a great pity you didn't become more domesticated both for your own sake and for Kingsley's," and she directed a sidelong glance at Evelyn Peterson, who was slouched in a chair with her dinner-dress pulled up to her knees. The firelight gleamed on her slim legs. "I have mislaid one of my needles. No use looking for another in this house."

"I know where your knitting-needle is," Marsh said.

Henry Arkwright lunged up. "Aha! Our little pianist! I was waiting for you to speak, my dear. What about some of your excellent music? You don't mind, Kate, do you? After all, King was very fond of music." He was across the room as he spoke.

Marsh finished her coffee and got up. "Your husband found your needle this morning, Mrs Arkwright. He picked it up in the ti-tree."

The lid of the piano fell back on the keys, making the strings vibrate.

Delia Arkwright turned her head. "You didn't tell me, Henry. Where is it? Henry!"

"Coming, my dear. Now, Dr. Marsh, is the stool right for you? You are such a tall girl. I might say I like tall women."

"You told me the other day you liked them small," Miss Peterson drawled.

"Give 'em to me big or little," Gair broke in cheerfully. He got up and went over to the piano. "You are making Marsh nervous," he told Arkwright, edging him away. "Take my comfortable bunk on the port side of the fire and enjoy the music. I'll conduct for you, Marsh."

"It won't be necessary," she replied coldly. "I'd prefer to be at the piano alone."

She bent her head and braced her fingers wide over the keys before deciding on a Bach fugue. Anything florid would be unseemly. She became interested in what she was playing as the pattern of the fugue unfolded. The strong recurrent phrase which dominated the smaller patterns throughout seemed curiously applicable when translated into terms of human thought and deeds.

Gair was watching her with an uncanny awareness as she came to the end; as though he had read the same significance into the fugue. He glanced over his shoulder at the group near the fire.

"Marsh Mowbray," he said softly. "You are a coward. You try to ignore the difficult and unpleasant."

"Go away," she muttered, striking a discord.

"Precisely what I mean. You are trying to avoid me because you are afraid that what I will say might cause your lulled conscience misgivings."

"My conscience is quite clear."

"Prove it. Listen to what I have to tell you."

She glanced at the others. Katherine Waring's face was in profile. "All right, Larry," she said quietly. "What is it?"

"Good girl!" he nodded. "Keep playing and we won't be suspected of anything more dire than flirting."

She drifted into an idle improvised melody.

"Listen carefully, Marsh. The night you arrived at Reliance there was a discussion at the dinner-table. Kingsley made quite a speech about it."

"I know," she cut in. "I was in the kitchen. I heard it."

"Smile at me, if you can. Arkwright is watching us," Gair said. "Putting King's speech crudely, he was threatening to denounce someone for a blunder made in his or her medical career. Sweetie, I said smile—not frown."

"He might have meant that," Marsh admitted, trying to remain non-committal.

"King and Dr. Kate were once in partnership. What made them break it? Choice or necessity?" He allowed time for his insidious queries to sink in before he continued.

"Now cast your mind back to the morning you found Kingsley.

Do you remember me hunting everywhere for his glucose? Had King been carrying it he would never have fallen in a coma."

"Well?" asked Marsh, meeting his gaze fully.

Gair glanced away, frowning. "Marsh, I must tell you. I'm sorry if it hurts, but Dr. Kate had his glucose. I saw King's snuff-box on her desk this afternoon."

"I gave the snuff-box to Dr. Kate," the girl announced calmly.

"You're lying," Gair said quickly. "Stop playing the cover-up, Marsh."

"No, Larry, I gave it to her. I found it on Sam's body."

"You are sure?" Gair's eyes narrowed. "How did Sam get hold of it?" He put up one hand and rubbed his lean jaw reflectively.

Marsh relaxed and watched him in silent triumph.

"Sam," he repeated slowly.

"Yes, Larry. Sam," the girl said. "I told you you were wasting your time."

"Am I!" he exclaimed, in an undertone. "Listen, my stubborn darling, not only was the unfortunate Sam a half-wit, but he also had the habit of lifting any bright or attractive object he saw. Kleptomaniac is a harsh word to pile on to half-wit, but Sam was the nearest approach to one I have ever seen."

"You can't blame an imbecile for the effects of his mischief," Marsh said, in an effort to retain the initiative.

"No," he agreed swiftly, "but you can blame the person who exercised a strong influence over a weak-brained boy."

"What do you mean?"

He leaned nearer, speaking rapidly. "Katherine Waring could make Sam do anything she wanted. She had him trained like an animal. You said something about her calling my bluff, but I am going to get in first."

"Larry," Marsh whispered with anxiety. "Don't! Please don't say any more." She put one hand on his, as it rested on the piano lid. His knuckles tensed under her fingers as though to hold her touch.

"The arts and wiles of your sex. No, my sweet, not even for that. She is not worth that beautiful stubborn loyalty of yours."

The girl withdrew her hand swiftly and gave him a look of hate.

"You can do your damnedest," she muttered, and began to play heavy sombre chords.

Gair straightened up. "How apt, Marsh," he observed cynically. "The death-scene music will improve the atmosphere."

Katherine Waring's head had turned sharply and there were startled expressions on the other faces, but she did not care. Gair moved across the room. He was smiling faintly, with perfect command of himself and of the situation he had precipitated. He even paused to pour himself a drink.

"Dr. Waring," he said, coming nearer with glass in hand. "I have been thinking for some time now about the tragic accident which took place today. We, of the medical profession, are inclined to ignore certain factors. We are so accustomed to dealing in terms of life and death that unconsciously we sometimes take the law into our own hands."

Katherine Waring was quite calm. "Yes, Larry? What are you trying to say?"

"A member of your household met with a fatal accident," he said bluntly. "Tomorrow I understand he is to be buried along with King. I consider that the police should be informed first."

Marsh's fingers, spread on the keys, became suddenly powerless. Her foot was pressed on the sustaining pedal, so that the one chord vibrated through the room. A long silence followed Gair's announcement. Dr. Waring sat like a statue, and as inflexible. Arkwright's mouth had fallen open and his eyes protruded. Evelyn Peterson had sat upright suddenly and remained with her knees held high and her feet not touching the ground.

Delia Arkwright was the first to speak. "Well, Katherine? I trust you owe it to Kingsley's memory to keep scandal away from his name? Dr. Gair, your suggestion is in very bad taste."

"Preposterous!" Arkwright exploded at last. "The idea!"

Into Evelyn's eyes flashed a tiny look of fear. She tried to laugh. "Really, Larry! How melodramatic of you!"

"Do you really think so, my dear? Dr. Kate, what about it?"

Katherine Waring's body seemed to relax. Without turning her head she said, "Please go on playing, Marsh."

Then she gestured with one hand as though to calm the others. She answered Gair with a cold courtesy. "You need have no worry, Larry. Whatever others may do, I still consider the ethics of our profession—and the law. I spoke to Walker this afternoon after I had examined Sam in Henry's presence. I also communicated the facts to Simon Morrow, and an inquest has been arranged for early in the morning. Marsh, you will be needed as a witness."

The girl released her gripping fingers and let her hands fall into her lap. "Very well, Dr. Kate."

Gair said: "I see. Then there is nothing more to be said. The local constable and the coroner will trust your judgment implicitly. "

She inclined her head without speaking. There was an edge of sarcasm in Gair's voice which escaped no one.

He went to the door. "I beg pardon for causing such a furore. I might have guessed Dr. Waring would make no mistake." He looked at Marsh as he stressed the last word.

The feeling Gair left behind him was uncomfortable. But beyond Delia Arkwright asking when he was going back to town, nothing was said.

Marsh shut the piano and got up. "I think I'll go to bed," she announced abruptly. "Good night, everyone. Good night, Dr. Kate."

She did not notice Katherine Waring's warm personal smile this time.

IV

The passage was dark as she felt her way to the stairs. The lamp on the bottom newel had burned low, and she had to trace her way across the foot of the stairs to the table where the candles were kept. A warm draught of air reached her as she felt in the drawer. She swung round quickly.

The door of the kitchen was open, and Michael Waring stood on its warm glowing threshold. He was swaying slightly and surveyed her with a dull concentration.

"I wanted you," he said, and his voice was thick. "I wanted to tell you something important."

"You're drunk again," Marsh said, in disgust. "You haven't been really sober all day."

"'Course I'm drunk," he declared arbitrarily. "Who wouldn't be drunk? Everybody is drunk in this house. But with me it is whisky. I am not drunk on blood."

Marsh lit her candle and took a step up the stairs.

The boy stumbled forward. "Stop a minute, damn you. Something to tell you. I've been thinking."

"You are in no condition to speak, let alone to think," Marsh replied. "Wait until you sober up, and then think before you speak."

Young Waring was in an ugly mood. He tried to heave himself at her, but the girl slipped up the stairs quickly. She looked down on him from the top. He was hanging on to the banister with both hands.

"Drunk on blood, that's what. Drunk on blood," he repeated in a rising tone.

Marsh went into her room and shut the door. She was trembling and the candle-flame wavered as she lit the lamp on the bedside-table. The grotesque shadows on the walls faded as the spirit caught fire. She sat down on the bed, her head in her hands. Her fingers ran through and through her short curly hair, trying to ease the thoughts in her mind.

For a long time she sat there, her brain twisting and turning as it tried to evade, reject and explain in bewildering rotation. Now and then footsteps sounded along the passage outside her room and doors were opened and shut. Minutes went by and then the last of the footsteps went by Marsh's room. They hesitated for a moment outside her door, and she raised her head. She jumped up when they continued on to the far end of the passage, and eased a crack in the door just in time to see Katherine Waring enter her own bedroom.

She shut the door again and leaned against the wall, closing her eyes wearily. A deep silence had fallen on the house. It was broken once by the sound of running water from the room adjoining her own, and then it settled again uninterruptedly.

Marsh opened her eyes. She moved carefully across the room and stripped off her long dress to don a pair of dark slacks and a matching pullover. The cuffs were pulled down so that only the tips of her fingers showed. Over her head she tied a scarf peasant-wise, leaving her forehead and cheek-bones in a deep shadow. On the table beside her bed lay the usual heterogeneous collection of articles. From them she selected two; a torch and the key to the laboratory Dr. Waring had given her. Extinguishing the lamp she sat down on the bed again, lighting a cigarette with fingers that were now quite steady. Deliberately she let the minutes go by, timing her vigil by chain-smoking.

After a long patient wait she got stiffly to her feet, and pulled back one cuff to shine the flashlight on the tiny face of her wrist-watch. The hands covered one another exactly.

"The witching hour," Marsh whispered, to break the tenseness of her mind and body.

At the door she waited for a few more minutes to pass before she slid the handle round. With her senses alert, she glided along the passage, one hand brushing the wall, until she came to the head of the stairs.

The journey down was eerie, as step by step she descended into the darkness. At the foot of the stairs she paused, trying to visualize the way ahead. There was a faint glow, hardly more than a tiny break in the blackness, which came from the embers of the kitchen fire, but it formed a guide as she proceeded along towards the door opening on to the verandah. It was locked and the noise as she turned the key seemed loud in the intense quietness. She waited for a moment, pressed hard against the wall.

It was then that she remembered Rex and a muttered "damn" escaped her. The dog's usual sleeping quarters were on the verandah. She would have to chance Rex, having got thus far. She spoke his name softly and persuasively, feeling a hearty dislike for the canine breed generally.

Nothing stirred and she heaved a faint sigh, which broke off suddenly. If Rex was not there then perhaps Michael Waring had taken him out. A stronger word passed through Marsh's mind. There were two risks now—Michael and Rex. She would still chance it.

Out of doors it was not so dark. Somewhere behind the heavy sky the moon was shining. She could distinguish the path to the scrub. Once in the shelter of the ti-trees she played the torchlight on the ground, as the track to the laboratory was still heavy with mud. She walked along with fair confidence, keeping her ears alert for any sound of a dog. She did not want to come up against Michael again, in his brutish uncontrolled mood.

As she drew near the laboratory she switched off the flashlight and continued the remainder of the journey in darkness. With the key held ready she traced the lock of the door with a forefinger. She was about to fit it when she heard movements inside the building. Her heart began to thud, but when the person within commenced to whistle softly she unlocked the door.

Shane narrowed his eyes against the full glare of Marsh's torchlight. He retaliated quickly by bringing his own to bear.

"My body-finding friend!" he said coolly. "Sorry I can't oblige you, but I am neither dead nor in the desperate throes."

"What are you doing here?" the girl demanded, from the threshold of the laboratory.

"Lower your voice and your light, girl. Or is your visit a legitimate one and it does not matter?"

"Never mind. What I want to know is why you are so interested in Reliance when you pretend not to be?"

"What a long and badly constructed question," Shane commented. "Don't elaborate. I get your meaning. What do you want there?"

Marsh had glanced her light round to fall on the filing cabinet. At the man's question she switched it off.

"Tell me why you are here," she repeated, "or I'll rouse the household."

Shane's face was in the dark again. He laughed softly. "I don't think you'd dare. But to save you an embarrassing situation, I'll tell you why I came."

"How did you get in?" she asked abruptly, remembering the key in her hand.

"I had a key. Kingsley Waring's key."

108

"He gave it to you? When did he give it to you?"

"Not exactly."

"You stole it from him," Marsh accused.

"Not so fast, girl. I took it from the ring left in his clothes at the golf shelter. I wanted to get back some property of mine that I knew was kept in here. You may return it to Dr. Waring."

"I don't believe you," Marsh declared, as she took the key. "Your behaviour has been suspicious all along. What is the property?"

"That, my dear Dr. Mowbray, is my business."

Shane's flashlight went out suddenly and he advanced across the room. Marsh fumbled for the button on her own.

"Don't show a light," he commanded in a whisper. His hand gripped her wrist and she started to struggle. "Stay still, you fool. I heard someone outside."

The girl held her breath and listened. "There is no one," she said, after a pause. "You only pretended so as to change the subject."

"When you will rely more on your conscious mind and pay less heed to what you want to believe, I will like you better. I never met a woman with all the signs of intelligence, yet so unintelligent."

"If you have taken anything from this laboratory I will tell Dr. Waring," Marsh threatened.

He laughed again. His arrogance, which she considered part of every male character, annoyed her more than his previous churlishness.

"She won't miss it. What I have is my own and something that I value. Think well on that, Mowbray. The night you played your Brahms I brought something to lend to Kingsley Waring; something he wanted the use of for a while. A man does not make plans and then overload himself with insulin. Good night."

He was out the door before she could see what it was he carried away from the laboratory.

Still standing in the doorway Marsh played the light around the room. There was a chance she might recognize a space in the order of articles she had first surveyed with Katherine Waring. Her flashlight rested on one object and then another along the bench on the far side of the room. Intent on her purpose she did not sense the hand that stretched out from behind.

Suddenly the torch was snatched from her grip and flung out into the scrub.

Marsh gave a quick gasp of fright and backed along the wall farther into the laboratory. "Shane?"

Someone was in front of her, crushing her against the cold stone wall, and the hand grasped her jaw savagely. She put up her hands and began to struggle. A stinging blow caught her on one side of the face, followed up by another. Her head sang and she sank to her knees.

She was jerked up roughly and more blows fell hard on her head. A violent push sent her staggering across the room, where she lost her balance and fell to the floor. There were a few hasty footsteps, and then the door of the laboratory banged.

CHAPTER SIX

I

The bang of the door penetrated Marsh's dazed mind as she lay sprawled on the floor of the laboratory. It conveyed something. The intruder had gone and could not get in again even if so desired, because she had the only keys to the Yale lock of the building; her own and the one belonging to Kingsley Waring that Shane had given to her.

She lifted her head in the darkness and listened. She had been mad to come on this nocturnal excursion. Ever since she had come to Matthews her standards of thought and action had been thrown into disorder. She, who had always been circumspect and unimpressionable, had been betrayed by susceptive faculties into all sorts of impulsive foolishness. She must get away from Reliance before her carefully nurtured characteristics became further impaired.

She tried not to think of the sudden brutal attack, because although her reason told her she was safe from further assault, she felt weak and frightened. She got up from the floor and began to feel her way about the room.

There was a surgery divan somewhere. How ghastly it must be to be blind. No, it couldn't have been anyone from Reliance; probably some drunken tramp, or Shane. He looked capable of beating up anyone who questioned his blasted male superiority. No woman would have done it. Why should anyone have done it, for that matter? At last, the couch.

Marsh eased her bruised and aching body on to it. It would have been foolish to attempt a search for the torch that had been knocked out of her hand; and more foolhardy still to make the trip back to the house without one. She was safe and more comfortable where she was until daylight. She tried to sleep.

Whoever it was, no mention must be made of the unpleasant

experience to Katherine Waring. Dr. Kate had enough on her mind without adding an assault to the trouble at Reliance. It had nothing to do with her and with the unfortunate deaths of both Kingsley and Sam, any more than there was any connection between Waring's illness and the imbecile's accident. But she would leave Matthews in the morning without fail.

Dozing fitfully, she remembered Mrs Bannister's request that she should go back to town and then Shane's suggestion. And Larry was only staying on because of her. Nobody wanted her to stay except Katherine Waring.

When Marsh awoke finally, the early sun was shining through the window of the laboratory. For a moment she was puzzled by her surroundings, for the bright sunshine had changed the laboratory from a place of darkness and pain to an ordinary cheerful room. Katherine Waring's forecast of fine weather looked like being accurate.

She sat up as she remembered what had sent her on the disastrous trip to the laboratory the previous night. Her head swam as she got to her feet and she stumbled across the room, lurching against the filing cabinet. For a moment she rested her throbbing head against the cold steel. Then she opened the long sliding drawers and began her search.

The drawers had been pointed out by Katherine Waring as containing a complete record of her husband's career and took the form of diaries neatly filed under yearly dates. Marsh lifted them out, and sitting down on the floor spread them about her.

The object of her search was the cause of the partnership break between Katherine Waring and her husband. If she could establish that the break had been happy to both parties, and this seemed to her the likely way to find out, then she could call an end to Laurence Gair's innuendoes and leave Reliance with an easy mind.

It would give her immense satisfaction to prove to Gair how wrong he was about Katherine Waring, and to expose him to himself as she saw him beneath his superficial charm; cynical, self-centred and childishly malicious. He had been like that even at the University when she knew him first. Cold-blooded, too. At the first post-mortem they had both attended, an epileptic attendant, in transferring the corpse from the tray to the table, had fallen down in a sudden fit, the body with him. Larry had led the betting among the student observers as to which body would come out on top . . .

She chose a diary from the middle of the pile and turned over its pages. It seemed like the record of any general practitioner, an inter-mingling of surgical and medical work. There was nothing strange about that. Few specialists had the good fortune to follow their bent from the beginning. But what Marsh did query was the fact that although the husband and wife were in partnership Waring did not apply himself to his surgery only, leaving Katherine to look after the medical side of their partnership.

Perhaps neither of them realized at the time in what direction their genius lay, and Katherine may have had her share of surgical work.

From frequent mention of a Base Hospital Marsh guessed that their practice must have been in some provincial city. Picking up the next diary she learned its name and that half its citizens must be walking around minus their appendices. There was only one break in the monotonous row of appendectomies and that was the entry—'attended inquest on Mrs Farmer'.

Very soon after this entry Kingsley Waring had let his diary lapse, and the remainder of the book consisted of blank pages. Marsh was not surprised, as the record had been quite ordinary—in fact, almost dull. How he had managed to maintain such a small-time flow of events without wearying, she could not understand. One would think that after long hours of work even the enthusiast would be too tired to add to the day the task of keeping a diary.

She opened the next book at the first page and her casual ex-pression changed when she saw it bore at the top a Collins Street address. She checked the date and found it was twelve years ago.

Twelve years since the Warings broke partnership in a provincial city and came down to Melbourne to specialize.

Marsh turned back to the previous diary, but the blank sheets told her nothing about the reason for the break. While before them was a row of appendectomies and dull routine stuff.

No, wait a moment! That inquest on some woman. Was that what she was looking for?

Frowning anxiously she went through the pages seeking some other mention of Mrs Farmer, but she found nothing to add to that single reference—'attended inquest on Mrs Farmer'.

She rose to her feet wearily and began to refile the diaries in the cabinet. Her head had started to throb again as the worthlessness and foolishness of her midnight adventure became more apparent.

Irritably she tried to fit the books into position. Something was preventing this and she put her hand right into the drawer to remove the obstacle. It was a larger-sized book than the diaries and bore on its old leather cover the title—*Life of John Hunter, F.R.S. 1728-1793*, by Drewry Otley.

The unique feature of the book was not its age nor the historical interest of its faded words, but the fact that Waring had used it as a scrap-book. The leaves had been cut to form an alphabetical index and odd cuttings pertaining to each index letter had been pasted in.

Marsh opened it and was startled out of her idle curiosity when her eyes caught the name Arkwright. This was contained in a letter which read as follows:

My dear Kingsley,

I received your letter and can readily understand your concern. I, too, was excessively shocked by Arkwright's faulty diagnosis. Had he called me in sooner I may have been able to do something. Frankly, I am unable to understand why blind obstinacy on the part of some members of our profession prevents them from consulting the more experienced man. Is it pride, I wonder?

In view of my regard for you, my dear King, and the fact that Arkwright is a connection of yours, I promise to accede to your request not to let the affair go any further.
Yours sincerely,
Charles Winthrop

Marsh raised her eyes from the letter and stared unseeingly across the room. Fragments of a past conversation came back to her.

"Medical errors should be acknowledged for censure. It is the duty of a colleague to expose mistakes."

The book drooped in her hands as she remembered the high, slightly sneering voice and Arkwright's blustering reply.

"You mean to say you would have the courage to denounce another man to the world."

"Or woman," Kingsley Waring had inserted with a certain emphasis.

Suddenly Marsh lifted up the book and ran her finger down the letters to W. She swung the leaves over so abruptly that the book slipped from her hand. As it fell to the floor a few loose sheets scattered around her feet. Even before she verified it she guessed what had caused the loose leaves. Someone had torn out the pages indexed W.

There was nothing for her to do after that discovery but to replace the diaries and to put Waring's scrap-book back where she had found it. She glanced around the room to ensure that everything else was in order. The cushion on the divan was indented with the mark of her head. She shook it up and adjusted it with slow deliberation before she left the laboratory, banging the door to lock behind her.

She reached her own room without an encounter and flung herself on to her bed. And because she was exhausted by the night's adventures and sick from disappointment and apprehension she began to weep. The tears poured down her face until in her utter weariness she fell asleep.

II

A sharp tapping at the door roused her nearly three hours later, and Katherine Waring's voice called her name. She started up guiltily and, catching a glimpse of her appearance in the dressing-table mirror, got right into bed.

"Come in," she called, pulling the sheets up to her chin.

"Didn't you hear the breakfast gong?" Dr. Waring asked. She

was dressed in a long tailored black coat and her face was shaded by a broad-brimmed hat. "Simon Morrow is picking us up at the road."

Marsh stared at her blankly.

"It will be quite an uncomplicated affair," the older woman went on, drawing on her gloves. "I suppose you have never attended an inquest before. You will be asked a few questions. Just answer them directly. Don't try to enlarge upon any particular one. I will wait for you downstairs. Don't be long, for the undertaker's men will be coming shortly."

As she turned to leave, Marsh said awkwardly: "I must go, after the funerals today. Thank you for asking me to Reliance. "

Dr. Waring smiled faintly. "I did not mean you to run into all this trouble, Marsh. Don't go. I'd like you to stay for a few days longer."

"I must go back to town," she repeated, trying to subdue a strange agitation.

"You can't leave," said Katherine Waring, and a note in her voice startled the girl. "Your car—the drive is still impassable. I want you to stay, Marsh." She went out of the room swiftly.

Marsh sat up in bed slowly, staring at her reflection. She had forgotten the mud that had sucked and clung to her feet when she walked through the ti-tree spinney. Half a mile of it lay between Reliance and the road. She had not known how much she had wanted to leave until now, when a natural hazard was stopping her.

"It will take a day or two to harden," Katherine Waring said, when they were skirting the drive on their way to the road.

A sleek grey coupé, not unlike Simon Morrow himself, was drawn up waiting for them. He smiled a little when Dr. Waring introduced Marsh, but made no mention of the incident at the Tom Thumb. He was a man born with a pleasant easy flow of small talk, and while Marsh was inclined to examine his remarks for a double meaning there was nothing she could put her finger on. Katherine Waring's attitude towards him was unimpeachable.

Marsh went through her part in the proceedings lifelessly. It was, as Dr. Waring had foreseen, a simple business. There was only one disturbing thought in her mind as she sat with Morrow in the local constable's office and waited for Walker to fill in papers; a minor recollection because she was beyond fighting against the major stream of events. And that was what Shane might do or say when he knew an inquest had been held without his being called as a witness.

From the police-station they went back to Reliance for the funerals.

The little cemetery lay over the rolling countryside away from the strong ocean winds. It was typical of a hundred others adjoining Australian townships, a lonely half-neglected spot where the earliest settlers in the district had been buried.

A place where lizards basked undisturbed on crumbling head-stones in summer, and the long brown grass rustled as the copper-headed snake slid on its sinister way.

Occasionally a freshly constructed monument could be seen, when people like Kingsley Waring chose to lie among the pioneers, united to them by sheer possessive love of one small corner of the earth.

"How nice for Dr. Kate!" Laurence Gair murmured to Marsh when he saw Morrow. "So comforting to have an old friend on hand at a time like this."

The girl ignored the thrust as Katherine beckoned to her.

"She must have remembered suddenly how King and Simon hated each other," Gair observed. "Your job is to hold him off while Katherine weeps at the graveside."

"Unapproachable and irreproachable," Simon Morrow said gently, as he permitted himself to be led aside. "I did not know that gate-crashing at a funeral was such a crime. I see I'm not the only offender, however."

Marsh paused as he did and glanced in the same direction. A tall heavy figure stood under one of the pine trees some distance away. It was Shane.

"Do you know that man?" Morrow asked.

"No," the girl replied shortly.

"Neither do I," he went on, "but there is something vaguely familiar about him. I tried ever so tactfully to find out yesterday at the hotel. A very reticent gentleman. Does Katherine know him?"

"I don't know. I think Mr Waring did."

"So he has come to pay his last respects. Very proper. So have I. I like to be proper, Dr. Mowbray." There was a faintly mocking tone in his voice.

The others were grouped around the graves as the coffins were lowered, but Marsh still detained Morrow aside. He pursued a soft commentary.

"They always say the most unnerving part of the burial ceremony is the thud of earth on the coffin. Where did Katherine find the reverend gentleman? 'Dust unto dust.' Katherine is always punctilious, but how Kingsley would have disliked it. He prided himself upon being a complete agnostic. Why are we proud of such an unproductive title, I wonder? The more most people see of death, the more they are convinced of eschatology. However, not Kingsley, I fear. Perhaps we doctors are inclined to deify ourselves. What do you think, Dr. Mowbray? We have such powers over life and death that remain unquestioned by the ignorant. Perhaps that is bad for us."

"Mr Waring said something like that," Marsh said suddenly. She had not intended to make conversation with this smoothly spoken, provocative man. "He said the illusion of infallibility should be destroyed because mistakes do occur in most careers."

"What an extraordinary admission," commented Simon Morrow, after a slight pause. "King had a certain genius for—er—beating others to the punch."

Marsh asked him quickly what he meant, but his reply was just as ambiguous and barbed. "My dear Dr. Mowbray, how intensely you speak! If you had known King as well as Katherine did, you would not ask me what I meant. Excuse me, I see that dissolute young boor creating a scene. His tortuous mind amuses me."

Michael Waring had not once gone near his mother during the ceremony. He had taken up a position at Sam's grave and his face was sad and bitter as he watched it being filled in. At the end he ostentatiously removed one of the wreaths from his father's grave and placed it on the imbecile's.

When Katherine Waring remonstrated he turned on her savagely. Then Morrow intervened and he strode out of the cemetery without waiting for the cars. The rest of the party drove back in silence.

III

Marsh went straight to her room with the intention of doping herself into some sort of sleep, so as to stop her mind from revolving and to ease the continuous ache near her left temple. She had drawn the shade to shut out the bright sunlight when a tap came at the door.

"Come in," she called unwillingly, and Evelyn Peterson entered. She regarded Marsh curiously.

"What happened? I saw the bruise." She pointed to Marsh's forehead.

Although she had not known until that moment that the skirmish in the laboratory had left some mark, she answered at once. "I ran into a door. The bathroom door—in the dark," she added, wondering if anyone else had noticed the bruise.

Evelyn said drily, "I suggest you comb that front curl down into a bang and no one will see it." She sat on the end of the bed and pulled a cigarette-case from the pocket of her exquisitely cut black suit.

Marsh watched her settle herself more comfortably. "What do you want?" she asked.

Evelyn turned the case over in her scarlet-tipped fingers. It was made of thin gold with her initials boldly inscribed in one corner. "King gave it to me," she announced, with a quick upward glance. "Shocked?"

"Not terribly. Your relations seem to have been fairly common knowledge."

The girl shook back her dark cloud of hair. "Not as common as you might think," she corrected. "Although I should hate it to become too well known. I wouldn't like to hurt dear Katherine's career."

Marsh had been experimenting with the comb. It was a new experience, but she turned away from the mirror at the nurse's ominously casual remark.

"What are you driving at?" she demanded.

Evelyn opened the case and took out a cigarette. "I have been in the medical game long enough now to realize that big-time doctors like to keep their peccadillos quiet. Scandal can ruin many an established position. I could blow the gaff so hard that Katherine Waring wouldn't have a patient left after the sensation hunters had left her. Furthermore—"

"Well?" said Marsh. The girl had paused and was looking at her under her lashes, the smoke from her cigarette spiralling about her head.

"Not only the established career. The up-and-coming doctor cannot be too careful. Supposing now I put it about that your attention at King's sick-bed hadn't been as good as it should; that King might not have died had a little more care been exercised?"

"What do you want?" Marsh asked, gripping the rail of the bed with both hands.

"As I can't have King back, I want the next best thing. My good name. Dr. Kate has some papers belonging to me. She stole them from King. I want them back."

Marsh let go the railing. "Why don't you ask Dr. Kate for them yourself?"

Evelyn sat up slowly, flicking particles of ash from her suit. "She is so damned sublime she probably wouldn't think I could ruin her. But you cannot afford to lose her patronage or risk a scandal. You realize the damage I could do. I want you to get those papers from her. Make her understand I mean business."

She stood up and looked Marsh over. "You're a fool, Doctor, to stick by that woman. She'll suck the blood from you. I know what she is. King told me."

"Just a minute," Marsh said, as she moved to the door with her graceful cat-like walk. "If I promise to do what I can, will you do something for me?"

The nurse looked back over her shoulder. "It depends on what you want."

"I want you to answer a few questions. Nothing important really."

Evelyn eyed her warily. "All right," she agreed, coming back, "but I've been around too much to be beaten by a double bluff. If you had been born in the slums and had to fight every moment of the way to get somewhere, you'd know I meant every word I said."

"I believe you," Marsh said coldly. "Your type hates everyone."

For a moment the girl's eyes glittered. Then she smiled. "And you most of all, Mowbray. Do you think I have forgotten the way you pushed me out of King's room? I hate you because you have never had to fight and snatch at every opportunity that came your way. When King died I thought it would be all up with me, but my type, as you call us, has learned never to give in. There will be other opportunities."

She gave a husky laugh at the look of disgust on Marsh's face. "Not necessarily what you are thinking, you poor frigid fool. Men don't mean a thing to you, do they? Yet Larry for one is crazy about you; just as King was crazy about Katherine. "

"Was he?" Marsh asked, startled.

"Sure he was. Crazy with love and hate for her."

"You sound like a cheap novelette," Marsh said coldly again.

The girl shrugged. "What is it you want to ask me?"

Marsh tried to collect her thoughts. This talk of violent emotions was repugnant and disturbing. "The Arkwrights," she asked directly. "What do you think of them?"

"Blow-me-down Henry? He's okay as long as he doesn't paw you too much. That wife of his is enough excuse."

"Did they like Mr Waring? Did they get on well with him?"

"Henry fawned a bit. I think King was attached to Delia. He certainly put up with her always treating the house and his rooms in Collins Street as her own. She'd pocket any money he gave her without a word of thanks, as if she had every right to expect it."

"What about Simon Morrow?" Marsh asked, without looking at her. "Did Mr Waring like him?"

"Hated his guts," Evelyn replied without reserve. "Did you see the way he has now started to come around Dr. Kate?"

"Leave Dr. Waring out of this," Marsh said swiftly.

Evelyn's lips curled. "She certainly has a hold on you. The few she does attract she gets properly. Betty Donne is positively besotted. That chattering fool, Jennet, is almost as bad. Though Michael tries to drag her the other way," she added reflectively.

"Michael treats his mother shockingly. Why?"

The girl shrugged again. "He is a bit neurotic. She wants him to be a doctor, and he doesn't, I think."

"And Mr Waring? What did he want?"

"Naturally he had to back up his wife's wishes."

"How long were you with him?" Marsh asked, nearing the climax of her questioning.

"About five years."

"Did he ever tell you how he began to specialize?"

"In a way it was your beloved Katherine's doing, but she never dreamed or intended he should become such a success. He found the constant interfering and managing impossible. Another thing, too—if Dr. Kate found a case becoming too involved, she would drop out gracefully and leave him to shoulder the responsibility."

"I can't believe that," Marsh said. "You only know the facts from one side."

"You asked me," the girl retorted. "Why don't you ask Dr. Kate yourself?"

Marsh was silent.

"You dare not," Evelyn challenged. "You have doubts about her, too. You are not quite happy about her."

"You are being absurd," Marsh said, but her tone was not convincing.

Evelyn threw out her hands. "Go and ask her for yourself. And when you do, find out how her husband happened to take too much insulin, and why he happened to be without his glucose."

"Be quiet! Do you want the whole house to hear you?"

Evelyn laughed scornfully. "You poor boob! As if we all don't think the same thing. And unless you get those papers from Dr. Kate I won't merely be thinking."

She went to the door and opened it. "Everyone is rather het up in this house at the moment. Take my advice and don't wander around in the dark or you may get a few more bruises." She slid out of the room.

Marsh turned back to the mirror somewhat disturbed by this parting shot. Then her hands slowly relaxed. She had got nothing of value from Evelyn in return for her promise to mediate between her and Katherine Waring, but she drew back the shades and replaced the tablets in their bottle with the intention of tackling the problem right away.

There were voices in the library when she reached the door. She could hear Henry Arkwright. "I know, my dear, it is purely your own concern, but I do think Morrow's attitude is a little compromising. People might talk. Don't misunderstand me, but dear old King did not think highly of him."

Then Katherine Waring's voice came calmly. "I don't follow you, Henry. In spite of a long-standing acquaintance I barely know Simon Morrow personally. As for Kingsley's opinion of him, it certainly would not apply to his work. Simon is a brilliant surgeon; one of the finest in Australia."

Arkwright coughed. "Don't take offence, Kate, but I think it better that Delia and I stay on for a while longer. Just in case the fellow annoys you."

There was a slight pause before Dr. Waring answered. "Very well, Henry. If that is to be your excuse, so be it. Would you mind? I have some letters to write."

"Certainly, certainly, my dear. Are you sure I can't help you at all? Were the funeral arrangements satisfactory?"

"Very satisfactory, thank you. Please close the door as you go out."

She looked up and saw Marsh standing on the threshold. "Do you want me, Marsh? Come in, my dear."

The girl edged past Arkwright, avoiding his straying hand. It just brushed her shoulder. She closed the door in his face and went over to the desk. "I am sorry to bother you, Dr. Kate."

"No bother at all. I am rather relieved to see you."

She got up gracefully. She had changed from her black dress into a thin grey linen, for it was now quite warm. "Will you have some sherry with me? You look pale. Is anything worrying you?"

The girl's lips twisted ironically, but the older woman had her back turned. She waited until Dr. Waring handed her the glass and then stood turning it round to catch the light on the diamond cuts.

"Go on, Marsh," Dr. Waring said, sitting down again. "What is the trouble?"

The sherry was dry and mellow. Marsh sipped at it quickly. "I have been talking to Miss Peterson," she said with an effort. "She came to my room."

"Yes?"

"She wants some papers you have which belong to her,"

Marsh blurted out. "She won't leave Reliance until she has them. And if you don't let her have them she'll—she will—"

"Will what?"

Marsh raised her eyes. "She thinks she can blackmail you," she replied in a low voice.

Katherine Waring was quiet. She got up and came slowly round the desk to Marsh.

"Dr. Kate," the girl said desperately. "Don't rely on knowledge of your own integrity. Peterson means what she says. I found her searching your room. Give her the papers."

"Did Miss Peterson say what was in those papers?"

Marsh shook her head.

"No, I didn't think she would. I will tell you. Evelyn Peterson once did something which, should it be known, would not only kill her chances as a nurse, but would also involve her with the law." She turned away and said vehemently: "Do you think I am going to let that girl go back to nursing again? No, Marsh. Tell her the answer is no."

"Dr. Kate—"

She raised one hand in remonstration. "Your career is an important affair, Marsh. I can help you a great deal. Please do not spoil your chances by listening to low gossip and innuendoes. Trust me, Marsh. You need me as much as I need you."

"You know I will always trust you," Marsh said quietly. She put down her glass on the desk. "Forgive my intrusion on this unpleasant business. Perhaps I should leave, after all."

Dr. Waring turned swiftly. "You heard me," she said, with the same undertone of vehemence. "I need you, Marsh."

Then she gave a little embarrassed laugh and her face went back to its usual impassive expression. She sat down at her desk and took up her pen.

Marsh stared at her bent head for a moment and then left the room.

She was wandering aimlessly along the passage when the telephone rang. As there was no one nearby she lifted the receiver. A man's voice asked for Michael Waring.

"I'll see if he is in." She went along to the living-room and put her head in the door. The Arkwrights were sitting there. Delia did not look up from her knitting, but Henry rose at once.

"Has Michael come in? He is wanted on the 'phone."

"He is not here," Arkwright told her. "He set off to walk home from the cemetery."

"Such an ill-mannered boy," Mrs Arkwright commented. "I can't understand how Katherine lets him behave as he does. He was never like that with King."

Marsh went back to the telephone. "He is not in. Can he call you back?" "No message," said the man's voice, and he rang off.

IV

After luncheon Marsh escaped from the house and wandered along the sloping cliff path on the village side of Reliance, where the golf-course ran down to the sea. During the meal Arkwright had extended an invitation to go sailing.

"I hope you don't mind, my dear," he said, in an audible aside to Katherine Waring. "It is more in the nature of medical treatment than a jaunt. Our young friend looks as though a good blow on the briny would do her good."

With Delia Arkwright's steely gaze on her, Marsh answered uncompromisingly, but now she watched a solitary yacht with a certain interest. It tacked across the rocky coastline about a mile off shore. A few white clouds sped about the sky, but the sun shone warmly and sparkled on the sea, which was now all shades of blue. She lifted her head to the slight breeze that forever blew in Matthews.

Her mood of almost pantheistic delight was broken when she saw Betty Donne standing on a jagged arm of land which formed the headland between the ocean and the bay. The nurse had not attended the funerals; neither had she waited at the luncheon-table as usual. Marsh began to walk towards her swiftly.

She was standing on an overhanging rock, her head bent to watch the breakers crash up beneath her, and did not hear Marsh's approach.

"There has been one accident," Marsh said curtly, putting one hand on the girl's arm to steady her. "Dr. Kate doesn't want another to happen. Come away from there."

The nurse twisted out of her grasp. "Leave me alone, damn you," she cried angrily, but she clambered back over the rocks to the path. "Did Dr. Kate send you to find me?" she asked, over her shoulder.

"No, I was just out for a walk." The girl tried to smile. "She didn't even know I was gone, did she?"

"I don't know," Marsh answered. "Where were you this morning? Why weren't you at the cemetery?"

"Did she say anything? Was I missed?" Her voice was pathetic in its eagerness. Then her eyes were lowered and her mouth dropped peevishly. "No, she didn't miss me. What did it matter if I wasn't there? She had you."

Marsh said awkwardly, "You are not so foolish as to be jealous, are you?"

Betty looked up, and her blue eyes blazed for a moment. Then she gave an odd little giggle. "You are the foolish one. What an idea! You are far more likely to be jealous of me. I went down to the hotel this morning. I knew Dr. Kate would not notice me gone. I was having a grand time with Todd Bannister while the rest of you were weeping crocodile tears at the cemetery. We get on well together, Todd and I," the girl finished defiantly.

"That's excellent," Marsh remarked, although she was frowning. "I think you need some new companionship. Don't you consider it would be a good idea if you had a complete change of scene? Leave Dr. Waring for a while. She could get in some temporary assistant. Get right away from nursing until your nervous condition improves."

Betty Donne veered into anger again. "You are trying to push me out," she said on a high note. "I won't go, I tell you. Dr. Kate needs me more than she needs you. I have seen the likes of you before. They come and go; get what they want from her and then leave. But I have stayed. I'm loyal. I tell you she can't do without me. If you try to push me out I'll get desperate. I'm warning you—"

"Quiet!" Marsh said, losing patience. "Be quiet, you little fool. No one is trying to push you out. But it is obvious you'll have to go soon."

Betty Donne stopped her muttering. "What do you mean?" she asked abruptly. "I insist on knowing what you mean."

Marsh eyed her for a moment. "You are becoming unbalanced," she informed her bluntly. "Mr Waring's death has been too much for you. Go while there is still the chance."

The nurse began to chuckle. She shook all over and tears streamed down her face.

"Too much? That's funny, that is. Too much for me?"

She collapsed on the ground and rocked to and fro with laughter. Marsh watched her, a troubled look in her eyes.

"I wish you'd go," the girl cackled. "Go before I die of laughing." She flung herself face down on the grey sandy soil of the path.

Marsh knelt beside her and tugged at one heaving shoulder. She had done this before, too. The firm yet gentle hand and the commanding bracing words. The combination was usually successful. But not this time. Betty Donne raised her dirty tear-streaked face from the ground. The naked hate in her eyes shocked Marsh.

"I said go away, Doctor," and Marsh went, extremely disturbed.

She crossed the fairways of the links with her head bowed and her hands clasped behind her back. The slight peace that the sight of the white yacht on the blue sea had given her was gone, and she felt the devil's caress once more.

A voice hailed her by name, and she looked up, startled out of her unhappy pondering. On a tee situated high on a rise, Todd Bannister stood. He held a golf-stick over his shoulder and his leather bag bulging with clubs lay at his feet. He was beckoning her eagerly.

"I nearly brained you," he called out. "Didn't you hear my pill

127

whistle by your shell-like ear? I yelled fore like mad. Come on up and I'll show you how to hold a stick."

He looked so gay and well-groomed in his grey slacks and canary-coloured pullover against the sombre green of the pine trees that Marsh climbed up to join him. She remembered that although he was just an acquaintance she had picked up on the road to Matthews, he had helped to chase the shadows away before.

"What a villainous collection of blunt instruments," she remarked with an effort, inspecting his golf-sticks. "Do you really need them all?"

"Of course," he insisted indignantly. "I say, how did the planting go this morning? Is the old basket really under six feet of sod?"

Marsh was kneeling on the ground, turning over the club heads. "I am relieved to see they are all numbered. You entertained Dr. Waring's nurse this morning, I understand."

"Who told you that? Was it frightfully wrong of me? Poor kid, she looked all in, so I fed her pink gins until she looked like one. Are you going to scold me?"

"On the contrary," she said, glancing up at his lively face. "You did a good deed. Do you think you could keep it up?"

"Pink gins? Sure! Come along."

"No, not me. Betty Donne. She is not altogether herself. You could help her to snap out of it." "What's the matter with her?" Todd asked suspiciously. "Lady Waring been beating her up?"

"Nothing organically wrong," Marsh said evasively. "She could do with some of your cheerful companionship."

Todd gave her an incredulous stare. "You don't mean nuts?"

"Not yet. She's over on the headland. Find her and show her how to play golf."

"But I wanted to show you," he said plaintively, thrusting his wood into the bag. He heaved it up on his shoulder. "If I play around with Betty, will you come out on the course with me one day? I don't see as much of you as I decided to."

"It's a bargain," Marsh promised, holding out her hand. Todd gripped it and then turned it palm upwards.

"So soft," he said wonderingly. "I knew you wouldn't be as hard to feel as you like to pretend sometimes. Friends, Marsh Mowbray?"

"More than friends," she replied, smiling at him warmly. "Go now, like a good fellow."

She watched him scramble down the slope and then turn to bow at her with a flourish. He called out something but the wind caught his words, so he blew her an airy kiss and strode away.

Marsh was still smiling. She felt better again.

V

Miss Jennet was at the telephone when she entered Reliance. Her hands were white with flour and she jogged from one foot to the other as she spoke. "Will you wait please? I'll see if I can find him."

She put the receiver down and saw Marsh. She smiled at her in relief.

"Who is wanted, Miss Jennet?"

"Michael. He is probably in his studio, and I have scones in the oven. Could you—"

"Where is the studio? I'll find him."

It lay in the ti-tree scrub in the opposite direction from the laboratory. Marsh approached it diffidently. She disliked young Michael intensely.

He was standing before a new canvas with a brush in his hand and was working with quick decisive strokes. When Marsh spoke he turned querulously.

"Damn you," he said, thrusting his brush into a bottle of turpentine. "Can't I have a moment's privacy from women? First Evelyn and now you."

"Sorry," Marsh returned crisply. "You are wanted on the 'phone. Someone rang for you this morning. Miss Jennet is busy so I came across to oblige her."

The boy's sullen look became guarded.

"Who is it?" he asked, stripping off his paint-bedaubed overall. Whatever the quality of his art might be, Marsh thought, he certainly looked the part.

"He wouldn't leave a message."

When Michael hurried out she did not follow. Canvases were stacked around the room. They were worth looking at; a little crude in technique but boldly executed. Many of them were portraits, which she studied with tolerant interest.

She was standing in front of the easel when Michael came back. The outline was enough for her to recognize his new subject. It represented a scene she herself had witnessed—the imbecile boy, Sam, standing before the kitchen range with a long knife in his hand.

"Well?" asked Michael harshly. "Do you like my pretty picture? Shall I give it to my mother when I finish it?"

The boy's eyes were bright and his dark hair hung untidily over his forehead. He seemed strangely exultant. When he reached for a bottle which stood on the window-sill his hands were quivering.

"Drink? Never mind. I am used to drinking alone. Go on. Unleash your gentle tongue. But do you mind if I continue with my work?" He selected a tube and squeezed it on to his palette.

"Why must you be so beastly to your mother?" Marsh asked in exasperation. "She is such a fine person. Now your father is dead she must need you."

Michael finished off his drink. "You amuse me, Doctor. You don't know what the hell you are talking about. You never saw my parents together. She doesn't need me or anyone else, unless she can possess them entirely."

He turned round, palette and brush in hand. His eyes were gleaming excitedly. "So far she has had everything her own way, but just wait a while. Just wait, Mowbray, you poor simpleton." His voice had begun to rise dangerously.

Marsh left him without another word. She was a bit frightened of Michael Waring when he became uncontrolled. He could so easily have been the person who had attacked her in the laboratory.

His eyes were still fever-bright when she saw him at dinner that night, but he drank only water at the table and refused a liqueur in the living-room.

Laurence Gair managed to draw her aside and murmured cynical surprise over his abstinence.

"Don't tell me the influence of a good woman has been the means of his refusing this excellent Benedictine. I saw you going to his studio. Did you point out the error of his ways, my sweet? Dr. Kate needs a strong manly son in her hour of trial. Was that it? Don't scowl so fiercely, Marsh, or she will notice and call you to her side under some perfectly unnecessary pretext. Smile distantly, so as to show her your interest in me is negligible. I arouse you neither to anger nor passion."

"Larry," Marsh said wearily. "The only emotion you arouse in me is doubt of everything true and sincere and honest. You try to corrupt everything you come into contact with."

He smiled swiftly down at her. "I will mend my ways when you come to your senses, Marsh. The seeds of doubt I have sown will ripen for your ultimate good. Then you may reform me. How are the investigations progressing?"

She frowned at him in warning.

"Still trying to deceive yourself, Marsh? You are investigating but you won't admit it even to yourself."

"Maybe I am trying to understand a few things," she said tersely. "But it is only to stop your foul insinuations. And when I do, Larry, I won't rest until I make you pay for your injustices. You are by no means in the clear yourself."

She was rewarded by a sudden change through his expression, as though she had sent him off balance. She pressed her attack. "Last night I went to the laboratory. I went to look for something which I thought might help my—my problems. Someone snatched the torch away and attacked me in the dark."

"And you think it was I?" Gair suggested gently.

"It may have been. You see how little I trust you, Larry."

His face darkened. "Marsh, you idiot!" he said, in an angry undertone. "You are not helping yourself any by accusing me."

"I am not accusing you, Larry. I merely stated that you yourself are not above suspicion."

He muttered something and went back to the coffee-table. Katherine Waring looked past him to Marsh as she handed him his cup and saucer. A sudden warm smile lightened her apathetic features, as though she knew that in the brush between them Marsh had gained the ascendancy.

Marsh then turned her attention to Evelyn Peterson. She knew that Dr. Waring did not intend to have any direct contact with the nurse, and that it was left to her to act as the intermediary.

Evelyn was sitting slumped back in a deep chair, staring into the fire sullenly and oblivious of Henry Arkwright's repeated efforts to engage her attention. She caught Marsh's eye and jerked her head almost imperceptibly towards Katherine Waring, but when the girl regarded her serenely her gaze became sullen again. The reflection of the flames danced in her dark eyes for a moment. Then she looked at Marsh once more and from her to Michael Waring. There was a world of meaning in that lazy speculative stare and the girl felt suddenly uneasy.

When she went to her room that night she did not immediately prepare for bed. Evelyn was certain to come, so she waited, smoking a cigarette restlessly and trying to make up her mind how to deal with the situation. Somewhere below the surface of her mind was a small feeling of resentment that Katherine Waring had given her the responsibility.

Evelyn came just before midnight. She was dressed in a negligé of apple-green chiffon which flowed softly about her, disguising her extreme slimness, and her dark cloudy hair hung around her shoulders. But her vivid mouth was set and her eyes were cold and hard.

"What's the verdict?" she asked at once, setting her back to the door.

"Dr. Kate refuses to give you the papers," Marsh said, and waited. She thought she could detect a look of fear behind the anger in Evelyn's eyes. Katherine Waring was not to be intimidated so easily.

"The woman's sticking her neck out. Did you tell her what I would do?"

"I told her," Marsh replied, watching the nurse closely. She was striding up and down, fierce short steps of impotent rage. She caught up the fragile material of her gown, wrenching it between her fingers.

Marsh said coldly: "Dr. Kate told me what was in the papers. She will not permit you to continue with a nursing career."

Evelyn stopped. "And if I promise that, will she return them?"

"I think she might."

The nurse laughed savagely. "You think wrongly. Katherine Waring will never let them go unless I force her. She will keep those papers and wait for the right moment. I know her, the cold-blooded devil."

Marsh was silent, waiting for the girl's anger to subside, and hoping that the problem would be taken from her shoulders.

Evelyn saw the cigarette-case lying open on the dressing table. She snatched up a cigarette, lit it with shaking fingers and continued her agitated pacing. Presently she began to smoke more slowly. Her dark eyes became veiled and a little smile twisted her mouth.

"Okay," she said nonchalantly, going to the door. "That's that for the moment. So far she has the whip hand, but we'll just see what happens later. Good night."

Marsh shut the door with a faint sigh of relief. Then her brows drew together. Something Evelyn had said disturbed her with its familiarity. Then she remembered that Michael Waring had issued almost the same warning that afternoon, and at the thought of Michael she experienced a sudden pang of fear. A fear that she had not felt before, even when Laurence Gair had poured his barbed hints into her unwilling ear. Michael was dangerous. His wildness and his unbalanced youthful outlook could do more harm than an adult approach to destruction.

And Michael was up to some immediate mischief, Marsh knew. His sudden politeness to his mother's guests, his abstinence and the air of restrained excitement which had followed on a mysterious telephone call all pointed to imminent danger.

She stripped off her long dinner-gown and climbed once more into her slacks and dark pullover, conscious of the fact that she was tossing aside her newly resolved principles. She smiled wryly when she remembered them and Evelyn Peterson's advice against wandering around in the dark, and then defended her action by thinking that this situation was different. She would be an observer, not a participant this time. Michael was up to something and needed watching. She was not being foolhardy.

She opened the door of her room slightly and crouched on the floor to wait. The boy's room lay opposite. She could see a light under his door, but after a while it was extinguished. Her crouching position soon made her stiff, but she did not move. After a half an hour of discomfort she was rewarded by the sound of a creak and caught a faint movement along the passage. She waited for a minute to pass before she, too, slid out of her room and proceeded cautiously towards the stairs.

A faint slit of light was being played about in the lower hall as she descended. It paused and she sank behind the banisters. Then Michael's head was visible as he bent over the lock of the door. As he went out Marsh moved quickly after him.

There was some scuffling on the verandah and a whine from the dog, Rex. She was near enough to hear Michael mutter: "Not tonight, old chap. You'd better go into the garage or you'll rouse the house."

She waited behind one of the pillars of the verandah until he had put the dog away before she ventured down the steps. Her rubber-soled brogues made no noise, but Michael was on edge. She could guess by the movement of the light that he was glancing over his shoulder, and she felt a slight nervousness in turn as she followed the light through the ti-trees.

When he reached the road Michael pocketed his torch and strode along briskly. The moon was up, displaying the landscape in half-tones of blue and grey, and the air was faintly balmy as the land breeze blew gently over the undulating countryside.

An ideal night for a walk, Marsh thought grimly, as she strained to keep Michael's figure in view. She dared not approach too close for fear he might turn round and see her in the moonlight.

They had gone some distance from Reliance when the boy left the metal road and struck inland away from sight. She ran along the road and found the turning. It was a narrow lane, its surface of hardened mud bearing the imprint of car tyres. Michael was visible for a moment as he topped the rise ahead. Then he disappeared the other side.

She hurried after him. But even before she reached the high point of the lane she knew where they were heading.

CHAPTER SEVEN

I

The white headstones of the cemetery gleamed in the moonlight. There was a terrible beauty about the peaceful scene which sprang from a sense of loneliness rather than from actuality. Marsh, who prided herself on her realistic attitude in her dealings with death, could not prevent an involuntary shudder. Some age-old part of her, linked with an era of superstition, almost caused her to run away. It was the whinny of a horse that brought her back sharply to the existing conditions.

From the shadow of the pine trees in the corner of the cemetery where he had stood that morning, Shane emerged. In either hand he carried a spade.

"He wouldn't dare!" Marsh whispered, aghast. "It's just not possible."

Michael had vaulted the low rocky wall of the graveyard. She saw the two meet and exchange a few words and then clamber across the graves to the newly turned piles of earth covered with their limp flowers.

Trying to quell a deranged idea that it was all a nightmare, that it could not possibly be happening, Marsh slid down into the ditch which bordered the road. The moonlight was so bright now that she bent double and worked her way along to the wall of the cemetery like an animal.

It was a ghoulish scene under the hard cold light of the moon with the breeze soughing through the pine trees. The two men were working without a word, digging at one of the graves. The earth broke easily under the steady labour. Once Michael paused and took off his coat, but the older man beside him kept up his rhythmical movements without a break. Only when the horse whinnied again and came stamping out of the shadows did Shane turn his head. He whistled once and the animal quietened and began to crop the weeds on the nearby graves.

Cramped and cold and nervous, Marsh waited behind the wall. She was both fascinated and repelled as she watched the preparations for an illegal exhumation. Her mind was too shocked to form any idea of what she should do or why she should even stay, but she could not move.

Presently Shane threw down his spade and went over to his horse, while Michael knelt beside the grave flashing his torch into its depths. When the older man came back there was a murmur of voices. Then Shane lowered himself into the hole.

Marsh bent her head on her arms, nauseated. When she looked up again the two men were straining at ropes on opposite sides of the grave. Slowly and painfully a coffin streaming soil came out of the ground.

It slipped back a few inches and Shane gave a sharp order. Both men were breathing heavily but they continued to work rapidly. The coffin was placed alongside the trench. Michael spread out a large ground-sheet while Shane prised open the lid of the coffin. Together they lifted the body out and laid it on the sheet, which was wrapped around it and tied with the ropes. The coffin was thrown back and the grave filled in. Michael was working feverishly now, and Marsh heard Shane say curtly, "Steady!"

He worked the grave over carefully and replaced the wilted wreaths. The horse was led across, jerking its head nervously and bringing up its forelegs a little as the clumsy bundle was slung across the saddle. Shane gripped the bridle above the bit as he adjusted the weight of the body.

"Put the spades over there," he ordered Michael, pointing to the hut near the pine trees. He started to lead the animal in and out the graves, muttering to it under his breath.

Marsh sank down behind the wall again. She waited until the others were some distance ahead before she crept back to the road. They made their way along the rough country roads, across country. Michael was talking excitedly but Shane was scarcely replying. Once

Marsh heard the boy laugh raucously and as the horse shied the man turned on him savagely.

It was a slow procession but at last the distant murmur of the ocean became stronger and they were back near the coast. The road was now little more than a narrow path as it entered the scrub, and Marsh lagged a few steps as Michael began to flash his torch again. She had no idea of their whereabouts so she had perforce to follow. The sea seemed right under their feet now.

Presently the scrub became sparser, to give way to bare land, sloping in folds and dents down the cliffs. From one of these folds rose a windmill, which twisted and whined lazily in the gentle air. The girl sank on the ground again and remained immobile as the men paused. She could see the dark bulk of a cottage below the windmill.

The horse, still carrying its burden, was tethered to the rail of the verandah and Shane went inside the cottage. Lights appeared at the unshaded windows. Then he came out again to help Michael carry the bundle inside. Crouched in the wiry grass, Marsh waited until Shane put the horse away in a shack near the creaking windmill. Then she crept forward to the cottage.

She tiptoed up the steps of the verandah and along to the windows. Her heart gave a sickening jump as Shane came towards them and she pressed herself against the wall. He drew the curtains, leaving but a slit for her to peer through. She could see the body wrapped in the groundsheet on a table, but both men were out of her line of vision.

There was a chink of glasses. "Drink?" Shane asked, in his harsh curt voice.

"Yes," Michael answered. "I mean no. Can't we start right away? It is getting late." The other man laughed shortly. "You'd better have something. Ever watched a post-mortem before?"

Marsh's eyes widened at the word. On the other side of the table was a bookcase. She could not read the titles of the books but some looked familiar. At the same time she remembered what Todd Bannister had said, "If you call everyone Doctor in Matthews you won't go far wrong," and then Simon Morrow's remark: "There is something vaguely familiar about him." It all added up to a fact that she was a fool not to have guessed much earlier.

Then they moved into her view. Shane commenced casually to undo the knots of the shrouded figure on the table. A cigarette was in his mouth and his eyes were half-closed against the smoke as he laid bare the body. It was Sam.

With a word to Michael he left the room for an interval and came back clad in a rubber apron and gloves and carrying a case of instruments.

"You can go if you're queasy," he suggested. "I'll let you know later what I find."

Michael was very pale as he watched Shane handling the shining knives. There were beads of sweat on his forehead and he put up one hand to his mouth. Shane began to whistle softly and Marsh, watching the scene tensely, recognized the tune.

"Stop that!" Michael cried. Then he ran his hand over his face. "I think I will push off now. There is no point in my staying. I'll come back in the morning."

Marsh moved swiftly to the shadows at the end of the verandah as the door opened, letting out a path of light. Michael stumbled going down the steps as the light was shut off. He began to run across the moonlit slope, but at the ridge he stopped and, bending double, started to retch. She waited until he had recovered himself and had gone out of sight.

II

The body lay still untouched on the table and Shane was again out of vision, whistling softly to himself. With a hard-beating heart Marsh went along the verandah to the door and knocked. The whistling broke off at once.

"Is that you, Waring?" Marsh opened the door. Shane stood quite still, staring at her incredulously.

"May I come in?" she asked, as coolly as her thudding heart

would allow. "Your first assistant is vomiting his way home. I offer my services instead."

"How the devil did you get here?" Shane asked angrily. "Did young Waring tell you?"

"I followed him from the house. This is all very illegal, colleague. If I told what I had seen tonight you would go to gaol."

The case of instruments between them winked evilly under the lamplight.

The man said softly: "If I thought you intended to do that, I'd cut your throat. What do you want?"

"I want to know what you are going to do with this body," Marsh replied, advancing towards the table. Shane watched her every movement.

"What are post-mortems usually conducted for?"

"Dr. Waring signed the death certificate," the girl said. "She examined the body herself. She would not make a mistake."

"You think that woman's opinion is infallible, Mowbray. It will give me immense pleasure to report the results of my examination to the right authorities."

His hands moved over the body deliberately.

"One moment," said Marsh quickly. "What has Dr. Kate done to you to earn this interference? And why did you bring her son into your low schemes? He was causing her enough trouble and pain before."

The man looked up. "Your reproaches leave me unmoved. I am beyond the age where my sympathy can be enlisted easily. I learned my lesson twelve years ago. I needed assistance in tonight's business, and young Waring served my purpose."

Marsh leaned over the table. "Why are you so bitter about Dr. Waring?"

"I detest all female doctors," he replied savagely. "They ask to be treated as colleagues but display all the weaknesses of their sex when it comes to a showdown. I am going to make up for my past chivalry now."

"You cannot urge the exhumation of a body already exhumed, if that is your intention."

"The body will be returned tomorrow night. Care to come and help?"

"But the post-mortem you say you are going to conduct! It will be obvious."

Shane put out a hand and pushed aside the case of instruments. "There will be no post-mortem. It is not necessary, but I wanted to be rid of that young whelp. Come round here and look at this."

Marsh edged round the table. Exerting pressure, he twisted the head of the corpse, and pinched the grey skin at the base of the skull.

"A vulnerable spot, my dear colleague. Inspect closely. That mark was no accident. A long thin instrument was inserted there deliberately. The unfortunate Sam was pithed like a frog."

"I can't believe it," the girl whispered. "Dr. Kate—"

"Either Katherine Waring is not the doctor you thought she was or else she ignored it on purpose. Well?"

She gazed at the mark between his fingers. "She wouldn't have missed it. She—I have seen her at work. She is thorough—painstakingly so."

"Then—" said Shane, with a sardonic tilt in his voice.

"No," she said fiercely, looking up at him. "I will not believe it."

He shrugged and replaced the head to its normal position.

Marsh clenched her hands together and walked to the window to stare out on the brightly lighted scene. "What will you tell Michael Waring? What are you going to do?"

"Young Waring? I will tell him nothing. The revenge is mine because I took the risk in exhuming the body. Had I been notified of the hurried inquest—clever woman, your precious Dr. Kate—it wouldn't have been necessary. As matters stand now I am going to photograph the area at the base of the boy's skull and send it to the police. The photograph having been taken prior to today's burial, of course," he added casually.

She swung round. "Supposing," she said in a hard voice, "supposing I got in first? You exhumed the body illegally in order to conduct experiments. That wound is just one of your experiments. That is the story I could tell. I think you have been in trouble before. Will your career stand it again?"

Shane eyed her for a moment. Then he threw back his head and laughed.

"Stop laughing," Marsh said. "I mean what I say."

"No one would believe you," he said, turning away to get another drink. "Will you join me?"

"I mean what I say," she repeated desperately. The instruments flashed in the lamplight as she moved nearer. "I mean it," she said, her voice rising. She snatched at the scalpel lying loose on top of the rest, but Shane was too quick for her.

There was a crash as he let fall the glass he was holding to grasp her wrist. The low hanging lamp was set in motion, knocked by his shoulder in his swift movement. Marsh's fingers splayed and twitched under the brutal grip. Her vision became clouded as the shadows stretched and shortened under the swinging lamp. Her brain felt clogged and irrational.

Shane's eyes held her bemused gaze until the knife dropped back on to the table. "You little fool, Mowbray! Get away from that woman before you lose your head completely."

At once his words reminded her of similar advice she had given Betty Donne and the thought of the nurse's mental state helped her to gain her self-control.

I must have been mad, she thought, looking down at the scalpel.

Shane pushed her into a chair and threw some twigs on to the dying fire. Then he mixed a drink and put the glass into her hand. She swallowed it in one gulp and coughed as it burned her throat.

"I don't know what came over me," she said, but Shane was silent as he watched her.

"I was tired—terribly tired when I came down to Matthews," she went on inconsequently. "And then everything happened. Such a lot of things have happened. Someone attacked me last night in the laboratory. I wanted to go away then. But Dr. Kate . . . Was it you?" She rubbed her wrist. The marks of his fingers were still there. "It could have been you."

"No," said Shane gently. "It was not I. Why don't you leave Matthews?"

Marsh was quiet for a moment. The whisky was circulating

warmly through her body. The lamp had stopped swaying and the fire crackled comfortingly.

"I can't leave yet," she answered stubbornly. "Please give me time. Wait for a little while before you do anything about—" and she gestured towards Sam's body. The man rose and covered it up.

"Please, Shane."

He turned back to her, frowning heavily. "You are either a brave woman or a very foolish one. What do you hope to achieve by time?"

"There is some explanation. I know Dr. Kate too well. I must stay by her until I discover that explanation."

He shrugged again. "Very well. I'll stave off Michael and give you three days."

"Three days! That is not long."

"I have waited twelve years," Shane said, his eyes and mouth hard. "Twelve years to repay Katherine Waring."

"Why do you hate her? Help me, Shane. Why am I talking like this to you? You are a stranger. There is something mysterious and furtive about you. I don't trust you."

His eyes gleamed for a moment. "I think you are a little drunk, my dear. Drunk from relief after an ordeal. Tonight's show was enough for the strongest stomach, even a hard-boiled woman doctor like yourself. Naturally you want to talk now. It doesn't matter to whom as long as it is a man, not a woman, and least of all Katherine Waring. You have been under a constraint of thought and word, and now you want to talk. Go on."

"Quite a psychiatrist!" Marsh said, her spirit reviving.

"I know women," he replied, his eyes running over her lazily.

"Tell me what happened twelve years ago," she asked abruptly, sitting up straight.

The man laughed. "Don't be scared, Mowbray. I am not going to insult you. Like all women, the thought was your own. Relax while I tell you my story. I'd like you to hear it, as it may make you see the light."

"I won't believe a word you say if it is detrimental to Dr. Kate," the girl declared, but her words sounded pettish in her own ears.

With that disconcerting and humiliating habit of suddenly

ignoring her, he did not reply. He leant his arm along the edge of the mantelpiece and stared down at the fire.

III

"Twelve years ago I was a resident at a Base Hospital in the country. Your sainted Katherine Waring and her late-lamented spouse were then partners in the town. They were mounting the ladder together in those days."

"Go on, please," Marsh ordered urgently, as he paused to reflect.

"One day there came into the wards under my supervision a woman who was a patient of theirs. She was ill but not seriously so, and we did all we could be called upon to do while waiting for information and instructions from the Warings. That information did not come. Then the patient died very suddenly. It was a complete surprise and shock, and the medical superintendent of the hospital, after the post-mortem, refused to allow the death certificate to be signed without an inquiry being made. The patient had received no treatment at all at the hospital and I was called in to be asked why.

"I told the superintendent I had received no information and instruction for treatment from the Warings. I was dismissed as Kingsley was shown in. The following day I learned that an inquest had been ordered which I was to attend as a witness.

"On the morning of the inquest I had an invitation from Waring to lunch. Being young and enthusiastic I jumped at the opportunity to form an acquaintance with the up-and-coming Kingsley. He was affable, very affable over lunch; clapped me on the back and called me 'my boy'. I was impressed but not suspicious. Over the table we discussed my career and he dropped out hints as to how he could help me. I was positively hero-worshipping by this time. Then with the coffee came the real motive for his affability.

"That unfortunate woman who had died. Frightfully bad luck, the whole thing. He had done his damnedest to avoid an inquest, but the medical super did not like him. Jealous, you know. And there it was.

"Here he glanced over his shoulder, leaned across the table and lowered his voice as I sat smoking one of his cigarettes and warming the brandy he had ordered for me.

"The patient had really been one of his wife's. Frankly, old boy, you can't go into the witness-box and say the patient had died from neglect. It would ruin Katherine's career. She was terribly upset and Kingsley had promised to do what he could.

"All along the same line. It all boiled down to this, though I was still bemused by Kingsley's eloquence and the fine-sounding promises he had made. I was to soften up on the evidence and to push the blame on to anyone but Kingsley and his wife."

Shane paused and smiled bitterly. "I did it well. In fact, I was so chivalrously disposed towards Kate Waring that I found the whole blame laid on myself. The coroner was quite nasty at the summing-up, but by then it was too late for me to do anything. After the inquest Waring slapped me on the back again and called me 'old boy' once more.

"It was white, damned white of me, and get in touch with him when I wanted any advice. I thanked him and then went into the nearest pub to get drunk.

"That night the superintendent called me into his room and threw a Melbourne paper across his desk. 'You damned fool, Shane,' was his comment.

"There it was in neat headlines on the front page— 'Doctor sharply reprimanded for neglect.'

"It was in the next day's papers, too, and the day after that there were letters of indignation to the editors. Either the public or the profession likes to make tin gods out of doctors, so such a scandal is all the more shocking.

"A week later the hospital board demanded my resignation.

"And that, my dear Dr. Mowbray, was what your cherished Katherine did to me without so much as appearing in the picture."

"What did you do when you resigned?" Marsh asked, watching his dark bitter face intently.

"I took a locum up country for a few months, hoping everything would quieten down. But when I came back my name was still notorious. I called up Kingsley Waring to see what he could do for me, but he and his wife had given up their practice and had gone to Melbourne. It took me three months to see him. He was still affable though he didn't clap me on the back this time. He had a nice set of rooms in Collins Street now and told me he was specializing in surgery. His appointment book was already overloaded. Katherine was also specializing.

"He discussed everything except my problem, and I left his office none the better but a great deal wiser for having called on him. Soon after that I heard of a job going as a ship's doctor on a liner for Great Britain. Don't ever be a ship's doctor, Mowbray. Ever tried looking after seasick patients when you are feeling lousy yourself?"

Marsh smiled briefly. "Have you been in England all this lime? Why did you come back?"

"I had an urge to see my own country again," he replied carelessly. "I have now enough degrees and experience to set myself up in Collins Street and knock most of the others out. I thought I'd take a holiday down here before I began."

"I see," said Marsh. "And Mr Waring met you here again."

"He called in one day to escape the rain. He had been out walking. I rather enjoyed our conversation," he added cryptically. "I even went so far as to offer to lend him some medical books that I brought out from England. I had them sent down from town and dropped them in to him the night you heard me on the verandah."

"Was that what you were after in the laboratory?"

"It was. Does my explanation tie up to your satisfaction?"

"Perhaps," she replied, and stood up.

Shane regarded her amusedly. "You are an odd girl. Because you are trying to smother your doubts about one person, you are suspicious about everyone else. Why won't you admit it?"

Marsh walked away from him. "Admit what?" she asked coldly.

"What you are trying to hide from yourself. That Katherine Waring is a murderess."

Marsh stiffened. She was at the door and her back turned. "Will

145

you keep your promise about Sam?" she asked, in an even tone.

He came up behind her and put one hand on her shoulder to turn her round. She faced him steadily.

"You run up and down the gamut, but your loyalty remains unchanged. I'd like to know more of you, Mowbray." He dropped his hand. "I'll stay quiet for three days."

"Thank you," she said, and slipped out of the cottage.

IV

The moon had passed its zenith, but Marsh had no difficulty in finding the path back to the road. The trip along the macadam was easy, too, but she shied when a rabbit shot its startled way across. It was only when she entered the drive which led to Reliance that she became conscious of nervousness. Until then her mind had been engrossed with plans to combat Shane's ultimatum.

Here the ti-trees were too closely growing to permit any moonlight, making it necessary to feel her way along. She was glad when she was through the scrub and the dark familiar bulk of her runabout under the pines could be seen. The house stood out as clearly as in daylight. She kept her eyes on it and, remaining as far as she could in the shadows, edged her way around the yard. A faint whine from the outbuildings meant that Rex was still locked in the garage. Either Michael Waring had forgotten to set him loose or else he had not yet come home.

She crossed the verandah and touched the door. It was open and slid inwards with a faint creak. She stood on the threshold, listening. The house was very quiet. Step by step she felt her way along the passage to the stairs and began to mount.

Suddenly, out of the darkness above a light was shone full in her face. She stood paralysed, gripping the hand-rail hard. She could neither move nor speak. Then the light was extinguished and a faint pad of footsteps sounded hurrying along the upper hall.

Swiftly she climbed the remainder of the stairs and found her bedroom door. She paused there, straining her eyes through the dark. She was breathing rapidly and her face was wet with perspiration. After a moment she backed into her room and locked the door.

Thus Marsh passed her fourth consecutive night of uneasiness.

It was playing on her, she knew. She was a good enough doctor to realize that, however adaptable and resilient human nature is, four days and nights of tension, doubts, and fears leave some mark on the mind and body. There is a tendency to jump at an unexpected noise, to regard with suspicion the most guileless of remarks, to interpret an innocent action as a furtive movement.

She had developed the habit of covertly inspecting the members of the household when they were all together, which was usually at meal-times. And now, with the ever-present awareness of Shane's time limit, her scrutiny, impartial before, had become a desperate aid to the theories her tired brain evolved. She was ready to use any means, however undependable.

Katherine Waring was not present at breakfast the following morning, and the others had lapsed into a morose silence, forgivable in the absence of the hostess. But towards the end of the meal she appeared at the door. She was dressed again in the grey linen as the day promised to be hot. It seemed exactly the colour of her fine eyes.

"Don't get up, Henry," she said, as Arkwright rose clumsily. "I have had breakfast. I thought you might like to know I will be reading King's will presently. Anyone may come in if they wish."

A little murmur went round the table. Marsh, noting the faint scornful smile on Dr. Waring's lips, made a mental resolve not to be present.

The older woman looked at her. "If you could spare a moment, Marsh, I would like to see you."

She got up at once and followed Katherine Waring out of the room. They went into the library.

"Sit down, Marsh. You look tired this morning. Didn't you sleep well?"

"Not very well," she replied, averting her face. She imagined that Dr. Waring's gaze was over-keen.

Katherine Waring picked up a pencil from her desk and drew it through her fingers. "You know, Marsh," she said, on a sigh, "of all the people here at Reliance, you are the only one I know I can trust." She paused and surveyed the girl silently. Marsh wriggled a little in her chair. "I trust you," she repeated.

The girl took out a cigarette and began to smoke quickly. Her nervousness was apparent and she tried to calm herself.

Dr. Waring laid down the pencil and sat on the edge of the desk, her fingers on a sheet of paper beside her.

"I know your innate integrity so well that I would never listen to anyone who might try to turn me against you. You are the type of person who would never let another down. Not only would I not listen, but it is my endeavour to scotch at once any unpleasantness connected with your name. Marsh, I want you to read this."

She picked up the paper, gave it to the girl and went over to the window. "Read it carefully," she said over her shoulder, "and tell me what you think."

The note was printed in distorted block letters on a sheet of plain paper. *Ask Marsh Mowbray where she was last night.*

"Well, Marsh?"

The girl fumbled for words, feeling sick and ashamed. Whoever it was who had flashed the light in her face was responsible for this. "Dr. Kate, I don't know what to say. An anonymous letter—"

Dr. Waring swung round. "An anonymous letter is a foul filthy thing," she broke in vehemently. "Tear it up, Marsh. Yes, do as I say. Tear it up and throw it in the waste-paper basket."

Marsh did so. As the last fragments fluttered to a resting-place, the other woman spoke. "I am not going to demean myself by asking you to answer the question, but there is something I would like to say. Believe me, I say it in all good faith. Emotional relations with the opposite sex are not for you. They could ruin your career. Take it from my experience that they will do you no good. If, by some chance, you should become involved in any way, remember always to weigh up your everlasting interest in your career with that of a fleeting unsatisfactory phase."

"You think," Marsh said in a low voice, "the letter meant that?"

"I don't think anything," she replied swiftly. "I told you I trusted you." She glanced over Marsh's head as the door opened. "Oh—Henry! I am not quite ready, but come in."

Relieved at the chance to escape, Marsh got up and left the room. Dr. Waring's supreme faith in her was almost unendurable under the existing conditions. She had an unshakable confidence in her, to which Marsh felt she had no claim.

At the foot of the stairs she paused to watch the others file along the passage to the library. Arkwright was already there, eager and anxious to know the will, but trying to cover up his expectancy. Michael sauntered in, careless and defiant, sure of his standing. Mrs Arkwright seemed certain of her position also. She went past Marsh, ignoring her.

But Laurence Gair paused at the sight of her. "Aren't you going to join the vultures?" he asked maliciously.

"I expect no pickings," she replied curtly.

Then Evelyn Peterson came up. There was a little knowing smile hovering about her mouth as she nodded to Marsh. The library door closed after them.

"There they go—the whole scheming bunch!" said a low voice in her ear.

Betty Donne stood behind her, her cheeks flushed and her hands clenched. "Aren't you going to stand by Dr. Kate? Aren't you going to protect her from them?"

"The will does not concern me," Marsh said coldly.

The nurse gave her a contemptuous look and then walked straight to the library. Marsh waited until the door had closed before she made her way down to the kitchen. Miss Jennet might be talkative and foolish, but her position in the house was a vantage ground that might be exploited.

V

The radio was on softly, as though Miss Jennet considered it improper to make a noise at such a grave time. Because of this, she was crouched up close to the speaker and either did not see Marsh come in or else was too absorbed in the forty-seventh episode. The breakfast dishes lay stacked on the table.

Marsh waited patiently until the episode concluded with a burst of atmospheric music. "Let me help you with the dishes. Miss Donne has gone to the library."

The little woman looked around at her, the rapt expression fading. "Why, Dr. Mowbray! I didn't hear you come in. No, please don't. You might spoil your frock. My, but that colour does suit you. I do like red on a dark person."

She sank a pile of dirty plates into the hot soapy water in the sink. Her small fat hands emerged pink and shining. "Poor dear Kate! I hope Mrs Arkwright won't be trying. I suppose her complaint makes her sour. And Michael—"

"I noticed Mrs Arkwright avoiding the sugar foods," Marsh interrupted casually. "Is she a diabetic, too?"

Miss Jennet nodded. "Such a business! It must run in the family. Now she has only one injection a day. Globin insulin. You see I know quite a bit about medical matters, Doctor. Kate always tells me anything I want to know. But King was different. Three times a day he would pass by that door and go up to the laboratory for his injection."

Without any difficulty or prompting she had got on to the subject Marsh had wanted to discuss. What was better still she did not seem to regard the girl's interest as out of the way.

"The day before Mr Waring became ill, did you see him go to the laboratory for his third needle? It was the evening I arrived. Can you remember?"

"Of course I remember," Miss Jennet answered reproachfully. "I was listening to *The Farmer's Family*. It was just as Merle was leaving the house to elope."

"Were you in the kitchen most of that day? I mean—whom else did you see going up to the lab?"

Miss Jennet pursed her mouth. "There was Mr Gair. I know he did because he had the key to lock up after dinner. Then Miss Donne said Kingsley was wanted on the 'phone for a Melbourne call—funny, that, because when he got to the 'phone there was no one there. He was quite annoyed about it, and sent me up to the laboratory to ask Miss Donne who had been calling him."

"You mean Miss Donne didn't come back to the house with Mr Waring after telling him he was wanted on the 'phone? She stayed in the lab?"

Miss Jennet nodded, and hurried on: "Then that Peterson person. She kept going whenever she thought King was in the lab. And I think Kate went once, but I'm not sure. I happened to be looking out of the window just as she was coming up the verandah steps."

Miss Jennet thought for a minute. "Oh yes, the Arkwrights, too. Certainly Mrs Arkwright, because she asked me where she could find an umbrella. It was raining hard that day. Isn't it funny to remember when it is quite warm now?"

Before she could enlarge on the whimsicality of the climate at Matthews, the kitchen door opened with a jerk and Betty Donne came in. She looked as though she had been crying, and stopped short at the sight of Marsh.

"Give me that towel," she said roughly. "You are doing my work." She snatched it away.

"Now, Sister! Don't be nasty to the Doctor. She was only helping. You'd better go now, Dr. Mowbray. Perhaps Kate wouldn't like it."

As Marsh left the room she heard Miss Donne say, "Dr. Kate doesn't mind you and I doing it, Miss Jennet."

Laurence Gair was coming along the passage as she shut the door behind her. He saw her, but averted his eyes and ran lightly up the stairs. Marsh followed, and as she passed the open door of his room he was throwing a bag on to the bed. She paused and leaned against the jamb, her brows raised.

"Leaving, Larry?"

He unzipped the bag. "Yes," he replied curtly.

"So suddenly? Were the pickings good?"

His hands faltered. "I'm satisfied. The others are still arguing downstairs." He strode over to the dressing-table and began to pull out the contents.

"Good heavens!" Marsh said, diverted. "You don't sleep in those, do you?"

Gair stuffed the gaudy pyjamas away. "Avert your maiden gaze, my girl."

"I'm too dazzled. It is a wonder you don't have nightmares."

The smile faded from his face. "Nightmares?" he echoed. "Come here, Marsh."

"What is it?" she asked, advancing cautiously.

He came to stand right over her, his hands hanging loose at his sides. He was frowning and his underlip was caught between his teeth. Marsh thought his manner betrayed some secret indecision. Larry, who was so certain of himself and who rarely allowed any weak emotion to escape through his suavity, was bewildered.

"Last night I had a nightmare. A horrible dream about you and Katherine Waring." He raised his hands uncertainly and then placed them suddenly on her shoulders. "Marsh, forget everything I said. Wipe it clean out of your mind. Leave here today—with me."

She twisted out of his grasp. "Rather sudden, aren't you, Larry? Two nights ago you threw out a challenge. I accepted it. Either you draw back or I don't leave here until I prove you were wrong."

"I said forget it." He turned back to the dressing-table. "Forget that challenge."

"You admit you were wrong about Dr. Kate?"

His eyes met hers in the mirror. "No," he said quietly. "In all honesty I cannot convince myself that I was wrong. But you are treading on dangerous ground and you must stop."

Marsh went back to the door. "I told you once before that your cynicism corrupted others. You force me to think only one thing."

"What is that?"

"Your pickings were good. I warned you that you yourself are not above suspicion."

A drawer was slammed violently. He swung round, his face dark with anger. "Marsh, don't be a fool. You know how I feel about you. I don't want you to come to any harm."

"I can't believe you, Larry. Self-preservation was always your strongest instinct."

For a moment they faced each other, both taut with anger. Gair was the first to relax. He went over to her, smiling.

"Maybe you're right. I'd rather keep out of strife than get into it. Come, say good-bye for the present nicely. I will see you in town before you sail. We will be able to talk more reasonably away from Reliance. These last few days have been enough to distort anyone's reason."

"Very well, Larry," Marsh said. She held out her hand.

He looked down at it. "What a poor farewell!" He tried to draw her nearer, but footsteps sounded along the passage and Delia Arkwright passed, giving them a steely glance. Gair made a face at her retreating back.

Picking up his bag, he said: "Perhaps I was wrong about Dr. Kate. Somehow I can't believe so. Be careful, won't you."

"It cost you something to say that much, Larry," Marsh replied, with a faint smile. "I know you are wrong. Good-bye."

He hesitated again. "Well, good-bye. Marsh—er—after I've gone see if I have left anything behind. Have a look through the drawers and cupboards. I may have missed something." He turned quickly and was gone.

Marsh remained still. She would miss Larry, she told herself. When they were together there was continual friction, but now she would miss him. She puzzled over this conflicting idea, and came to the conclusion that Larry's departure made her feel not so much lonely as more alone. There was now one less at Reliance. She did not like the feeling.

Mrs Arkwright came by the door again. She saw the girl alone.

"Has Dr. Gair left? Such a lucky young man," she remarked, with disapproving envy. "Kingsley took such an interest in him, but to leave him his practice like that! I really can't understand Kingsley's motives. And two enormous lump sums to persons I have never heard of. Katherine must contest the will."

She went away when she saw that her complaints were falling on deaf ears.

Marsh commenced to tidy the vacated room. She straightened the counterpane on the bed and pushed drawers to. She took the vase of flowers through to the adjoining bathroom, throwing the faded blooms into the waste-can and emptying the water down the basin. Then she opened the cabinet above the basin to see if Larry had forgotten anything. There were one or two odds and ends—then her hands stopped and she stood quite still. Wedged behind a group of bottles was a sheaf of papers.

She drew them down fearfully, for at once she had recognized them as belonging to Kingsley Waring's indexed scrapbook.

CHAPTER EIGHT

I

Marsh's immediate reaction was the thought that Larry had intended her to find the papers. As she stood staring down at them in her hand there came the sound of a car being driven away from Reliance. He had given himself a good start.

The bathroom was white and still. There was a faint aroma of brilliantine or soap associated with Gair in the air. Steps along the passage made her start guiltily. She shut the cabinet and went quietly through to the bedroom. The door was still open as Gair had left it. She looked out just in time to see Surgeon-Commander Arkwright entering his room. She hastened across the passage.

"Dr. Mowbray!" Arkwright had seen her. She opened her door quickly and threw the papers on the floor as he came back.

"You were trying to run away from me," he declared, his bulging eyes reproachful. "I have been looking for you. What about our sail today?"

She gazed at him blankly for a moment. He came a little nearer. "What is it, my dear? You look startled. You know, I have been observing you. You haven't looked at all the thing. The responsibility of King was too much for you."

"You told me that before," she said curtly. "I'm all right."

"I was talking to Kate about you," he pursued, trying to wedge himself into her half-open door. A corner of paper showed under it. "She thinks you should leave."

"Did Dr. Kate say that?"

He fondled her shoulder. "Not precisely, but you know what Kate is. She never says much. The most enigmatic woman of my acquaintance. But I'm certain she agreed with me."

Marsh slipped away from his hand. "I will leave when Dr. Waring wants me to go; not before. Will you excuse me now, please?"

His eyes bulged still more with apprehension. "You sound offended. Don't let my clumsiness upset you. You are all on edge. A good blow on the briny will fix you. What about after lunch?"

Anxious to be rid of him, Marsh agreed. When he attempted to nudge the door wider she slipped through the opening and locked it in his face.

"After lunch then," Arkwright said through the wood.

She waited until his footsteps went along the passage before she picked up the papers at her feet and took them to spread out on the bed.

In questioning Katherine Waring's integrity, Gair had based his attack on the cause of the partnership break between the Warings. Like Marsh he had anticipated finding the answer in the diaries, and had stumbled on the scrapbook. He could have removed the pages under W even some time before her foolhardy expedition to the laboratory, and taken them to his room to study more closely.

Filled with apprehension Marsh examined the sheets. On them were pasted several yellowing newspaper cuttings, a creased letter written in an uneducated hand and another typewritten one, obviously a duplicate, unsigned and typed on thin plain paper.

She read the newspaper cuttings first. One had a block heading which stated 'Doctor sharply reprimanded by Coroner'. The words seemed to waver across the page under her bemused gaze.

This was the story Shane had told her. The inquest on a Mrs Farmer that Kingsley Waring had noted in his diary. The inquest which had disgraced Shane was the cause of the partnership break, brought about, according to both Shane and Waring, by Katherine.

The scrapbook was Kingsley's recorded evidence of mistakes made by colleagues, and Mrs Farmer's death from lack of proper medical attention was Katherine's big mistake.

With trembling fingers Marsh picked up the letters. The handwritten one was evidently from the husband of the dead woman, who had been unable to resign himself to the tragedy. It was full of a pathetic helpless abuse, and contained wild accusations and threats.

It was your fault, not the hospital's. I will tell everyone it was your fault. The same sort of thing covered nearly two irregularly written pages.

The typewritten letter was a duplicate copy of the reply. Deepest regret was expressed, but a stern warning was issued against repeating such unwise remarks. The Coroner's finding must be accepted as final, and, even allowing for understandable grief, if there was any further communication on the matter, or repetition of such foolish and exaggerated statements, the matter would be put into the hands of a solicitor.

Marsh sank on her knees beside the bed and buried her face in the counterpane. Her whole being cried out at this unmerciful shattering of her dream of Katherine Waring's inviolate character.

I can't believe it, she thought to herself. She wouldn't neglect a patient. *Perhaps that is why she is always so over-scrupulous with patients now*, a voice suggested in her mind.

"No, no," Marsh whispered. "Dr. Kate would never threaten anyone—least of all a simple grief-ridden relative."

Haven't you found that ruthless streak in her? the voice said slyly.

Marsh got up and paced about the room to beat off the devil's caress.

There must be some explanation, she thought, clenching her hands together. There must be something. Larry wanted me to find the cuttings, but he wasn't triumphant or malicious about her when he left. He was—why, he was fighting against his previous convictions; whereas I am fighting the other way. There must be something that he did not tell me, but he has given me the chance to find out.

She darted back to the bed and picked up the typewritten letter. Did Katherine Waring really write this?

Then her face changed and she became calmer—no, actually, she did not write it. The nurse or someone they employed at the time typed it under instructions. Her initials were at the foot of the letter. If she could only find that nurse she might be able to learn the true facts of the case.

She gathered the papers together quickly. They must not be found lying about in her room, but must be returned to their rightful place in the laboratory where Katherine Waring would one day come across them and destroy them. She put them into her handbag and went to her door.

The passage was empty and the house quiet and cool as Marsh walked down the stairs and along the lower hall to the verandah. She blinked when she emerged into the hot sunshine, and headed for the laboratory. The track was drying in cracked flakes and the heat had hatched a thousand flies.

As she drew near the building she heard the sound of voices and prepared to turn back. No one must see her replacing the cuttings. They were hard feminine voices, raised in anger. Then there came a crash and a splintering of glass. She hastened towards the laboratory door.

On either side of the room stood the two nurses, eyeing each other fiercely. The remains of a test-tube lay near Evelyn Peterson's feet and there was a wet stain on the wall behind her head.

"What on earth are you doing?" Marsh demanded, from the doorway.

Miss Peterson did not remove her gaze from Betty Donne's. "Just in time to referee, Doctor," she said, an ugly smile curling her mouth.

Before Marsh could move, she was across the room and the two girls were buffeting and scratching at each other. They fell on the floor together, their arms threshing wildly. Evelyn's hair was all over her face as the other nurse tugged at it. Then Marsh saw her draw her fingers cruelly across Betty's cheek.

"For heaven's sake, stop!" Marsh cried, stamping her foot impotently.

They took no heed, but Betty, with her face bleeding and her hands clutching the dark hair, panted out, "You keep out of this."

She struggled to her knees, throwing Evelyn off and lurched towards the work bench. Her hand closed over a bottle.

Evelyn was still struggling to her feet, but she saw the bottle coming and put up one arm to protect her head. It broke, cutting the back of her hand. Betty started to laugh. Her face was heated, but three red scratches stood out across her cheek. Her eyes were red-rimmed and wild.

She looks mad now, Marsh thought.

Evelyn was swearing softly. Blood was dripping from her hand as she advanced slowly towards Katherine Waring's nurse, who was weak with hysteria. There was murder in her dark eyes as she deliberately planned her next attack.

"Miss Peterson," Marsh said sharply. "Stop at once. Get over there behind that table. The girl isn't responsible. Do as I say."

At Marsh's words, Betty Donne turned on her in a fury. She rushed at her blindly, screaming in rage. Marsh grabbed her arms hard above the elbows.

"Hold her," Evelyn shrieked. "Let me get at her."

Marsh raised one hand swiftly. She dealt the girl two sharp blows on either cheek, and, clenching her fist, drove straight to the point of her jaw. Betty crumpled to the floor.

Rubbing her knuckles, she turned to Evelyn. "I have never learned boxing," she said evenly, "but I shall experiment on you, too, if you like."

For a moment Evelyn eyed her. Then she shook her head and began to grin, raising one grimy hand to brush the hair out of her face.

"All right," said Marsh. "Now help me up with this girl. "

Together they managed to drag her across to the divan and dumped her roughly on to it. Marsh went over to the cabinet to find cotton wool and antiseptic. She dabbed at Betty's face with water until her eyes opened. She looked straight up at Marsh and there was hatred in the stare, but she submitted to having the antiseptic applied to her scratches.

"How do you feel?" Marsh asked crisply. She had been a little worried about the results of her amateur boxing.

Betty did not speak at once. Then she turned her head aside and said in a tired voice: "I'll go back to the house. I want to lie down."

Marsh tried to help her up. "Keep your hands off me. I can manage." She got to her feet shakily and limped towards the door. Marsh moved between the two girls warily.

At the doorway Betty turned, touching her torn cheek. "We haven't finished yet, Peterson."

Evelyn replied cheerfully, "Next time I'll tear your guts out."

"What happened?" Marsh asked, shutting the door against any

further exchange of threats. "What did you two mean by behaving like animals? If Dr. Kate—"

"Oh, Dr. Kate!" Evelyn said disdainfully. "I'm sick of that woman's name being for ever thrust at me." She fumbled in the pocket of her torn sports-dress for a cigarette.

"You'd better let me look at that hand," Marsh said. "Then we'll clean the place up. It looks a shambles."

Evelyn said, giving up her hand: "Did you see that hellcat with her bottles? If she'd had a knife to hand she would have thrown that."

"You'd be well advised to leave Reliance," Marsh said, pulling her towards the sink. "I'll have a word with Dr. Kate about Betty. Go today before she sees you again. You were like two she-cats fighting over a tom."

The nurse laughed. "I did not think you could be so vulgar, Doctor. Your description is just about right. Only that particular she-cat doesn't want the tom. I do."

Marsh looked at her sharply. "Michael Waring?"

"Guessed it in one," she replied shamelessly. "Quite bright, aren't you? Betty was all for protecting her saintly Katherine's unsaintly son. I don't see why. He's fair prey."

"What's your game?"

Evelyn shrugged her shoulders. "Dr. Kate won't give me what I want. Okay, I'll take Michael instead—plus the money King left him. I wonder how she will like that."

"And Michael?"

"He's responding nicely, thank you. I may even marry him. I could develop quite a fondness for him. Part of our natures seems identical."

"You'll break Dr. Kate's heart if you ruin Michael."

Evelyn laughed raucously. "It will give me the greatest pleasure, always supposing she has a heart."

Marsh dropped her hand. "Personally I consider young Michael a rotter, and it will do him good to get into the clutches of another rotter."

"You're very complimentary, I must say," she observed, without resentment. "Luckily for you I am in such a mellow mood. I enjoyed my scrap with that besotted half-wit, especially scratching her face. It took me back to the old days. I saw my mother do that once. Class will out, won't it, Doctor?"

Marsh bent down to pick up her handbag. "Who was with Mr Waring before you?" she asked abruptly.

"Some desiccated wench he'd had for years. I don't remember her name."

"Try and remember," Marsh argued.

"Why should I? I know she trained at the Queen Vic."

There was a speculative look in her dark eyes before she lowered them. She strolled over to the door.

"You know, Doctor," she said, over her shoulder. "You are rather obvious. We all know damn well what you are up to. Even Dr. Kate must by now. You'd better be careful," she added, as she stepped out of the laboratory.

Marsh stared after her in dismay. The warning was decidedly disturbing. She thought she had been discreet. Perhaps she had not been wise in questioning Evelyn a second time, but the others and Dr. Kate could not possibly know. Evelyn was only bluffing.

Quelling a tiny tremor of fear she put the thoughts aside as she tidied the room and carefully replaced the cuttings in the filing cabinet. Then she left the laboratory and made her way through the ti-trees to the road.

II

The sun was high and strong and the road shimmered in the heat. She could feel it through the thin soles of her sandals. Across the golf-course the sea broke lazily against the rocks. It was a deep steady blue. A slight breeze came from it, but Marsh lost its relief when she reached the village, which lay in a hollow. The loose sign on the red-brick hotel hung unmoving in the still air. Brushing the flies away irritably, she crossed the road.

Only a few fishermen were in the bar, while the private parlour was empty. The mushroom population of Matthews had departed with the week-end. The parlour was cool and dim after the heat outside, and Marsh sank wearily into a chair.

Mrs Bannister put her head in the door. "Oh, Dr. Mowbray," she said uncertainly. "Todd's out. He went down for a swim."

"I didn't come to see Todd," the girl replied. "Can I have a gin and lemon, please? And I want to make a 'phone call to town."

Mrs Bannister nodded to the telephone in the corner and withdrew. Without standing upright, Marsh dragged her chair towards it. She rang the local Exchange and booked her call. She was waiting to get through when Mrs Bannister brought in her drink.

"You look tired, Doctor," she remarked, with a sidelong glance, "and not very well. I heard you have had an upsetting time at Reliance."

Marsh nodded. "It hasn't been too happy."

The woman fidgeted about the table. "We hear things down here in the village."

"Do you?" the girl asked coldly. "What things?"

The telephone rang and she picked up the receiver. Mrs Bannister went out of the room. "Hullo? Queen Victoria Hospital? I want to speak to Sister Gullett, please. Yes, I'll hold on."

She waited, sipping her icy drink and holding the receiver at her ear. There was quite a long interval before someone came to the line.

"Hullo, Sister Gullett? This is Marsh Mowbray. I'm at Matthews."

Amelia Gullett's voice came over sonorously. "Doc, you fool! I told you not to go down there. You've run into a pretty upset. What do you want?"

Someone had come into the parlour behind her. She lowered her voice. "Sister, find out the name of Kingsley Waring's nurse for me, will you?"

"I can tell you. A little slut if there ever was one."

"I know her. She's here at Matthews. I want the one before. She trained at the Queen Vic. She shouldn't be too hard to trace. No, don't ask me why. Just find her name and how I can contact her."

There was a pause before Sister Gullett said, "I'd like to know what you are up to."

"I'd like to know myself. You'll do as I ask?"

Sister Gullett grunted. "I'm going on night-duty tonight."

"I'll call you up tomorrow morning early then. Do your best. It's important." She hung up the receiver before the ward sister could protest further, and turned to finish her drink.

Only a table away, Simon Morrow sat. He smiled at her. "Good morning, Dr. Mowbray."

"Good morning," she returned ungraciously, wondering how much he had overheard. His blandness and extreme courtesy aroused her distrust.

"How is everybody at Reliance?" he asked, taking off his gloves. An affectation in such warm weather, Marsh thought. "Is Henry Arkwright supporting Katherine in his usual treacly way? So anxious to be leaned on, poor Henry. And the tortured Michael? How is he? I see King's young partner has left. Katherine must feel her last link with King broken."

Beneath his suavity, Marsh thought she detected a question. "Dr. Kate read the will this morning," she informed him. "The party is breaking up."

He inclined his head. "The corpse is left denuded of its flesh. How soon do you go?"

"When Dr. Kate asks me," Marsh replied evenly. "Is there any message you want me to convey?"

His hands paused as he was opening his cigarette-case. The lid flew back suddenly. "I can wait until I see Katherine," he said pleasantly.

Marsh dropped some money on the table, nodded and went out. She found Morrow's conversation irritatingly abstruse.

III

Luncheon was in progress when she arrived back at Reliance. Katherine Waring glanced up briefly as she entered, but she did not smile or reply to Marsh's apologies. She seemed distrait and did not speak much during the meal. She had withdrawn herself farther away from the others.

In sharp contrast to his mother, Michael Waring was in good spirits. The morning's bequest was the cause of his animation. Evelyn Peterson had easy material to work on. Marsh watched her effortless inveiglement with a certain grim amusement. There was, as Evelyn had said, an identical streak in both natures; a bold insensitive trait. They were making plans for a bathing expedition that afternoon.

Surgeon-Commander Arkwright, his eyes goggling at the girl's behaviour, turned to Marsh. "Don't forget our little cruise on the briny, will you."

Evelyn heard him, and, to test her power, cried: "Sailing! I would love to come."

Michael's face darkened and he glowered across the table.

"No, no," Arkwright said, flinching under the fierce gaze directed on him. "The ship will only fit two. Comfortably, that is. Some other time."

The girl opened her eyes at him, registering disappointment.

"You're swimming with me," Michael declared angrily.

Evelyn gave him a sidelong glance, and smiled until the angry gleam left his eyes.

Surprisingly Delia Arkwright came into the conversation. "Henry, you must take Dr. Mowbray out. She deserves a pleasant outing for a change. So many unpleasant outings you have had, haven't you, Doctor?"

Marsh stirred her coffee and started to reply casually. She really did not care whether she went with Henry or not, and was in the middle of saying so when something in Mrs Arkwright's stare and a delayed reaction of her words made her stop.

She faltered, holding her coffee-spoon poised over the cup. She had a quick conviction that it was Mrs Arkwright who had seen her returning to Reliance the night before. She was glad of the slight disturbance when Betty Donne came in to eat a belated meal.

The nurse had been serving and was now ready for her lunch, as the others rose. Dr. Waring's eyes were on the three red lines across her cheek. She paused beside her chair as she went out, and murmured something in the girl's ear. Betty, who had been sitting stiffly at the table, suddenly relaxed and a smile of pure gratitude spread over her face. She looked up at Dr. Waring and touched her hand fleetingly. She reminded Marsh of a dog to which its master had unexpectedly given some attention.

On their way out, the telephone rang from its position at the foot of the stairs. Marsh had difficulty in restraining from darting forward to reach it before Dr. Waring. If it was Sister Gullett there was a chance she might recognize the voice. She felt a moment's panic when Katherine Waring asked who was calling.

"For you, Marsh," she said, holding out the receiver. "Mr Bannister."

Todd Bannister's voice held an injured note. "Say, she has a nerve asking who was calling. Does she usually check on all the calls?"

"What is it you want?" Marsh asked, one eye on Dr. Waring.

"You, my sweet surgeon. I shall die if you don't come out with me this afternoon. I was completely prostrated to know I'd missed you this morning. Though Mother was pleased. She really must learn to like you, Marsh."

"I can't come," Marsh said. "I have an appointment."

"Who is he? I demand to know. Marsh, there is a mirror just nearby and I can see myself. I'm positively green. I'm tortured with jealousy. Can you play golf with me tomorrow?"

Katherine Waring was going up the stairs slowly.

"I may be able to. I'll let you know. But do something for me."

"My life is yours. Mother's life, too, if you like."

"Speak to Betty," she whispered cautiously.

"Oh, Marsh, my dearest! You'll have me going neurotic, too."

"I think you are already," she replied teasingly. There was a pause. "Todd? Are you still there?"

"Yes, I'm here."

"Hold on a minute."

She put the receiver down and went back to the dining-room. Betty was just sitting at the table, the smile still on her lips.

"Todd Bannister wants a word with you," Marsh said.

The nurse looked up vaguely. "Who? Oh, tell him I'm having lunch. You talk to him," she suggested slyly.

"I already have," Marsh retorted. She went back to the telephone. "Hullo, Todd?"

"Todd has gone," said another man's voice. "Is that Dr. Mowbray?"

"Who is that?" Marsh asked. "I was speaking to the Tom Thumb."

"Shane. What's the progress?"

Marsh glanced about her. "You shouldn't have called here," she said nervously, lowering her voice. "I will try to see you later."

"What progress?" Shane repeated inexorably. "And don't ring off, please."

"A little," she whispered. "But I can't tell you now. Please be patient."

"You have only one more day."

"No," she said hurriedly. "Listen carefully, Shane. I can't speak any louder. Someone might hear. It is impossible to work quickly. Already people are suspicious. Trust me." It cost her pride an effort to say that.

"Why don't you ask for an explanation, instead of trying to discover one?"

"I can't," she said desperately.

"You mean you dare not," he rejoined. "You have only tomorrow." The receiver was replaced in her ear.

She went upstairs to her room, trying to subdue a sudden sensation of panic. The knowledge that she was working against time and that Shane was harassing her made a clear and level vision difficult to maintain. She began to get ready for the expedition with Arkwright, and her movements were stiff and clumsy as she tried to hurry. She put on a bright yellow shirt and rolled up her slacks to just below the knee.

A more open inquiry was indicated, as speed was necessary. It was Evelyn Peterson's opinion that everyone knew of her investigations. If that was the case then she would start a direct attack at one on Henry Arkwright.

He was waiting for her at the foot of the stairs, singing a sea charity in a wobbling baritone.

"Hullo!" Marsh called, and ran down the stairs in her canvas sneakers. With a stupendous effort she added, "Ship ahoy!"

Arkwright beamed happily. "Aha, my shipmate! All ready for the decks? Shall we splice the main brace before we go on board?"

"Not for me, thanks."

He had been drinking heavily before and after lunch. His eyes were slightly bloodshot. His walk, too, was not quite steady, but Marsh put that down to his capacity for make-believe. He already felt a rising deck under his feet.

Once out of the house he came nearer and she let him slip his heavy hand under her elbow, smiling grimly to herself. That she of all women should descend to relying on her sex to attain an end!

"This is really very jolly," he declared, encouraged. "I'm glad we are able to fit in our little jaunt before we leave Matthews."

He is still trying to get me to go, Marsh thought. I must find out the reason.

The Waring's boat-shed was the one built into the cliff on the other side of the cove where she had found Sam. This meant they had to follow the track that led towards Shane's cottage.

She was thinking of him bitterly when Arkwright said: "That's an odd sort of chap who lives over there. Who is he?"

Marsh replied carefully, "Beyond his name I know little about him."

"You have met him, then?"

"Only by chance. He directed me to Reliance when I arrived here. He also helped me with Mr Waring and he was with me when I found Sam."

She kept a close watch as she told Arkwright of the meetings. They did not sound like coincidences when listed like that.

But beyond stating, in his conservative dogmatic way, "I don't like the fellow's manner," he did not appear suspicious.

She was led down a steep path cut in the side of the cliff. Sheltered from the wind, it was now very hot. At the end of the mole, a yacht was lifting in the swell. Arkwright directed her on to it, to a position where she would be out of the way. He then seated himself at the tiller and commenced to raise sail. They cast off and moved slowly across to the rocky entrance of the cove.

IV

Marsh waited until they were past the reefs and Arkwright's attention was not wholly absorbed in the handling of the little boat.

"This is an ideal place for a talk," she said presently. "There is no chance of being overheard. I want your help."

Arkwright immediately reached out to pat her bare leg. Nothing delighted him more than being asked for advice by a woman.

Balanced forward, Marsh watched his unquestionable skill with the ropes, crouching now and then as he altered course and the boom swung over her head.

"When I said I knew nothing about Shane it was not exactly the truth," she said. "He is a doctor."

"Are you sure, my dear? I have never heard his name before."

"He has spent most of his career abroad," she replied, and then added in a steady tone, "He is not satisfied that Sam's death was an accident."

The gunwale near her feet skimmed the water before the little craft straightened.

"My dear, what are you saying? What does this fellow Shane know? I don't believe he is a qualified man at all. Just a sensation-mongering quack. His suggestion is downright appalling. Why, Kate herself—" He found it difficult to speak.

Marsh looked over the blue water to the cliffs. From far out they seemed to rise straight from the sea, with only a thin curl of white around the base to denote the breaking of the slight swell.

Arkwright became more articulate. "Katherine examined the unfortunate boy herself. I was with her in the room. There was no hint of foul play. I suppose your friend Shane means foul play."

"You examined the body yourself?"

"A cursory glance. It wasn't a pretty sight. I must confess I was amazed at Kate's sang-froid."

He began to splutter again. "What right has Shane to say the boy's death was intentional? Morrow was satisfied and so was Walker. It was well known that Sam spent a good deal of his time climbing around the cliffs. The wonder is he didn't fall before this."

"He wasn't killed by falling on the rocks," Marsh said, watching him closely. "He died from a stab in the base of his skull."

The boat tilted again, and she caught at the mast.

"In other words," she said loudly, "Sam was deliberately murdered."

"Murdered!" Arkwright shouted the word.

"Yes, murdered." Somehow, now that she had spoken the word instead of smothering its very shape in her mind, Marsh felt a curious relief. She had broken her own self-imposed reticence and could view facts more dispassionately.

After his first startled shocked exclamation Arkwright was quiet. He avoided her glance and gave all his attention to the course. His protrudent eyes were narrowed and his fat pink face was firmly set. His hands no longer wandered in search of shoulders or knees. One gripped the tiller projecting under his arm, while the other held the sail ropes as sensitively as a rider clasps a horse's reins.

"Shall we go back?" Marsh suggested. "I'm afraid I've spoilt the afternoon."

"No, no," he protested hurriedly. "Let us stay here until we have thrashed this matter out. As you said, it is a good place for a talk."

"You don't believe what I have told you, do you? Or rather, you are trying not to believe it."

Arkwright ignored her shrewd remark. "How is it you found Sam at the foot of the cliffs? He had been marked by the rocks and had all the appearance of being drowned."

Marsh clasped her knees and rested her chin on top.

"Whoever did it," she said musingly, "tried to make Sam's death look like an accident. I am inclined to think he may have been killed in his bungalow while he was asleep and then carried to the cliff's edge and thrown over. His room is only a few yards away, I believe, The currents are strong and his body was washed into the bay, where it became caught in the rocks."

"Does Katherine know about this—this story?"

The girl turned her head. "I have not said anything to her."

There was a pause, and then Arkwright spoke abruptly. "Go on. Who did it? And why?"

She returned her gaze to the cliffs. She did not like looking at Arkwright. His face and actions had changed. He was quite a different Henry Arkwright from the one who pressed heavy sympathy on Katherine Waring and hurried to do his wife's bidding.

They were nearer the cliffs now. She could see miniature figures playing on the golf-course. Arkwright began to alter his course again. The yacht turned in the direction from where they had come; away from those toy figures, which might pause on the tees before driving off to gaze down on the little white boat on its plain of blue.

She tried to calm herself and to answer Arkwright's question. Now that she had begun an open attack there was no turning back.

"I think Sam was killed because he knew something about Mr Waring's overdose of insulin. He was a feeble-minded boy, but there was the risk that he might let drop some remark that might be taken notice of. In his pocket I found a snuff-box belonging to Mr Waring. It was his custom to carry his emergency glucose in it, but he did not have it with him the other night. That is why he could do nothing to stop the coma."

Marsh forced herself to look at Arkwright. The sun was full in her face, and she shaded her eyes with one hand. But he did not speak or take his attention from the boat.

"You do understand, don't you? Mr Waring died from pneumonia. I signed the certificate. But pneumonia was the direct outcome of his lying in a coma all night on the wet windy golf-links. And that coma resulted from someone strengthening his insulin and seeing that he carried glucose that night. That someone knew something about diabetes. Either it is a doctor or a nurse or a fellow-sufferer of diabetes."

A slight sound, almost a groan, came from Arkwright. "A doctor, a nurse, a diabetic—it covers everyone at Reliance. Who should want King dead? I was attached to him. I admired him. I relied on him. He was my wife's brother."

Still watching him, Marsh said: "Mr Waring inferred that it was his duty to disgrace publicly those doctors who had made an unforgivable mistake in their careers. I know of yours," she added abruptly.

Arkwright's hold on the mainsail slackened. The boom wavered behind the girl's head. "Who told you? Kate?" His fat jowls were quivering slightly.

"No, not Dr. Kate."

"That little fiend, Evelyn, then?" he said, beginning to shout. "What King didn't tell her, she found out. I did my best—my level best. I even tried to call in a specialist, but it was too late. I hadn't handled a case like that before. You must believe me. King said he did. King—"

Marsh gazed at him steadily, not attempting to check his flow of indiscreet rage.

Arkwright had lost control of himself. His face was almost purple. He was careless with the boat. It jerked and twisted and once shipped some water. They were nearing the narrow rocky opening to the cove, where he should have been giving it his closest attention.

"I hated King. I always have hated King. So damned superior," he went on, spluttering in his anger. A stream of saliva was coursing out of his mouth. "It was Kate's fault. She egged him on. It's all Kate's fault. I could—I could—" He stopped abruptly, and wiped his mouth with the back of his hand.

"It was Kate. She killed King and that idiot. She and King were always wrangling for power. Kate won. She's trying to push the blame somewhere else. She always did that. I've seen it happen before."

"Dr. Kate had nothing to do with it," Marsh said fiercely. "She has done nothing."

"Kate!" Arkwright sneered. "You're crazy about her. She'll use you the way King always did with others. Kate is a—"

"Shut your mouth!" Marsh shouted, losing her grip of the situation at his jibes. There was a baling-tin near her. She picked it up.

"What about the steel needle I found? The one you took from your wife? A long thin instrument made that incision in Sam. And

171

why were you so keen to attend Waring? You were afraid I'd pull him through. You dare accuse Dr. Kate! You fat swine!" and she threw the tin at Arkwright.

It caught him on the side of the head and fell into the water to bob away on the swell. Marsh stopped aghast. Arkwright's eyes were queer. They were terrifying. His whole face seemed to quiver.

"I warned you," he said. "I warned you. Surely you guessed that the night in the laboratory. I knew you were up to something, poking and prying and questioning."

The laboratory, Marsh. thought quickly. Arkwright. He has been wanting me to leave all along. He even tried by beating me up. He'd try anything.

"You little fool!" Arkwright burst out, and his hands moved quickly.

The boom swung over and caught her across the shoulder-blades. She staggered and slid over the sloping deck. The next minute she was in the water.

CHAPTER NINE

I

She came to the surface with one shoe off and her slacks billowing about her legs. The first thing she saw was the cliff, dark and forbidding and quite close—frighteningly close. It seemed to be coming nearer. Then she saw something else. Someone on the cliff. A man on horseback, immobile against the brilliant blue sky, watching her as she kicked and threshed against the current.

A call came from behind and she turned. The boat looked very large as it bore down, the wind filling the sail. For a moment she had a desperate fear Arkwright intended to run her down, and with an effort lifted one heavy arm from the water to point to the horseman on the cliffs. He would not dare do anything if he knew they were being watched.

But the murderous expression had gone from Arkwright's face, and his eyes now looked like an anxious cod's. He drew near and reefed sail, shouting and giving directions; too many for Marsh to follow coherently. She grasped the side of the boat. They were too close to the rocks for Arkwright to leave the tiller, but he coaxed and shouted her on to the deck. She made a tremendous effort to heave herself up and succeeded at last in sprawling across under the boom with her feet over the side. She lay there panting with her eyes closed.

Above the sound of the sea and the breeze filling the sail she could hear Arkwright's voice, anxious, apologetic, defensive, whining. But only when they came into the cove did she open her eyes. It was quieter, and intensely hot after the ocean.

She was too dazed and tired to speak to Arkwright, to answer his questions and allay his anxieties for his own skin. She did not hear them but only the tone of his voice. At the mole she pulled herself up heavily and climbed on to the landing, her one shoe squelching water and her clothes clinging to her body.

He called to her to wait until he made the boat fast, but she plodded ahead and started to limp up the path. It was rough under her bare foot, and she kept her gaze on the stony ground trying to pick the smoother parts. Arkwright was still calling but presently she lost the sound of his voice as she came into the breeze at the top of the cliff.

A man spoke her name, and as the voice was not Arkwright's it jolted her out of her dazed condition. She looked up bewildered.

Shane stood barring the path, the horse's bridle over his arm. He said something, but she heard only one word. She began to laugh.

"Accident!" She bent double as a stitch caught her side. "Accident! What is that trite saying? 'Accidents will happen in the best regulated circles'? Yes, an accident—like poor Sam, like Kingsley Waring's overdose." She laughed and then turned to vomit up some salt water.

Arkwright was coming. She could hear him panting and whining up the path. She looked at Shane. He was closer and asking her a question.

Certainly she'd ridden a horse before. When she was ten. She had bolted into an orchard and had her face scratched by branches.

Shane smiled and put his hands to her waist. For one extraordinary moment she felt utterly helpless. She remembered that same time in the orchard when her father had lifted her from the ground and had held her against his shoulder, so firm and familiar and secure. Then she was high above the ground and staring at the coarse long hairs of the horse's mane. She put out one hand and twisted her fingers into it. There was a slight jolt and Shane had mounted behind her. The horse lifted his head and moved along the cliff path.

She jogged uncertainly away from the main centre of the animal's movement as she tried to lean forward from Shane. But she was pulled back to where it was admittedly more comfortable.

"Spare my horse as much discomfort as you can, my dear."

It was amazing to hear a man's voice so close to her ear, and to feel his breath on her cheek. It was a singular experience to Marsh. She murmured childishly, "I hate all men."

Shane's brusque laugh, familiar before but intimate now, startled her, too.

"After this afternoon's event I can't blame you," he said. "What possessed you to go out with that land-lubber?"

Marsh, always just, said: "You're wrong. He handles a boat expertly. I was trying to get him to talk. He had a knitting-needle. A long, steel, sharp-pointed needle."

The horse jumped under a twitch on the reins. "You little fool!" Shane said. "It's a wonder you weren't drowned. Why did you do it?"

His rough words made her a little tearful. She felt disconcertingly feminine and tried to beat off the weakness. She might not like men but she despised women who behaved girlishly.

"It's all your fault," she told him. "I had to do something. You must give me more time."

"Mowbray, stop feeling sorry for yourself. I'm taking you back to Reliance. Have a bath, have a brandy and go to bed to sleep. And don't start thinking again until you have done all three. I'll count this as time off. Recreation time."

She sat up. "Sit still," he ordered. "Don't you think this is very pleasant?"

"No," she replied crossly. "I'm most uncomfortable. Let me down now. I must have left Arkwright far enough behind and—"

"And—?" queried Shane, as he drew rein. "You don't want anyone to see you, do you?" He helped her lift her leg over the horse's neck and slide down, but he did not dismount himself. "What would your precious Dr. Kate say if she could see you now?" he said, looking down on her tired face.

She did not appear very attractive with her hair streaked over her forehead, but she seemed very young. He lifted his hand, touched the horse's flank with his heel and cantered along the soft ground which bordered the road.

Marsh turned towards Reliance with a sigh. Shane had an uncanny way of getting to her subconscious thoughts.

She tried to creep into the house unobserved, and had even gained the upper hall, when inopportunely Delia Arkwright came out of her room. She saw Marsh, glared, and hurried forward.

"Where is Henry?" she demanded. "What has happened? Really,

Dr. Mowbray, your appearance is scandalous. What happened to you?"

"I fell into the water," Marsh replied, edging along the wall. "I must go and change. Your husband is coming."

She got into her room, slammed the door and locked it.

II

When she came back after a bath Mrs Arkwright was outside her door again. She had intercepted her husband there.

"It's the look of the thing, Henry," she was haranguing him. "She came in looking—well, looking as though you had attacked her."

"Oh, I say, Delia!" Henry protested. "Do be quiet. Everyone will hear you."

"And a good thing, too," she continued loudly. "I've had enough of your philandering, Henry. First that Peterson creature, but she has cottoned on to Michael now. And talk about damaged goods! Part of King's legacy, I presume. And now this doctor of Katherine's. We leave tomorrow."

"And I've had enough of you," Arkwright burst out. "If I liked, I could make things pretty sticky for you."

There was a pause. Marsh stopped brushing her hair and frowned at her reflection.

"I'm sure I don't know what you mean, Henry," Mrs Arkwright said acidly. "Go and get out of those stupid clothes and try to act like a reasonable adult. And bring down my knitting-bag when you come."

Arkwright was breathing heavily. "I trust, my dear," he said, with ponderous significance, "that you haven't been mislaying your needles again."

There was no reply from Mrs Arkwright, and Marsh heard her steps going down the hall.

Arkwright knocked at her door. "Dr. Mowbray, are you there? I must speak to you. Let me in."

The door handle turned but Marsh watched it silently.

"Please open the door. I've something to tell you. I want to explain. You've got all the wrong idea."

Still Marsh remained quiet. For several minutes Arkwright kept up his plea. She could visualize him, his eyes bulging with apprehension and his pink face bedewed with perspiration, cringing outside her room. She was not so frightened of him now, but she was not ready to risk being alone with him.

"Henry?" said a cool voice, in the form of a question.

"Why, hullo there, Kate! Did Delia tell you about our misfortune? I was just about to inquire how my shipmate is. She took an uncomfortable ducking. A most regrettable accident."

"Most regrettable," agreed Katherine Waring's smooth voice. "I can't understand how it happened, Henry. You are such a careful person as a rule."

There had been a slight nuance in her tone, which caused Arkwright to mumble and stumble.

"Yes, Henry?"

"I think I'll go and change," he said, at last.

She waited a moment before she knocked at Marsh's door. It was unlocked at once. After the frightening incident with Arkwright, Marsh felt closer to Katherine Waring. Her passage at arms with another had brought her back to the one whom she had previously mistrusted.

Dr. Waring surveyed her with a faint smile. "Good girl," she nodded. "You've had a bath. Get into bed. I've brought you a drink. All three should take away that nasty feeling."

Marsh, her barrier of reserve down, laughed shakily. She could say what she liked to Dr. Kate now. Arkwright's blunder had done that much for her.

"All three already prescribed by Dr. Shane," she said, slipping off her robe. She got into bed and held out her hand for the glass. Then she saw Katherine Waring's expression.

"Dr. Shane?"

The girl's face closed suddenly, too. "He saw us from the cliff. I lost a shoe, so he let me ride his horse back to Reliance."

"You did not tell me he was a doctor before. Should I know this mysterious Dr. Shane?"

"I think so," Marsh faltered. "He knew your husband a long time ago."

"Very often King did not introduce his friends to me. Drink your brandy, Marsh, and then try to sleep for a while." She went out of the room quickly.

Marsh stared at the closed door. Tomorrow the Arkwrights were going and Gair had already left. That left—how many besides herself and Katherine Waring? She began to count.

But it was Arkwright who had attacked her that night in the laboratory and again that day. Once he had gone she would have no fears. It was ridiculous to think of the departures as strands of rope being slowly unravelled between herself and Dr. Kate.

Anyway, there was Betty Donne. She would not leave. She was Dr. Kate's nurse. And Miss Jennet who prepared the meals. No, she would never be quite alone with Dr. Kate. She could leave soon now. After all, her boat sailed in another three days. There was always the excuse of final arrangements to be made. She would never be alone with Dr. Kate. She must never be alone with her.

III

She dozed fitfully, stirring when footsteps went along the passage outside now and then. Shane's ultimatum had been transcended by something stronger. The instinct of self-preservation was just as powerful in her as it was in Laurence Gair. Blurred with weariness and fear she thought that no loyalty or ideal had a claim over personal safety.

She started from her sleep when a knock came at her door.

"Who is it?" she called, her voice fogged.

There was no reply and she raised herself on one elbow. A small white note lay just inside her room. She got out of bed and picked it up. The writing was an agitated scrawl.

I must see you. I am very sorry about today. I lost my head. You are wrong. Let me explain everything. I'll wait in my room until I hear from you. Don't be afraid of me, please. I wouldn't do you any harm. I just lost my head this afternoon.

The note was unsigned, but she could guess the writer.

And how am I to know you won't lose your head again? she thought grimly, crumpling the paper in her hand.

She went over to the dressing-table to get a cigarette. With the same match she burned the note in the ash-tray. It was so traditionally the thing to do that she smiled even as she crushed the ashes with a dead match and then emptied the tray out the window.

Outside it was still warm although it was nearly sunset. The sky was vivid, an indication of a still warmer morrow. The landscape was hushed and somnolent and bathed in a glowing light. For a while she stood looking out. Then with a sigh she turned away and began to dress.

She went to her door and opened it. At once she saw Arkwright standing just outside his own room. He had his eyes fixed on her door, so that when Marsh opened it their eyes met in a startlingly direct gaze. He did not move, but put out one hand in a pleading gesture. She surveyed him thoughtfully for a moment and then, inclining her head in slight encouragement, she walked to the stairs. Arkwright followed humbly.

They met Delia Arkwright going up to change.

She said, "I hope you feel better, Dr. Mowbray," without much concern, and to her husband six steps behind, "You're ready early," in an acid voice.

Marsh replied conventionally, but Arkwright did not speak.

In the lower hall he ventured closer to the girl. She flinched away, even though she knew he was frightened.

"Not here," he muttered. "I can't talk in the house. Come outside. Someone might hear."

"Very well," she agreed, and led the way to the verandah. Rex, the dog, rose and padded towards her.

"Come farther away from the house," Arkwright urged. "Yes, come this way. I will be able to explain better there." He nodded to himself, looking more assured. As she hesitated he tried to smile and put out his hand to her shoulder. She moved away adroitly and, catching a glimpse of the dog's leash hanging on the wall, clipped it on Rex's collar.

"I don't like that brute," Arkwright observed, as she was dragged down the steps. "He has been badly trained. Too many masters—King, Kate and Michael."

"Where are we going?" Marsh asked, as she followed him round the house.

Below the cliff the sea was an unbelievable sapphire touched with gold. The sky was a molten hue and gulls winged their way across the approaching sunset. The sun slid in and out of the flat-banked clouds towards the rim of the sea. She saw a white sail cutting across the water, shivered in spite of the warm air as she heard the lazy lap of the sea against the rocks just below her feet.

Arkwright did not take her far from the house. On the other side of the garage a bungalow was built in the scrub. The dog suddenly stopped and refused to go farther. A growl came from his throat.

"Leave him," Arkwright said urgently. "We must hurry. We might be missed."

But Marsh bent to the dog cajolingly. Reluctantly Rex rose and padded along uncertainly as though against his instinct. Arkwright pushed open the door of the bungalow and stood aside. She went in.

It was immaculately and simply furnished as a bedroom, and was lit by the full crimson glow from the sun. Inside it was hot and airless, for it had not been inhabited for several days now. There was a plain iron bedstead with a curious addition of parallel bars extending from one end to the other. She was reminded of a ship's bunk.

Another odd feature was the combination school-desk and bench in the centre of the room. It faced one wall to which a blackboard had been attached. On a table nearby was a heterogeneous collection, all carefully laid out; shells, seaweed, a brightly coloured handkerchief, some odd empty tobacco tins and even some fragments of coloured glass.

"Sam's room," Arkwright said, and she drew in her breath quickly.

The dog had crouched on the floor between them, his ears pricked. He watched Arkwright's every movement.

"Kate thought she could teach him," Arkwright continued, "but he was a thieving slobbery creature. I hated to look at him. See those things on the table? That handkerchief belongs to Evelyn. He stole it. He would steal things and then weep and whine if he was found out. Like King's snuff-box—I knew about that before."

"Why did you bring me here?" Marsh asked directly. "What is it you want to tell me?"

"It's Delia," he whispered, trying to light a cigarette with shaking fingers. "My wife. I don't know for certain but I think she killed the boy. It was the needle. You're a smart girl. But it would have been better . . . I did try to warn you. And when Delia told me you'd been out all night I wrote an unsigned note to Katherine. I thought she'd want you to leave. Why did you start all this? Where is it going to end?"

"It is too late for reproaches," she answered sharply. "Sam took the snuff-box. What comes next?"

He lowered his eyes. "I didn't know Sam had taken it. Delia told me. After you brought King home I saw it amongst her things. I was horrified but she didn't seem so concerned. She said she had found Sam with it and had taken it from him. She intended giving it back to King. When I knew King's condition was serious I was worried. I realized that if anyone ever knew Delia had his emergency glucose they might start thinking things. So I decided to put it back in Sam's room. It was the morning after King's death. I woke early. I'd been worrying about the box all night. I crept out of the house and down here."

Arkwright dropped his head into his hands. "I thought Sam was asleep. I meant to slip in, put the snuff-box on the table there and get back. But I couldn't hear him breathing. You saw Sam, didn't you?"

She nodded.

"He snuffled and slobbered when he breathed. But this room was quiet. Deathly quiet is the phrase, isn't it? It was just light and I went over to the bed."

Arkwright realized he was sitting on it and got up hastily.

"Then I saw the knitting-needle sticking out of his neck. I couldn't take it in at first. It was so unbelievable—so impossible."

"What did you do?" Marsh asked, as he paused to stare down at the bed.

He roused himself. "I don't quite remember at first. I couldn't think for a while. But I do remember pulling the needle out and examining it. It was slimy to feel. It felt horrid, and I wanted to be sick. Then I remembered Delia and the snuff-box. There they both were—the snuff-box that Delia said she had taken from Sam and her needle. I was afraid because she hated King, too, though she never admitted it. Delia never does show her real feelings. I wanted to be sick when I saw Sam dead," he said again. "He looked worse dead than alive."

"Go on," Marsh said. "Hurry. What happened then?"

Arkwright shuddered. "I dressed the body. His clothes were lying over there. It was heavy and slack and still warm from the bedclothes. I kept the knitting-needle but put the snuff-box in the pocket of Sam's jacket. Then I dragged the body out of the room to the edge of the cliff. The sun was just coming up as I rolled it over the cliff. The tide was in. I heard the body hitting the rocks going down. It sounded horrible—horrible." He shuddered again.

"When it was quiet I looked over. I could see Sam floating against the rocks. A wave would come up and submerge the body and then it would be left. I thought it would never go. I had to wait a long time before it disappeared. Then I went back to the bungalow.

"There were marks through the scrub where I had dragged him, and I had to destroy them. Then there was his room. It was a hideous job but I finally finished straightening it and went back to the house. Delia was still asleep when I got to my room. I remember standing over the bed staring at her and wondering if she were a murderess.

"She stirred and moaned in her sleep as though she knew what I was thinking. She looked extraordinarily like King. Handsome, you know, in a determined ruthless sort of way, whereas King had something more. Personality or something—like young Gair."

A charm, Marsh thought suddenly. An irresistible charm like Larry's, which covered a self-seeking individualism. A power to attract which was used to disguise a deep-rooted egoism.

"I thought of King," Arkwright went on. "Delia is a diabetic, too. Although she is on globin insulin she knew enough about insulin to tamper with King's hypo. Supposing"—he dropped his voice

to a whisper through the red haze in the imbecile's bungalow—
"supposing when she took the box from Sam she decided to increase his dose? She knew King's habits; his walk after dinner. He didn't eat much that night. Supposing—"

"Hush," said Marsh, raising her hand. Rex had got up and had gone to the door.

Arkwright's eyes were frightened now. "What is it?" he asked in a whisper. "We mustn't be found here. Someone might tell Delia."

It was a mere crack of a twig against the background of softly mewing gulls, the breeze in the ti-trees and the growing sound of the sea against the rocks. But it was the small ominous noise of another presence.

Marsh listened with a thumping heart for other tell-tale sounds. She moved quietly to the door, holding Rex by the collar although the dog seemed quiet enough. Presently she peered out. The sky was still radiant, but the sun had sunk and the land looked gloomy.

"Did you see anyone?" Arkwright asked. He was breathing quickly.

Marsh shook her head. He came nearer and she shrank instinctively behind the dog. "Don't!" he said thickly. "I told you not to be afraid of me. It's Delia. Anything I've done was because of her."

"What are you going to do now?" Marsh asked. "She said you were leaving tomorrow. Will you go with her?"

He seemed faintly surprised. "Of course. Where else can I go? My naval appointment will be finished in another year. I have no practice, but with the money King left Delia I might be able to fix something up."

"You believe she is a murderess and yet you will use her blood-money?"

"What else can I do?"

"That is for you to decide," Marsh said unhelpfully. She took up the dog's leash and went to the door.

Arkwright called after her. "What will you do? You mustn't let this business go any further. We will all be ruined professionally. Everyone at Reliance will be implicated. It must be hushed up. After all, you have no proof and in another few weeks that wound in Sam's neck will be untraceable. Why, even Kate missed it."

She felt a surge of relief at his words. Relief slightly tinged with disillusionment. She comforted herself with the reflection that it was better to discover her goddess with medical rather than with moral clay feet.

"You are going abroad soon," Arkwright persisted. "You will be able to forget all these suspicions."

Taking her silence for compliance, he became more like his former self. "It will be all for the best, my dear, don't you agree?" he said pompously.

She stepped out of the bungalow without replying, and walked swiftly back towards the house.

IV

During dinner that night Marsh pondered on Arkwright's story as she covertly kept Delia Arkwright under observation. She appeared to the girl no different from the first time she had seen her. There seemed no change in her frigid austere demeanour. She still watched Henry's fidgetings with an acid eye and Evelyn Peterson with an outraged glance. Her attitude towards Katherine Waring remained faintly superior and Marsh she continued to ignore. She took up her knitting after coffee and Marsh stared with a fascination at her steel needles flashing to and fro under the lamplight.

Arkwright broke out when he saw her. "I wish you'd stop that infernal knitting all the time, Delia." Whereat she merely bent a still more sour glance on him and disdained a retort.

"Henry," Dr. Waring interposed with her unfailing tact. "Delia says you are leaving tomorrow. Perhaps it is as well. It has been a trying time for us all."

Marsh sat wondering how she could let Shane know of Arkwright's story, and what he would do when she told him. He was so bent on Katherine Waring's destruction that he might not accept it. She looked at Mrs Arkwright again. Strange to sit quietly in a room with the windows wide to the warm hazy night in the company of a likely killer.

Death means so little to us, Marsh mused. A murder politely covered up with the trappings of an accident is just another death. There is nothing frightening about it as long as it is so disguised.

On the verandah overlooking the ocean were Evelyn Peterson and Michael. Their laughter and cigarette smoke floated into the room. Dr. Waring had now opened up an intricate patience, her long fingers hovering over the cards. Betty Donne sat nearby like a statue, her eyes never leaving her. Arkwright moved about the room, helping himself to too many drinks. He was the only one drinking tonight, for again Michael had not touched the liquor tray.

He seemed less uncouth now that Evelyn had begun to interest him, Marsh noted with faint approval. That he should fall for the nurse's obvious charms when they were directed to him was to be expected, but she had not considered it would improve him. He had almost lost the bitter antagonism he displayed indiscriminately.

Evelyn regarded him with a mixture of contemptuous affection and possessive pride. Marsh felt a slight liking for the girl and a certain respect for her adaptability, even though Dr. Waring showed more dislike for her than she had ever done. She had tried to separate the two during dinner and glanced now and then at the window with a tightening of her mouth.

Presently they came in and Marsh, seeing Michael's face, thought he looked older. Before, he appeared dissipated in a pretence at being adult, but now that his face was clear he seemed more mature.

He addressed himself to Surgeon-Commander Arkwright. "Could you give us a lift up to town tomorrow? Evelyn and me?"

Arkwright coughed and glanced from Katherine Waring to Miss Peterson, who was surveying the room half-amusedly and half-defiantly. "Well now, my dear boy—" he began.

"Will you or won't you?" snapped Michael.

Dr. Waring swept her cards together and began to shuffle them expertly. "Why do you want to go to town, Michael?"

He glanced at her briefly. His eyes were no longer full of hate, Marsh noted. "I am going to resign from the University first. Then I will try the Gallery to see if they can fit me in as a student. I've had enough of pretending to become a doctor. Now I have my money I am going to do exactly what I want, and what I am fitted for."

Katherine Waring commenced to layout the cards again. "And Miss Peterson? Why is she going with you?"

There was an awful silence. The nurse might have spoken, but Michael restrained her. "That," he said, "is entirely our business. Well, Uncle?"

Mrs Arkwright said, surveying Evelyn with extreme distaste as though she were drawing her skirts aside: "We have no room for two extra in our car. If you want to come, Michael, you may, but—"

"I see," said Michael. "Nice pure Auntie! Or are you jealous of Evelyn?"

Mrs Arkwright shook with rage.

"I must leave soon—maybe tomorrow," Marsh heard herself say. "I can give you a lift."

"Well!" said Michael, surprised. He came forward, holding out his hand. "You are not so bad as I thought. Thanks a lot. Good night, everyone. We must go and pack."

Why did I say that? Marsh thought dismally. Why did I offer? I don't approve of them that much.

She dared not look at Dr. Waring. She got up from her chair and muttered good night before anyone could speak.

When she reached her own room she got ready for bed quickly. She had her light extinguished just as the first footsteps came up the stairs. She lay in the dark, listening.

She'll never let me go tomorrow. She doesn't want Evelyn and Michael to go off together, but she can't stop them. But she'll find some way to stop me if she can.

The footsteps did not pause at her door. Marsh sighed with relief and began to make her plans. She would go and see Shane first thing in the morning. Tell him about Delia Arkwright and then leave before lunch.

Oh, dash! There was Todd Bannister. She had promised to play golf. She would drop in at the Tom Thumb and tell him—say goodbye. Rather mean after his friendliness, but there it was.

She smiled when she thought of Todd; his boyish whimsicality, his outrageous philandering and the absurd awe in which he pretended to hold his mother. It was a relief to think about a person like Todd. Someone who was gay and alive and not haunted.

Suddenly Marsh opened her eyes wide. The door handle of her room was being gently turned. She had not locked it. If Katherine Waring had found it locked she would have known that Marsh was trying to avoid her. She probably knew in any case, but the unlocked door was a sort of pretence that no confidence was lacking between them.

There was a faint light showing under the door and along the edge. It widened and someone came into her room. Marsh closed her eyes and began to breathe steadily.

"Marsh?" asked Katherine Waring softly. "Are you awake, Marsh?"

She did not answer. She tried not to tense her body or to alter her breathing. She felt the light on her face, but her eyelids did not quiver. Presently she heard a long sigh and then Katherine Waring went quietly away.

V

Marsh was awakened early the next morning by someone's hand on her shoulders. She started up at once. Miss Jennet's plump amiable face was looking down on her.

She spoke in a whisper. "Someone on the 'phone, Doctor. They said you wouldn't mind if I awakened you."

That would be Gullett, Marsh thought.

"Thanks, Miss Jennet," she said, throwing off the covers. She hurried downstairs, tying the sash of her robe.

"I put the line through to the library," Miss Jennet said. "It's so draughty in the passage." She beamed and nodded and withdrew to the faint sounds of the early morning radio session in the kitchen.

Marsh went along to the library. She took up the receiver and heard Sister Gullett yawning into it.

"The things I do for you, Doctor, when I'm nearly dead," she complained. "An emergency op. last night. The patient should pull through."

"Did you find out that name for me?" the girl asked urgently.

"The Warings' nurse? McNeil. I remember her now. She came into a packet and bought a private hospital in the bush somewhere Western District way."

"Can't you remember where? Think hard. Western District is a large area. Hamilton, Warrnambool?"

"None of those. Doc, don't worry me. I told you I just had an emergency op."

"It's important, Gully."

"So's my breakfast and bed. Good-bye, Doc." Before Marsh could speak she had rung off.

"Marsh!" She dropped the receiver and swung round.

Katherine Waring stood in the doorway. She wore a dark blue house-coat and her hair hung around her shoulders. Her face was pale and lined as though she had not slept.

"What are you doing? Was that Sister Gullett? Has anything happened at the hospital?"

"No. Yes," Marsh stammered. "An emergency operation last night. Gullett says everything is all right."

Dr. Waring advanced into the room. "Why was she ringing you? You are no longer in residence at the hospital."

Marsh searched for an explanation and found none.

"Marsh, what are you doing? You've become so secretive. You, who were always so frank. Don't turn away from me."

The girl tried to meet her eyes. "I'm sorry," she burst out. "Perhaps it will be better when I go today."

"Why did you offer to take Michael and Evelyn? You know how I feel about her. And whatever he has been, Michael is still my son." She picked up the dangling receiver and replaced it carefully.

Marsh took a deep breath. "Dr. Kate, if you let Michael go with Evelyn it may mean the making of him. You can see for yourself how he has stopped that heavy drinking. If you stop him he may learn to hate you for ever."

Her eyes were bitter. "Yes, he hates me. My own son. I hoped now King was dead he might change."

Marsh shivered at her words, but she repeated, "Let him go."

"Evelyn planned this, didn't she? I wouldn't give her the papers so she took my son. Is that right, Marsh?"

She nodded reluctantly. "Give her the papers, then," she urged. "I'll ask her to let Michael alone."

"No," said Katherine. "No, Marsh. Don't ask her that. Michael must come back to me of his own free will. They can go. I'll persuade Delia, but you must stay, Marsh. Stay for another day. Please."

"Very well," she agreed, in a hopeless voice. She did not try to fight. She had known as early as the previous night that she would not be leaving. It was not worth even attempting to fight. When the Arkwrights went there would remain only herself, Betty and Dr. Kate. One more day.

Soon after breakfast she left to go to Shane's cottage. She went furtively, fearing Katherine Waring's surveillance. She found Shane in the small outbuilding which served as a stable, grooming his horse. He saw her coming across the hill and raised one hand, holding the curry-comb in a stiff greeting.

He went on with his work silently as she blurted out Arkwright's story. When she finished he was still silent.

"Well?" she asked defiantly. "What now?"

"What do you mean—what now? According to your story Katherine Waring knows nothing of the real cause of the imbecile's death. My efforts at revenge are of no avail. You want me to forget what I know. Is that right?"

"Yes," said Marsh.

"My good girl, hasn't it occurred to you, cold-blooded female that you are, murder has been done and it is up to me as a good citizen to report my suspicions? Furthermore, Dr. Waring may not have inserted the needle in the boy's neck, but she missed it on the post-mortem and such carelessness should not go unpunished."

"It was a mistake—an omission," Marsh said, without conviction.

"A doctor should not make mistakes."

"I understood you would not do anything if I proved Dr. Kate had nothing to do with Sam's death," Marsh said, in a shaking voice. "If you want to carry out your petty revenge and ruin us all you can, but I warn you I'll fight to the finish."

Shane laughed. "I make no doubt you will, my little virago. And while I am about it I'll tell the police about the scalpel you tried to use on me."

She strove to control herself. "Listen carefully, Shane," she said with an effort. "I warned someone else of this. You yourself are not above suspicion. Remember that, for when I say I'll fight I'll use every movement you ever made in connection with Reliance. By the time you are through ruining Katherine Waring your own name will be smeared again. You will never practise in Australia. Good day."

She walked swiftly away, fighting her strong agitation. Shane was not like Larry. He was intolerant and hard and there was no personal attraction between them on which she could play. His stubborn desire for revenge might make him capable of sacrificing even his career to obtain expiation.

The sort of thing a man would do, Marsh thought bitterly.

She wished desperately for an opportunity to speak frankly with Katherine Waring. She would know what to do with Shane. And yet when the Arkwrights, Michael and Evelyn left after lunch she felt a growing apprehension of being left alone with her. She was afraid of what a tête-à-tête might bring forth.

She went with them as far as the township, wedged into the back seat of the Arkwrights' car along with suitcases and Michael and Evelyn. They all said good-bye formally as Marsh got out at the hotel to keep her appointment with Todd Bannister.

Henry Arkwright dodged her gaze as though he was saying: "You needn't be afraid of me. I only told you so that you wouldn't be afraid. But you won't let it go any further, will you?" While Miss Peterson's brazen wink meant, "I didn't do so badly after all, did I?"

Marsh watched the car as it climbed the rise out of Matthews and vanished on the road back to town. There remained only Betty and Miss Jennet at Reliance now.

It was hot again; a strange still heat for Matthews. The sky and sea were the colour of lead. Only the tops of the pines bent to the wind from the north, for the township lay protected in its hollow. A storm was brewing. It would break soon or maybe not for several hours. Weather conditions along that rocky coast were always unpredictable.

Marsh went into the hotel and along the passage which led to the parlour. Mrs Bannister was in the tiny office under the stairs. It was ill-lit and musty with yellowing papers.

"Todd is expecting me," the girl said, pausing at the door.

Mrs Bannister got up from her chair with her mouth open as though to speak. "What is it?" Marsh asked, irritated. The woman's continual inarticulateness annoyed her.

"Come in for a moment," said Mrs Bannister.

She closed the door behind Marsh. The little room was stifling. "You haven't gone yet," she remarked hesitantly and the girl showed her impatience.

"Dr. Mowbray, I wish you wouldn't encourage Todd. No, please—don't misunderstand me. Listen awhile. Todd is my only son. I understand him. No one else does or ever will. He has become too interested in you. It is not good for him—or for you," she added in an undertone.

"You are presuming too much," Marsh said coldly. "I barely know your son. What is it you are always trying to say?"

The woman fiddled with some papers. "Don't go with Todd today. Please end your acquaintance with him. Go back to town. He doesn't like doctors."

Someone was coming down the stairs over their heads. Mrs Bannister looked up at the low ceiling. "It's Todd. Please tell him you're leaving now—right away. Leave Matthews, Dr. Mowbray—before the storm breaks."

They could hear Todd's voice calling. Marsh said: "Mrs Bannister, I find you very ambiguous. If you could only be more explicit—"

"There is no time," she replied, going to the door. "Are you going?"

"No," said Marsh. "No, I'm not."

The door burst open. "Marsh, my medical mentor!" Todd said, standing on the threshold. "I saw you arrive from upstairs. Has

Mother been hiding you away from me? Are you ready for your first lesson in golf?"

She turned to Mrs Bannister uncertainly. "Perhaps we could talk later," she suggested. The woman regarded her expressionlessly.

"What's this?" Todd asked, taking Marsh by the arm with one slim brown hand. "Talking about me behind my back?"

"Don't be ridiculous," she said, puzzled by the shadow that passed over his face. "Let's go now."

"Todd!"

He turned back. "Yes, Mother?"

Mrs Bannister's face looked pale under the combination of daylight and lamplight. "There is going to be a storm. Do you think you should go out?"

"It will hold off long enough."

She came nearer. "The bar is busy. I may need your help."

But Todd, with his hand still on Marsh's arm, called over his shoulder, "Tell them to help themselves."

"Mother doesn't like girls who like me," he confided to Marsh when they got outside. "Come along, sweet one! To the links we go."

He walked swiftly, with his lithe graceful movement.

"Don't rush so," she protested. "It's frightfully hot."

The hand on her arm was as cool as water. In the other he carried two irons. "Enough to begin with," he explained when she remarked on the paltry display. "Now if we start at the fifth we can always shelter if it begins to rain. Mother doesn't like me to get damp feet."

Marsh laughed. "Why do you talk like that about your mother? As though you were frightened of her?"

"So I am, Marsh dear. Terrified. I'm frightened of everyone. But I'm brave. I hide my fears under the gay mask I wear."

"You sound like a case for a Hollywood psychiatrist. Someone to trace the source of your hidden fears. Think, Todd, think! What is it you are hiding deep down in your subconscious mind? You must try to remember!"

He laughed, but turned his neat head away from her. "What has Mother been saying about me?"

"Oh, only that you are a bad boy. You drink too much and you flirt with all females."

"I'm all that, too. Noggins and Nellies. Did Mother really say that? No, you're joking. You don't take me seriously. Why don't you take me seriously?"

She laughed up at him as he pulled her up to the rise on the fifth tee. Then her carefree smile vanished.

"Todd!" she exclaimed. He had peeled off his sport coat and was folding it with deft movements to place in the shelter. "Todd, can't we go somewhere else? This is where—" She stopped.

"Good heavens! I forgot. But you don't care, do you? Do you think we might see His Majesty's ghost?"

"I'm not a sensitive soul as a rule," Marsh said, wandering over to the shelter-shed and looking down at the place where she had found Kingsley Waring. "But somehow I just don't like it today. Unpleasant vibrations, or something."

"Nonsense, my little one. Now come along like a good girl and Uncle will show you how to hold a stick."

She took an iron from him and surveyed the white ball he had placed on a heap of sand.

"Oh dear!" Todd said, regarding her grip on the stick sadly. "Do you mind if I'm bold? Stand still." He put his arms around her and guided her hands. "Now, is that comfortable?"

"Very," Marsh replied, smiling.

"That's bad luck. Let me show you another grip."

"No, this one will do nicely. Surely it is the easiest thing in the world to hit this white ball."

"Try and see," he suggested. "Give it one hell of a nudge."

She did so and he let out a whoop. "Extraordinary fluke!" he exclaimed, watching the ball's flight. "But, dear Marsh, your shoulder, your elbow and above all that dainty foot of yours. Dreadful!"

"Well, I hit the thing. And sent it some distance. That's the general idea, isn't it?"

Todd closed his eyes with a pained expression. "Golf, my dear Marsh, is a science. If you are to go round saying Todd Bannister showed you how to play you must do as I say. Come on, try again."

Marsh tried again and again and again and then threw down the stick in disgust. "What a stupid business. I did much better when you didn't show me how."

She flung herself down on the grass and looked up at the heavy sky. Seagulls were hurrying across the links.

"How quiet it is!" she said. "Even the sea seems to have stopped moving."

As Todd sprawled gracefully beside her, she asked, "Have you a cigarette?" He groaned. "No, don't get up. In your coat?"

She leapt up lightly and went into the shelter. As she entered it there was a sudden rise of wind and some drops of rain spattered down. She held her breath. For a moment she swayed and caught hold of one of the uprights to steady herself. The wind rushed through the dried ti-tree walls of the shed. It was a memorable sound. Todd's tweed sports coat lay neatly folded on one of the benches. She looked down at it and felt some inexplicable fear.

"In the inside pocket," Todd called. "Can't you find them?" But she did not move. The coat was as carefully folded as Kingsley Waring's had been that wet windy morning.

"What's the matter?" Todd asked, beside her.

She started and tried to smile at his clear handsome face.

"Vibrations?" he asked.

"I think it must be," Marsh said slowly.

She watched him stoop over and get his cigarette-case from the coat and then refold it again. Her own clothes had come back from the hotel as systematically arranged. She moved quickly away as Todd had his back turned, and started to walk swiftly along the track which bordered the links at the cliffs' edge.

"Hey there, Doc!" Todd called after her gaily. "Where are you going?" He hurried after her and slipped his cool hand through her elbow. "I know how you feel."

"You know?" Marsh asked, startled.

"All golfers feel like throwing themselves into the sea. It is the hallmark of the true player."

The wind blew up again, but this time there were no raindrops. The storm was holding off.

"The sea is starting to move again," Marsh said, stopping and watching it far below her. The sudden gusts of wind had cut into the heavy leaden swell. It swirled and widened in circles below them.

"Marsh, what did Mother say to you?" Todd's voice held a note of anxiety.

"She wanted me to leave Matthews," she replied slowly. "I couldn't understand what she meant, but I think I do now."

Todd was standing immediately behind her. He put his chin down on her shoulder. "Marsh, I may sound like a facetious sort of chap, but I'm not really. Mother hates me to become too friendly with any woman. Jealous, I suppose. She knows I like you very much and she doesn't care for the idea. You can't blame her in one way. She's had a hard life. My father—"

"Your father?" Marsh prompted, her eyes going sideways, trying to see his face.

"Well, the truth of it is my father committed suicide. Rotten for Mother, you know. It happened years ago. She has never spoken of it to me."

"Suicide? Why?"

"Unsound mind. That's the usual, isn't it? He had been in bad health. It preyed on his mind until he really did become unsound— or so Waring said."

"Waring?" Marsh said. "Kingsley Waring?"

"Oh, come on, Marsh. Let's go back. I don't want to remember."

"No, go on," she said strangely. Her gaze was on the churning mass of sea below. She felt that if she kept watching it move, Todd would go on talking.

Todd's face touched her crisp hair. The wind blew again and rocked them on their feet. "There's nothing else to tell," he said.

"Is that why you are frightened of doctors?" Marsh asked. "Because Kingsley Waring wanted to certify your father?"

"I'm not frightened of you, Marsh sweet. Don't go back to town yet."

"Is that why you hated Waring?" she asked.

"I suppose so. Don't let's talk of him." His face was touching her cheek. "Marsh, I feel as though I were standing on the edge of the world with you."

"Is that why you wanted Waring to die, Todd?"

"I can't say I was sorry when he did. Poetic justice is always satisfying. Marsh, do you think we could stay here for ever? There is something wildly exciting about standing on the edge of a cliff waiting for a storm to break. I do hope it holds off for a while longer."

"Todd, did you hate Kingsley Waring enough to make him die?"

The grip round her waist was tightened. Todd's voice was vibrant. "This is wonderful! Father must have felt like this."

"Your father?" Marsh asked, with another sidelong glance.

"Yes. Before his plunge into eternity. A sense of exhilaration, of clarity of mind, of inviolateness."

"Todd," Marsh said, trying to speak calmly. She was very frightened. "Do you want to know what your mother said? She told me I will never understand you and that I am not good for you. Todd, do you know what she was trying to tell me? She was trying to warn me, because you, too, are like your father. Your mind is also sick and unsound."

With a tremendous effort Marsh jerked herself out of his grip and climbed to higher ground. Todd was below her. He turned slowly, and lifting up his small handsome head began to laugh.

The wind blew up again and held steadily. Raindrops as large as pennies fell heavily. The sea commenced to heave and roll. And Todd, his lithe graceful figure braced against the wind, laughed madly up at Marsh.

CHAPTER TEN

I

Abruptly he stopped laughing and into his face came an expression of great sadness. His eyes, so often crinkled with quizzical mirth, now enlarged with melancholy. The whole structure of his face altered so much that Marsh found it hard to recognize the gay jesting Todd of her first meeting.

She held out her hands to him in a sudden gush of sympathy. "Come here!"

He hesitated, looking below him into the sea.

"Todd!" she said firmly. "Come. I want you."

He clambered up the slope and took the hands she held out. The wind buffeted them and she braced herself against his weight as he trembled all over. Gently she guided him back to the links and to the shelter-shed where she had found Kingsley Waring.

Todd shrank close to her as she sat on a rough bench. "Don't leave me," he begged. "It will pass off. It always does. Marsh, don't ever leave me. I want someone; not just Mother. I want you. I would be all right if you were with me all the time. Promise me you'll stay."

"Hush," she said gently. "We'll talk about it later. I want you to answer some questions."

Todd went on. His words were slurred, so quickly did he speak. "I don't expect you to marry me. I wouldn't think of suggesting that. But stay in Matthews. Couldn't you practise here? There is no local doctor. You could, couldn't you, Marsh?"

Sick at heart she listened to his pleading. He was like a child in his fears.

"It's not impossible," he urged, looking into her face as he crouched against her. It was raining gustily now, and he shivered as he spoke.

Marsh reached for his neatly arranged coat and put it around his shoulders. "No, not impossible," she agreed softly. "Todd, what do you know of Kingsley Waring? Tell me what you did. No one can harm you in—" She broke off. She was going to say 'in your state of mind' before she remembered she was dealing with a wayward brain and must proceed carefully.

"I'll tell you, Marsh darling," he said eagerly. "You know I'd tell you anything. It was the day I met you. Remember? When you told me you were a doctor I couldn't believe it. I'd seen women doctors before. Most of them dress like charwomen." His voice took on its lilting note momentarily. "But you, my very sweet, looked like an intelligent mannequin. So slender, so sure of yourself and so strong. I'd hated all doctors until I saw you. But when you told me you were going to Reliance I hated Kingsley Waring all the more. I didn't know you were a friend of his wife's. Why didn't you tell me, Marsh?

"All that night I wanted to tell him how much I hated him. I thought out a marvellous speech—a perfect flood of vituperation. It was so well prepared that I felt I had to find him so as to use it. Do you understand, Marsh?"

She pressed his arm. "Go on," she urged quietly.

"Bruce Shane was at the hotel that night. He usually rides into us for his meals. One of his horse's shoes was loose, so he left Saracen in our shed to be fixed in the morning and walked back to his cottage. I knew Waring went for a walk every night. He was always walking around Matthews as if he owned the place; the beach, the sea, the golf-course and the wind. I told you about the wind that first day, didn't I?

"Mother thought I had gone to bed, but I sneaked out to the shed and saddled Shane's horse. I was really enjoying myself. I hadn't had such fun for years. It was all like an adventure. I rode out to Reliance and left Saracen in the scrub near the house. Then I crept nearer, so as to watch for Waring to come out. There was a car parked under the pines."

"Mine," Marsh said. "I saw you from the window."

"I didn't speak to him then. I thought what a good idea it would be to give him a bit of a fright. Let him know someone was following and watching him. That he did not own all Matthews after all. I got back to the horse and then the stalking began. He kept stopping and glancing over his shoulder. I'd stop, too. He heard the horse whinny and called out Shane's name, but I didn't reply. He tried to find me in the dark, but I eluded him.

"It was then that I noticed he was acting oddly. He kept staggering and fumbling in his pocket. We were out on the links by then. It was raining and cold. I didn't feel cold though. I was warm all over. But Waring was flapping his arms around him. The wind was making him unsteady on his feet. He lost his balance once from fumbling in his hip-pocket. I thought he must have been drunk.

"I was still on Saracen. I watched Waring, but I didn't feel sorry for him. We were half-way across this fairway when he started to call out for Shane again. I could barely hear him above the wind. At the foot of this tee he fell again. I rode right up close and watched him. He was face downwards in the grass but he roused himself and said something. Then I told him who I was.

"I told him about my father and how I hated him. I enjoyed orating from the back of a horse with the wind and the rain beating down on me and Kingsley Waring huddled at my feet. He tried to drag himself up this slope. Just outside the shelter he collapsed completely and remained still.

"I slipped off the horse and shook him. I wanted him to hear what I had to say, but he would not move. Then I thought of taking off his clothes instead, and how cold and wet and humiliated he would be when he woke up."

"Oh, Todd!" Marsh said, in a low voice. "Why didn't you go for help? He was ill."

He pressed closer to her. "I didn't know," he whispered. "He was so arrogant and healthy when my father was ill. Don't blame me, please, darling. I did fold up his clothes and put them in the shelter. That was when Saracen got away and spoilt things. I had to walk home in the wet.

"I don't think Mother knew about it. She has never said anything. That night I slept so well. Marsh, I think I dreamed of you. I woke up thinking of you, I know. I'd forgotten about Waring. Then you came for help and I remembered in a vague faraway sort of manner, as though the night before had been part of my dream about you. Even when Shane found the horse-shoe I still didn't realize fully that I had been with Waring the night before. But when I left you I began to think and the incident became more real. Then there were whispers about the village."

"What whispers?" Marsh asked, stiffening.

He seized her hand and started to stroke it. "You know what small townships are, darling. And the Warings hadn't made themselves liked amongst the natives. Then there's Simon Morrow. It's well known about him and Katherine Waring."

"Dr. Kate avoids him," the girl said sharply. "What foundation has that malicious rumour?"

"None probably," he answered soothingly. "But, believe me, Marsh, those who are close to the soil and the sea know more of human psychology than your greatest psychiatrist. I'm telling you what I know. Don't be annoyed."

"We must go," Marsh said, disengaging herself. "The rain has eased a little. It must be getting late."

She got to her feet and looked down at Todd. There was nothing to be gained by prolonging the conversation. It was typical of Marsh, who, unlike most women, had no desire to turn Todd's confession over and over. What he had done he was not responsible for.

"Don't go back to Reliance," Todd said, one hand around her wrist. "Come back to the hotel and have dinner with me."

There was an amazing strength in the slim brown fingers. His possessive touch irritated her a little.

"Go back to your mother," she replied, trying to hide her impatience. "She knows how to look after you. I'll come and see you before I go."

The grip on her hand increased. Todd stood up. "But I want to talk to you, Marsh. You must have dinner with me. I need you to talk to."

"Oh, Todd!" she exclaimed, exasperated. "I can't do as you want just because you find me sympathetic. It's no good pretending. I'm leaving Matthews tomorrow and I am not coming back. I'm sailing for England at the end of the week. I shall probably be away at least two years. Perhaps we may meet again when I come back."

He was very pale. The skin was taut and shining over his cheekbones. "You mustn't go," he said, slurring his words again. "You said before it was not impossible. I thought you meant it."

Marsh searched for something soothing to put him off, but he noticed her hesitation at once. He seized her by the arms just above the elbows.

"I wish," he said, in a low shaking voice, "I wish I'd pulled you off the cliff with me. I wanted to because we'd both be much happier dead. Now I wish I'd done it because . . . damn you, you're like all doctors. A desperate case is of great concern and moment, the convalescence a time of retrospective triumph and the cure a signal for disinterest and search for another desperate case in order to boost the professional ego. Be damned to you all!"

He released her so abruptly that she staggered and lurched against the wall of the shelter. He picked up the two golf-sticks they had set out with so blithely and in a childish gesture of angry despair broke one in half. The two pieces were sent spinning over the cliff. Then he started off across the fairway alone.

"Todd!" Marsh called after him half-heartedly. He broke into a run, but did not glance back. Shrugging slightly, she turned towards Reliance.

II

The wind blew again from the ocean side of Matthews. It rushed along the road cold and fierce, just as it had on the evening of the girl's arrival. The leaden sky had broken into heavy masses of blue-grey clouds. It was a long hard walk back to Reliance, but as she drew nearer Marsh felt no anticipatory sense of relief.

She entered the silence of the ti-tree scrub. The wind only touched the tops of the scraggy bushes, its sound smothered. The abrupt break from the blustery road to the quiet track brought home to her the isolated position in which Reliance stood. When the house was crowded she had not noticed it, but now only the hostile neurotic nurse and the ineffectual Miss Jennet remained with Katherine Waring.

She fancied that the silence and the loneliness meant something; that she would not come out of both untouched—that they were a prelude to some hitherto intangible fear becoming definite.

Her fancies became more real as the house came into view. It was rain-swept, dark and cold-looking. There was no smoke blowing wildly from the kitchen chimney-stack. Even Miss Jennet's radio was silent. Rex was missing from his customary place and the leash which usually hung on the wall was gone. His sleeping-mat had been kicked into a corner.

It is like a deserted house, Marsh thought. And she shivered as she mounted the verandah steps.

But as she entered the house she could hear voices; a low murmur from the library. On the table at the foot of the stairs lay a tweed cap with a pair of pigskin gloves thrown negligently across it.

Marsh was no longer led by reason. During the last days her self-discipline had gradually given way to impulse. Her spirit, weakened by doubt and fear, could not fight against the desire to overhear the conversation between Katherine and Simon Morrow.

She crept along the passage to the half-open door.

"Where is she?" Morrow was asking.

"In the laboratory." Katherine's voice was hard and clipped, unlike her customary mellow tones.

"You're taking a terrible risk." Morrow's voice was different, too. It sounded angry and apprehensive. "Why don't you get rid of her as well?"

"I dare not. There has been enough talk about Reliance already. Perhaps later something may be—contrived."

The man's laugh and reply made Marsh shrink back. "You have already contrived so much. You are a remarkable woman, my dear. I think I am half afraid of you."

Then she trembled suddenly as her own name was spoken.

"What about the little Mowbray? I have already warned you of her activities."

"Marsh?" said Katherine softly. "Ah, yes, Marsh! You may leave her to me, Simon. You had better go now. It would not do for her to find you here."

Marsh backed hastily to the stairs and fled up them silently.

In her own room she stood with her back against the door panting, her eyes moving wildly around. She crossed to the window. The sloping roof of the verandah lay outside. The drop from the roof to the ground was steep, but there was a water-tank she could get down to first. She gazed longingly at her little car under the pine-trees.

She put one leg over the sill, half-turning towards the room. In doing so her distraught gaze was caught by a white envelope propped on the dressing-table. Her name was on it. For a long moment she sat astride, staring at the tantalizing white square.

Part of her mind said: You're panicking. There is a saner way out of all this. Read the letter and then take action.

But the instinct for immediate escape was strong. Even as she vacillated, footsteps sounded coming up the stairs. Quickly she swung her leg back, snatched up the letter and hid it in a drawer. Then she drew a deep breath and, walking to her door, deliberately opened it.

Katherine Waring was standing at the head of the stairs where a low lighted lamp made the shadows move grotesquely on the walls about her.

"I did not know you had come in, Marsh," she said, smiling at her. But to the girl the smile seemed forced, and the grey eyes above cold and speculative.

"I came straight up," she answered huskily. "I was caught in the rain."

"Change your clothes and then come down to the library. I will serve dinner in there as there is only the two of us."

"Where is Miss Jennet?" the girl asked, waiting for Katherine to turn away first.

"Jennet went back to town on the mail-car this afternoon."

If only she would not stare at me so closely, Marsh thought. Her nerve was nearly breaking.

"And Miss Donne?"

At last Katherine Waring glanced away. "Betty went with her," she said over her shoulder. "Will you be ready in twenty minutes?" This time Marsh was certain she was lying.

Back in her own room she opened the letter with wet shaking fingers. It was from Betty Donne. She read it hurriedly.

... *warning you* ... *Dr. Kate* ... *evil through and through* ... *all her fault* ... *if anything happens to me she is the cause.*

A little moan escaped Marsh, a sound of fear and despair. She clung to the dressing-table for support.

Then sheer animal courage—an instinct for survival made her brace herself. She had twenty minutes before Dr. Kate would come looking for her. She would not know that Marsh had overheard her telling Simon Morrow that Betty was in the laboratory. She had enough time to release the girl and get away to safety.

The climb from the window was accomplished easily. She crept among the outbuildings until she reached the shelter of the ti-tree. It was dark now. Night had come earlier with the low inky clouds, and she had to feel her way along the path to the laboratory.

A faint glow came from the window. She approached it cautiously and peered in. A shaded lamp stood on the bench revealing faintly the outline of a figure lying on the divan.

Her hand shook as she fitted her key into the lock—the key Shane had given her.

"Betty!" she said softly and crossed the room.

But the woman lying asleep on the divan was not the nurse but Miss Jennet. Marsh stared down at her in fear and perplexity. Katherine said she had gone back to town on the mail-car.

"Miss Jennet! Wake up. Where is Betty Donne? Why are you here?"

But even as she asked the question she remembered Simon Morrow's "Why don't you get rid of her, too?" Miss Jennet was a menace to their safety. She knew too much—just as Betty Donne had.

The woman was stirring. "Is that you, Kate? I had a lovely sleep. What was it you gave me? Oh, it's you, Dr. Mowbray."

Dr. Kate must have drugged her, Marsh thought. "Quickly, Miss Jennet, we must get away from here."

Miss Jennet smiled up at her. "I don't quite understand. Kate told me to stay here until she came for me."

"Please, Miss Jennet, come quickly. I can't explain now, but you mustn't stay here."

"Did Kate say for me to go with you?" she asked doubtfully.

"Yes," lied Marsh unhesitatingly. "Please hurry. Here, let me help you up."

She took the woman's arm and shepherded her to the door. "Don't talk until we get to the road," she ordered. "And try and walk quietly."

"I don't understand," Miss Jennet said again. "Are we running away from Kate?"

"Hush!" said the girl. She dragged her unwillingly through the ti-tree.

On the windy road she asked: "What happened? Where is Betty?"

"Miss Donne? Why, isn't she at home with Kate?"

A sudden coldness gripped Marsh's heart. She shook her head.

"That's funny," Miss Jennet observed. "I hope Kate is managing about dinner all right, because she said when she tucked me up in the laboratory this afternoon that Miss Donne would cook it."

"Why did Dr. Kate drug you?"

"Drug me? Did she? She gave me something because she said I didn't look well. Can we go back now, please?"

"No, you mustn't go back. I know you don't understand, Miss Jennet, but please trust me."

"Where are we going, then?" the woman asked plaintively. "It's cold and wet here."

Yes, where? Marsh thought, looking around her mechanically. There were the marks of a horse's hooves in the soft ground bordering the road. "Shane!" she said aloud. And at once the panic and perplexity left her.

Shane was so strong and direct and unafraid. She remembered his air of indifference to those he met and his imperturbability in crises and dangerous undertakings like the exhumation of Sam's body. His very unpleasantness had won a sort of respect and liking from her. Shane would know what to do next.

205

"We will go to a—a friend of mine," she said. "He lives in a cottage the other side of the cove. He knows all about Dr. Kate."

The sudden bitterness in her voice made Miss Jennet say timidly, "Have you and Kate quarrelled?"

Marsh laughed shortly and patted her arm. "No, we haven't quarrelled. Don't worry yourself about things. This way, and stay close to me."

III

Together they struggled against the wind and rain. It was a silent tiring journey, broken only by Miss Jennet's panted complaint that she was missing the twenty-seventh episode of *The Mystery of Mallow House.*

Presently they saw a light flickering through the rain and heard the clang and whine of the windmill belonging to Shane's cottage. The light shone from the tiny sitting-room. It looked warm and golden to Marsh as she crossed the verandah and peered in. Shane sat at the table, his head bent between his outstretched arms. A glass, half full of whisky, was beside him.

"Shane!" she called, tapping at the window. "Open up. I must talk to you."

The man stirred, rolling his head to one side. His eyes were half-closed. Why, he's drunk, Marsh thought with surprise and disgust.

She called his name louder and banged against the wall of the cottage. Shane's eyes opened slowly. He sat up, stretching out a fumbling hand for the tumbler. Then he saw Marsh at the window.

"Open up!" she ordered again. She waited until he had got to his feet unsteadily and then went to the door. She pressed against it, ready for the bolt to be removed. It was opened with a jerk so that she and Miss Jennet stumbled across the threshold on top of him. He reeled backwards and started to laugh idiotically.

"You would be drunk tonight," the girl said bitterly. "Tonight of all nights. I never thought you capable of it. Why do people spring their unpleasant surprises at the worst possible moments?"

"I was celebrating," he said, slurring the word. "Celebrating my return to the medical world of Melbourne. Going up to town tomorrow. Since you're here you can be the first to welcome me back. Two's better at this game. Do you good to get drunk, Mowbray. Take some of the starch out of you. Come on, what'll it be?"

Although her mind was on more urgent matters, Marsh observed him curiously. "I believe you're afraid. That's why you have been drinking."

The glass slipped from his hand, and rolled towards the edge of the table. He surveyed her resentfully. "Damn you!" he said. "Come on, what'll you drink? Let's drink hard for tomorrow I face the medical moguls of Collins Street again. Will they remember Bruce Shane or not? That's what I'll be thinking. Of course I'm afraid. What happened once might happen again."

"Nonsense," she said bracingly. "There's nothing to be afraid of. Like all men you exaggerate your petty hurts. One minute you're all bombast, then some trivial thing will send you into a weak huddle. Forget your paltry complex, for I need your help."

Either he was using his annoying trick of ignoring her or he did not comprehend what she said. Refilling his glass he lay outstretched on the couch. Another few drinks and he would be sodden and insensible.

Marsh shook his shoulder urgently. "Listen, Shane! You were right about Dr. Kate. I know now. I think I knew all along. But tonight I overheard her talking to Simon Morrow. She has done something to her nurse, Betty Donne. Then it was to be Miss Jennet here, and—and possibly me."

Into his dull eyes came a gleam. "Katherine Waring? By tomorrow night she'll be in gaol."

Miss Jennet let out a faint scream. "Try and be calm." the girl urged her quietly.

"But did you hear what that nasty young man said? My dearest Kate in gaol! Oh dear, whatever can I do?"

"Quiet!" Marsh said impatiently. She went over to the couch and tried to rouse the man. "No use," she said at last. "We'll have to stay here until he sobers up."

"Stay here? But why? Can't we go back to Kate now? I really feel we must warn her about this horrid person."

Marsh set her teeth against her rising irritation. "Listen, Miss Jennet. I know all this seems puzzling, but you can't go back to Reliance. It's not safe for you."

"Safe? But Kate has always looked after me. I'd always be safe with her."

"Not now. One day soon she would make you drink something or give you an injection which would kill you. And when you were dead she would say it was an accident like Sam's death or due to illness like her husband's."

"Oh no, Doctor," Miss Jennet replied confidently, "you're wrong. Kate would never do that to me."

Marsh gave up. She settled herself in a chair at the table to watch Shane. Miss Jennet chattered to herself under her breath and made clicking noises of expostulation.

"He looks like a dead man," she whispered presently, peering over the girl's shoulder.

"He'll be all right," Marsh answered shortly.

"You know, Doctor, I've been thinking. If he were dead he wouldn't be able to talk about putting Kate in gaol, would he?"

Marsh sighed resignedly. "No," she agreed.

"Don't you think—I mean, I wouldn't mind a bit going back to the laboratory in the dark to get whatever you need. Perhaps you could make it look as though he died from drink. That was the way Isabella killed her husband in *The Widow of Westlea*."

"Don't talk foolishly," the girl said harshly. "We're not living in one of your erotic radio serials." She glanced over her shoulder. Miss Jennet's plump face was bedewed with perspiration and her eyes were excited. "You must face facts," she told her more gently. "Katherine Waring has already murdered two people—her husband and Sam. Maybe poor Betty is another victim, but there must be no others. When Shane recovers we'll go with him to the police. He has positive proof that Sam was murdered that will make Walker believe our story."

"Oh no, no!" the woman whispered.

Marsh sank her head into her hands. "I'm sorry. There is no other course to take. Please try not to be distressed."

"You can't do it!" Miss Jennet moved about behind the girl's chair in agitation. "I must think. What will I do? What—" she broke off.

Marsh stared dully at the wall in front of her, where the woman's shadow was thrown. She saw the shadow come across hers and only comprehended what the upraised arm meant as something struck the base of her skull. She sank forward over the table, unconscious.

IV

When she came back to her senses she was still sitting at the table, but her arms had been hooked around the chair and tied together. She opened her eyes and saw that Shane was now awake, but heavy-lidded and blinking dazedly at the rope that secured him to the couch as he lay.

Before Marsh had time to speak, Miss Jennet came bustling into the room carrying a jug of water.

"You've come to, have you? I was getting worried. I was just going to try throwing water over you both." She giggled. "Shall I? I've always wanted to do it to someone."

"Undo my hands at once," Marsh ordered coldly.

The woman cocked her head on one side, her eyes bright with a silly mischief. "No, I won't. You think you've been awfully clever, Dr. Mowbray, but you've been very stupid really."

"Shane!" Marsh said. "Tell her about Sam's death. Tell her how serious the position is."

"Oh, I know all about that beastly boy. I should." She gave a sly sidelong glance.

The girl's mouth went dry. The pieces of the pattern had suddenly been whirled into confusion. "What do you mean?"

Miss Jennet held up one plump hand, inspecting it nonchalantly. "I killed him," she announced.

Marsh was stunned with shock, but Shane let out a short laugh.

"It wasn't funny," the woman reproached him. "It really took all my nerve. You see, he knew I had taken Kingsley's box of glucose. In fact, he took it from where I had hidden it behind the radio. To make matters worse, that nasty Arkwright woman made him give it up to her. But I paid her out for her interference by using her knitting-needle to kill Sam. I wanted her to get the blame. She was always annoying Kate, you know. But Commander Arkwright threw Sam's body in the sea. I overheard him telling you that in Sam's bungalow," she added, turning to Marsh.

Marsh tried to moisten her dry lips. Almost at once she had realized the position she and Shane were in. The pattern had fallen into a simple outline after that first confusion. She had been blind—stupidly blind. Miss Jennet was the real killer. Katherine Waring had been protecting her.

"Mr Waring," she managed to ask. "What happened?"

Miss Jennet seated herself comfortably near the door. "Yes, we may as well get things straight," she said in a satisfied tone. "I tied you up very securely and no one will even come within shouting distance of us. I am glad you suggested coming here, Doctor. Now, let me see! Oh yes, King. You know, I really hated him. He treated Kate abominably and was always so rude to me. I heard him speaking so unkindly about me to Kate. He said I was simple—like Sam." Her voice was incredulous.

"He was an unkind person," Shane said, and caught Marsh's eye as he had intended. She gave him a look of sullen despair and he frowned. "Go on," he urged Miss Jennet.

She wagged a finger at them. "Now don't you two start exchanging glances," she warned them brightly.

"You don't miss anything," Shane observed, in a complimentary tone. Dully Marsh hated him for his sang-froid.

"Nothing," Miss Jennet agreed in delight. "It was because of the chance seeing Betty tampering with King's hypodermic that my whole plan started. Betty wasn't really the cause of King's death, you know. I think she only wanted to give him a fright. I did most of the work—the vital part. I even prepared the wrong dinner, so that he didn't eat much. I need hardly tell you how insulin works on an empty stomach. I told you I knew a lot about medical matters once, didn't I, Dr. Mowbray?"

Marsh nodded. Her long fingers had been trying to reach the knot in the cord that tied her wrists.

"I nearly died laughing sometimes," the woman recalled. "Time and time again I let something fall that you should have noticed. Remember your first morning when I gave you a cup of tea in the kitchen? I counted the cups and named everyone but King. I knew he'd be dead by then—or just about. And then when you were asking me about the ones who went to the laboratory. You didn't seem to think it important that I was one. But I mustn't waste any more time chattering. Where do you keep the oil for your lamps?" she asked Shane.

He stared up at her, quite sober now. "Find it yourself," he said coolly.

She leaned over him and slapped him across the face sharply. "I've always wanted to do that, too," she said, and giggled uncontrollably. "I bet it is in your kitchen."

"What are you going to do?" Marsh asked, trying to keep her voice steady. "You can't possibly get away with—with—"

"Oh yes, I can," Miss Jennet nodded. "I have a wonderful plan this time."

Marsh put all the force of command into her voice. "Stop this nonsense at once. Do you think Dr. Kate will keep on protecting you for ever?"

The woman opened her eyes wide. "Of course. Years ago when Kate took me in she said: 'Don't ever worry about anything, Jen. You are my responsibility and I will always look after you.'"

"Miss Jennet, you must not—"

"Oh, let her go," Shane interrupted wearily.

Marsh turned her head. "Do you know what she is going to do? Can't you guess?"

"Shut up, girl!" He lowered his voice. "Listen closely. Is there any chance of getting your hands free?"

She reached for the knot desperately, and then shook her head, slumping against the table edge.

"The chair is heavy, I know, but you should be able to edge nearer to me, so that I can get your hands undone. We'll have to wait until that crazy creature goes or she may see our plan and cap it with one of her own."

"There won't be much time," Marsh said, her voice quivering.

He looked at her closely. "Time enough for you to get out."

"No, Shane. I can't do that. I'll get you free somehow."

"Don't be a fool, girl, and do as I say. Get back to Dr. Kate and tell her I made up for thinking ill of her all these years by saving your life."

"Ah, don't joke!" Marsh said, with a little moan. "We have such little time."

"Do you want me to indulge in heroics? Hush, here she comes."

Miss Jennet came in carrying two kerosene tins. "You shouldn't keep them with your horse," she said reproachfully. "Supposing something happened and his shed caught fire?"

"Miss Jennet," said Marsh, breathing quickly. "You must not do this terrible thing."

"I must, I must!" she cried shrilly. She opened the front door and the wind swept in, making the hanging lamp swing. "See! I will start it on the verandah and the smoke will soon suffocate you. You won't feel the fire." She carried the tins outside.

Marsh struggled in her chair. Her face was wet with a sweat of fear; a fear such as she had never conceived possible.

"Don't, girl!" Shane said gently. "You've got a chance, a good one. Don't panic."

"I won't leave you," she replied, through her clenched teeth.

"You're a fool. I never thought I'd admire a fool." Then he spoke sharply. "Start moving. Quickly!"

A soft explosion had sounded, then a crackle as the dry old weatherboards caught. A weaving mist of smoke rushed into the room. They could hear the crazed woman calling: "You won't feel a thing. It will all be over soon."

Marsh lunged sideways to get free of the table. Her movement was too fast and, bound to the chair, she fell heavily.

"Up!" Shane ordered. "Hurry!"

The crackle of fire was louder now. Smoke gushed into the room. Slowly and laboriously Marsh dragged herself to her knees and edged forward. She was at the other side of the table now, where Shane's bookcase stood. The chair was heavy and awkward on her back, and she fell on to her face again as one leg caught in the table. She tried to pull herself free, but the passage was too narrow.

"I can't get through," she cried, coughing. It was becoming difficult to breathe. She glanced back. The door of the cottage was edged with flames. "It's no use, I can't move."

Her head started to drum unpleasantly and black shadows seemed to creep up the corners of her vision. Somewhere, far away, she heard Shane's voice, but she did not try to follow what he was saying. The smoke was suffocating her as Miss Jennet said it would. She fell forward for the last time, unconscious.

CHAPTER ELEVEN

I

It was so good to breathe the fresh, salt-laden air again. Marsh sighed and turned her head on its pillow from side to side.

"Marsh!" said a voice above her head. She opened her eyes, but everything was dark. "I can't see," she whispered, very afraid.

Katherine Waring's cool hand took hers in a gentle clasp. "It's all right, my poor brave child. You are quite safe. It's only dark because it is night."

Then she realized she was lying in the open outside the burnt-out cottage. There was a coat over her and another under her head. She struggled to sit up, her head swimming. Dimly through the dark she could see Shane and Simon Morrow standing a little way off. Between them on the ground lay another figure, silent and shrouded.

She turned back to Katherine Waring, whose grip on her hand had tightened. "Miss Jennet?" she asked jerkily. The other nodded, but did not speak. Later Marsh learned what had happened.

Not long after she had escaped from Reliance, taking Miss Jennet with her, Katherine discovered their flight. Sick with fear at the danger the girl might be in, she called Simon Morrow.

It was Morrow's idea that the girl would have gone to Shane's as the only place possible. Her car was still in the yard, and he himself had just returned from the Tom Thumb where Betty Donne had fled in a fit of hysterical self-pity. A discreet call to Walker proved that Marsh had not gone to the police, and as the mail-car had left the township in the afternoon the chances were that she and Miss Jennet were still in Matthews.

After these inquiries they both set out for Shane's cottage, Katherine hurrying ahead with an instinct of impending disaster.

The sight of the cottage with the verandah ablaze drew from her a gasp of horror.

"Jennet!" she screamed wildly, running forward.

"In through the back way," Morrow ordered. Neither of them paid any heed to the whinnying, plunging horse in the adjoining shed. They thought the terrified screams came from the house.

Miss Jennet had left the kitchen door open. Covering his mouth and nose with his hand, Morrow dashed through to the smoke-filled room where Marsh lay unconscious on the floor.

"Get a knife from the kitchen," Shane managed to gasp through the suffocating atmosphere. "We're tied up. The girl is here on the floor."

The flames were creeping into the room, making it intensely hot. With the sweat pouring from his face, Morrow managed to free Marsh.

"Get her out first," Shane said. "She's fainted, I think."

Katherine bent over him, slashing at the cords that bound him. Through the smoke he looked up at her set face. The flames crept nearer but she did not falter.

Then Morrow was behind her, a wet handkerchief tied over the lower part of his face. "Outside." His muffled voice was curt.

He had Shane free just as the front wall of the cottage collapsed, showering them with sparks. Slapping at their clothes, the two men dived at the door.

"Saracen," Shane said, as soon as they were outside. "He's mad with fright. I'll have to get him out. The shed will catch soon."

Morrow followed him. The door of the stable was ajar and the horse, eyes rolling and ears laid back, was dashing himself against the barrier of his stall. The glow of the fire lighted the inside of the shed with an ominous red.

"Look!" said Morrow, clutching the other man's arm. Just inside the stall lay a dumpy, huddled shape. Even as they saw her, Saracen reared up again. One hoof came down on the blood-soaked hair.

"She must have been trying to get him out," Shane said in a hard voice. "She didn't mind us burning to death, but the horse touched her sentimentality."

"You know, then?" Morrow asked quickly.

Shane nodded, and began to coax the terrified animal.

Morrow stood aside as he led him, kicking and plunging, into the cold free air. Then bending down, he gently gathered up the battered body and carried it outside to Katherine.

II

Simon Morrow took Shane to his own house, but Katherine and Marsh went back to Reliance. There, exhausted and grimed, the girl was unable to rest until she knew the full story.

"All my life," Katherine explained to her, "I have had responsibilities thrust on me. Sometimes I accepted them as tributes, precious to anyone's ego, but other times they have been burdens. Either way I regarded them as obligations. The habit to shoulder other people's mistakes and problems became so strong that it formed part of my existence.

"I have tried to be patient, just, farseeing—and above all, tolerant. Such an existence earns few friends and many enemies, for the world does not accept the ideals it seemed to force on me. It sneers at them, jibes at them and whispers maliciously.

"And yet I could not change and would not change, for in that way I thought I was happy.

"Kingsley was my greatest responsibility. In many ways he was like a child; anxious to know and do everything, ignoring the confusion he created, the mistakes he made, and shelving responsibility. King's talent lay in only one direction, medically speaking. He was a surgeon, and nothing else. Time and time again I covered up for him, when he wantonly dabbled outside his métier—as in the case of Sam.

"King brought this imbecile into the house. I don't know where he got him, but it amused him for a while trying to develop that poor brain. Very soon the novelty faded and I had to step in to carry on when King suddenly lost interest.

"A similar incident happened with the case Dr. Shane told you about. That patient was King's and not mine, as he told Shane. Again I covered up for him, but I made it the end of our partnership. A patient had died and a young doctor's reputation had been smirched without any sense of guilt or responsibility on King's part. I could not continue with him professionally.

"He was terribly hurt at my decision and the reason for it. He never would admit later that our break was the starting-point of his successful career as a surgeon. He harboured a grudge continually and never lost an opportunity to try and revenge his wounded pride by sly slandering and subtle innuendoes.

"This almost diabolical cunning lost me Michael, friends and even nurses I employed in my rooms, for he had a tremendous charm which most people took for integrity.

"I could do nothing, for time and time again he would come back asking forgiveness and making liberal promises. Perhaps I knew he would never change, but he was my responsibility and I accepted him.

"Then he became poor in health. He hated that. That was why I thought he had planned suicide. I was shocked and bewildered at first. For a moment I even considered it might be better to let him do what he wanted. But when he died thinking I had caused his death, and then Sam was killed immediately afterwards, I knew what had happened. The new responsibility was mine, for in effect I had caused both murders.

"To Jennet, my life with King seemed intolerable and Sam an unnecessary obligation. She had killed them both for my sake. What could I do but protect her from the consequences of her drastic thoughtlessness? Once all the talk had died down, my idea was to get her away to some remote spot where she could do no further harm.

"And there was Betty, too, to consider, for although she played a part in King's death she never had the intention to murder him. The shock when he did die almost unbalanced her. She became so bad that I decided to make her hate me. In that way she lost the guilt complex which was associated only with her adoration. Simon says she seems to have settled down with the Bannisters."

A short silence fell between them, to be broken by Marsh saying carefully: "I don't want to disturb you by reviving unhappy memories, but there are one or two matters I would like explained. On my first night at Reliance I heard someone crying. It seemed to come from outside. Who was it?"

"I heard it too. It was Sam. I went down to his bungalow and tried to coax him into telling me the trouble. He was bewildered and distressed but he would not tell me. Evidently Jennet had threatened that I would send him away if he ever told about the snuff-box."

Marsh nodded. "Michael said someone must have frightened him. Another thing, Dr. Kate. What did Mr Waring mean when he said that about denouncing those members of the profession who thought they had got away with mistakes?"

Katherine's sad face lightened. "Henry was being extra pompous that night. King loved to deflate his ego."

The girl smiled, too, before she glanced away. "I came across a scrapbook in the laboratory," she said hesitantly. "There were cuttings in it about that inquest in which Dr. Shane was involved. At the time I thought you were connected with it."

"I don't blame you for arriving at that conclusion," Katherine replied gently. "Unless you had known King well, you could not understand the queer twisted streak in his character that would cause him to retain such evidence. He used to threaten to reveal those errors—his own as mine—in order to make me stay with him. It was Larry who tried to poison your mind against me, wasn't it, Marsh?"

The girl bowed her head, conscious of how far Laurence Gair had been successful. "Before he left, his belief in your guilt was shaken. I think it had something to do with Mr Waring's will. All I know of that is what Mrs Arkwright let fall—that two sums of money had been left to persons she had never heard of."

"Yes, she wanted me to try and stop those bequests, but I would not. It was conscience money that King left—to Bruce Shane and to the nearest living relative of the patient who had died. Larry must have heard King's account of that affair, but when he learned about the bequests he began to doubt him. Do you remember trying to find that nurse we had before our partnership was broken? Yes, Marsh. I knew what you were doing. Simon told me. The money for the hospital she bought in the Western District was put up by King—hush money. She knew that patient was his."

"Mr Morrow seems to have been a great help to you," the girl said, and there was a faintly jealous note in her voice. When Katherine only smiled without replying, she felt a strange resentment. Although the intense strain of the past few days had been lifted, she was conscious of a vague sense of loss. Katherine, aloof and unapproachable, was someone to be worshipped. But the woman who had poured forth her intimate troubles and laid herself emotionally bare was, after all, only another human being.

Marsh did not know that this was precisely what Katherine had intended.

III

She would not allow the girl to leave Reliance until she had in some part recovered from the ordeal in the cottage. Morrow called the next morning to discuss the inquest on Miss Jennet. The verdict would probably be 'death by misadventure', with no mention of the circumstances leading up to their being on the premises or of the real cause of the fire.

"I have fixed it so that you need not appear," he told Marsh. "Your trip need not be interfered with. Katherine has told me of the ambitious programme you have planned. But don't let your career swamp everything else that is worth living for," he added, with a mocking smile to temper the seriousness of his words.

The girl flushed with annoyance, but Katherine did not intervene. When Simon had gone she turned and said impulsively: "Don't go, Marsh. Simon is right. A career isn't the only thing that matters."

Marsh felt betrayed. "That isn't what you thought once," she answered stiffly.

Without speaking Katherine turned back to the window where

Simon Morrow's straight figure could be seen in the distance. She did not appear to notice when Marsh slipped out of the room and went upstairs to pack her cases.

She left the following morning, Katherine and Simon standing on the verandah of Reliance together to wave her good-bye. She had not seen Shane since the night of the fire, and for some reason she could not bring herself to mention his name. All she knew was that he was staying with Simon, but had refused the offer of Morrow's influence and reputation in establishing himself professionally.

Marsh felt a warm glow when Morrow ruefully confessed this rebuff. Unbidden recollections passed swiftly through her mind as she drove away from them without a backward glance. Shane, so brusque and impatient of quibbling. Shane helping her with Sam—mocking her in the laboratory at Reliance—holding her like a child in front of his horse. And lastly, Shane, lying across a table in his cottage, drinking to shut out the fear of disgrace and failure.

She thought of Larry and her lip curled; and of Todd with a sad and pitying kindness.

The little car was climbing the hill which overlooked Matthews when she saw the horseman reined in ahead, blocking the road. An odd little sound came from her throat as she slowed to a standstill.

Shane slipped from the saddle and came over to the car. "I only learned this morning that you are going overseas," he said. He sounded angry. "Why keep it a secret?"

"I did not know you would be interested," she replied, smiling.

"Do you really have to go?"

"Yes," she said, quietly. "Try to understand. I think you will. For years I have worked and saved for this trip. It means a lot to me. Probably it won't later on, but I can't change my plans or ambitions overnight. We have learned a great deal about each other in a few days, Bruce, but it is not sufficient. Let me have these two years. You will want them, too."

He was silent for a moment, frowning at the whip he pulled hard through his fingers. Then he took her upturned face in his hand gently. "Of course, you are right. I was being unreasonable. Good-bye for the present, my dear." Turning, he remounted his horse.

Marsh started the car. For a while the rider kept pace beside her until she gathered speed. Then with a last gesture of farewell they parted.

THE END

MORE FROM JUNE WRIGHT

MURDER IN THE TELEPHONE EXCHANGE

"A classic English-style mystery . . . packed with detail and menace."—*Kirkus Reviews*

June Wright made quite a splash in 1948 with her debut novel. It was the best-selling mystery in Australia that year, sales outstripping even those of the reigning queen of crime, Agatha Christie.

When an unpopular colleague at Melbourne Central is murdered – her head bashed in with a buttinsky, a piece of equipment used to listen in on phone calls – feisty young "hello girl" Maggie Byrnes resolves to turn sleuth. Some of her co-workers are acting strangely, and Maggie is convinced she has a better chance of figuring out the killer's identity than the stodgy police team assigned to the case, who seem to think she herself might have had something to do with it. But then one of her friends is murdered too, and it looks like Maggie is next in line.

Narrated with verve and wit, this is a mystery in the tradition of Dorothy L. Sayers, entertaining and suspenseful, and building to a gripping climax. It also offers an evocative account of Melbourne in the early postwar years, as young women flocked to the big city, leaving behind small-town family life for jobs, boarding houses and independence. *(336 pages, with an introduction by Derham Groves)*

SO BAD A DEATH

When *Murder in the Telephone Exchange* was reissued in 2014, June Wright was hailed by the *Sydney Morning Herald* as "our very own Agatha Christie," and a new generation of readers fell in love with her inimitable blend of intrigue, wit, and psychological suspense – not to mention her winning sleuth, Maggie Byrnes.

Maggie makes a memorable return to the fray in *So Bad a Death*. She's married now, and living in a quiet Melbourne suburb. Yet violent death dogs her footsteps even in apparently tranquil Middleburn. It's no great surprise when a widely disliked local bigwig (who also happens to be her landlord) is shot dead, but Maggie suspects someone is also targeting the infant who is his heir. Her compulsion to investigate puts everyone she loves in danger. This reissue features an introduction by Lucy Sussex, plus her fascinating 1996 interview with June Wright. *(288 pages)*

DUCK SEASON DEATH

June Wright wrote this lost gem in the mid-1950s, but consigned it to her bottom drawer after her publisher foolishly rejected it. Perhaps it was just a little ahead of its time, because while it delivers a bravura twist on the classic 'country house' murder mystery, it's also a sharp-eyed and sparkling send-up of the genre.

When someone takes advantage of a duck hunt to murder publisher Athol Sefton at a remote hunting inn, it soon turns out that almost everyone, guests and staff alike, had good reason to shoot him. Sefton's nephew Charles believes he can solve the crime by applying the traditional "rules of the game" he's absorbed over years as a reviewer of detective fiction. Much to his annoyance, however, the killer doesn't seem to be playing by those rules, and Charles finds that he is the one under suspicion. Duck Season Death is a both a devilishly clever whodunit and a delightful entertainment. *(192 pages, with an introduction by Derham Groves)*

PETER DOYLE

Peter Doyle's crime novels, featuring irresistible antihero Billy Glasheen, brilliantly explore the criminal underworld, political corruption, and the explosion of sex, drugs, and rock'n'roll in postwar Australian life, and have earned him three Ned Kelly Awards, including a Lifetime Achievement Award in 2010.

"Peter Doyle does for Sydney what Carl Hiaasen does for Miami."
—Shane Maloney

"Think of a hopped-up James M. Cain."—*Kirkus Reviews*

THE DEVIL'S JUMP

August 1945: the Japanese have surrendered and there's dancing in the streets of Sydney. But Billy Glasheen has little time to celebrate; his black marketeer boss has disappeared, leaving Billy high and dry. Soon he's on the run from the criminals and the cops, not to mention a shady private army. They all think he has the thing they want, and they'll kill to get hold of it. Unfortunately for Billy, he doesn't know what it is . . . but he'd better find it fast.

GET RICH QUICK

Sydney in the 1950s. Billy is trying to make a living, any way he can. Luckily, he's a likeable guy, with a gift for masterminding elaborate scenarios—whether it's a gambling scam, transporting stolen jewels, or keeping the wheels greased during the notorious 1957 tour by Little Richard and his rock 'n' roll entourage. But trouble follows close behind—because Billy's schemes always seem to interfere with the plans of Sydney's big players, an unholy trinity of crooks, bent cops, and politicians on the make. Suddenly he's in the frame for murder, and on the run from the police, who'll happily send him down for it. Billy's no sleuth, but there's nowhere to turn for help. To prove it wasn't him, he'll have to find the real killer.

THE BIG WHATEVER

As the swinging 60s turn into the 70s, Billy's living a quiet life. He's in debt to the mob so he keeps his head down, driving a cab, running some low-level rackets. He may as well have gone straight, it's so boring. Then one day everything changes. He picks up a trashy paperback left in his cab – and its plot seems weirdly familiar. The main character is based on him! Only one person knows enough about his past to have written it—Max, his double-crossing ex-partner in crime. But Max is dead. He famously went up in flames, along with a fortune in cash, after a bank heist. If Max is somehow still alive, Billy has a score to settle. And if he didn't get fried to a crisp, maybe the money didn't either. To find out, Billy has to follow the clues in the strange little book—and soon discovers he's not the only one on Max's trail.

"An absolute gem . . . a marvellous read and a truly distinctive piece of Australian crime writing."—*Sydney Morning Herald*

G.S. MANSON

COORPAROO BLUES & THE IRISH FANDANGO

Written in the spare, plain-spoken style of all great pulp fiction, G.S. Manson's series featuring 1940s Brisbane P.I. Jack Munro captures the high stakes and nervous energy of wartime, when everything becomes a matter of life and death.

BRISBANE, 1943. Overnight a provincial Australian city has become the main Allied staging post for the war in the Pacific. The tensions – social, sexual, and racial – created by the arrival of thousands of US troops are stirring up all kinds of mayhem, and Brisbane's once quiet streets are looking pretty mean.

Enter Jack Munro, a World War I veteran and ex-cop with a nose for trouble and a stubborn dedication to exposing the truth, however inconvenient it is for the -powers that be. He's not always a particularly good man, but he's the one you want on your side when things look bad.

When Jack is hired by a knockout blonde to find her no-good missing husband, he turns over a few rocks he's not supposed to. Soon the questions are piling up, and so are the bodies. But Jack forges on through the dockside bars, black-market warehouses, and segregated brothels of his roiling city, uncovering greed and corruption eating away at the foundations of the war effort.

Then Jack is hired to investigate a suspicious suicide, and there's a whole new cast of characters for him to deal with – a father surprisingly unmoved by his son's death, a dodgy priest, crooked cops, Spanish Civil War refugees – and a wall of silence between him and the truth, which has its roots deep in the past. Friends, enemies, the police – they're all warning Jack to back off. But he can't walk away from a case: he has to do the square thing.

"Great historical detail of wartime Australia mixed with the steady pace of sex and violence . . . keeps the pages turning."—Brisbane Courier-Mail

"Rough and gritty, but also vital."—The Age

CPSIA information can be obtained
at www.ICGtesting.com
Printed in the USA
LVHW041913140219
607610LV00001B/1